# *Our Love's Rivalry with Religion*

Michael Wright

ISBN: 978-1-7364114-6-9 (sc)
ISBN: 978-1-7364114-7-6 (e)

The book cover was designed using graphics provided by www.canva.com.

This is a work of fiction. All characters, events, organizations, as portrayed in this novel, are products of the author's imagination or are used fictitiously.

All Scripture quotations come from the World English Bible, which is in the public domain.

# ACKNOWLEDGMENTS

I gratefully acknowledge the extensive feedback and suggestions provided by Soukaina Tarraf, Ahmet Basagalar, Shirley Bull, Sandra Hall, Kathy Holgate, and Suzie Swickard Donner.

# New Job — First Day

Sarah Jefferson, Human Resources Director, smiled and extended her hand to Adeelah El-Sayed. "Welcome to the City of Waynesboro."

Adeelah carried a leather briefcase in her left hand and unconsciously fiddled with her hijab (headscarf). With a nervous smile, she extended her clammy hand to shake hands with Sarah and replied with a barely imperceptible quiver in her voice, "Thank you. I'm anxious to get started."

Adeelah El-Sayed, age 26, had just accepted an employment offer as Finance Director for the City of Waynesboro, Georgia. Today, a pleasant day in March, was her first day. She had formerly worked as assistant finance director for the City of Augusta, Georgia, and she was pleased to be accepted for this position of greater responsibility. This was a major move for her. While she knew she was qualified and had the necessary background and experience, this nevertheless would be a big challenge for her.

Moreover, Waynesboro is a small city with a population of just under 5,800 people, made up of 70 percent black and 26 percent white residents. So, it concerned her she just might be the only Muslim employed by the city. With so many things on her mind as she started this new job, she had no idea today would mark the beginning of a chain of events which would define her destiny.

During the interview process, Adeelah found that she liked Sarah, and hoped to become good friends with her. Sarah was very professional, but she was also friendly, spontaneous, and enthusiastic.

In Sarah's mind, Adeelah was simply heads and shoulders above the other candidates for the finance director position. In addition to her top-notch experience and professional achievements, Adeelah, early in the interview process, responded to Sarah's questions confidently, with conviction, and showed herself to be idealistic and highly principled. Sarah also found it striking that her extroverted personality and her talent for connecting with other people made her stand out from the stereotypical personality of the average accountant.

Sarah gave Adeelah the typical paperwork which new employees must complete when they start their employment with the city, and Adeelah sat in a conference room to wade through the numerous forms she had to fill out. Some forms required information, which she brought with her in her briefcase. When she finished, she returned to the personnel office. The receptionist took the paperwork and explained, "Ms. Jefferson is interviewing another prospective employee. She shouldn't be much longer, and she requests you wait here. Can I get you a cup of coffee or something?"

"Do you have tea?"

"Sure. How do you take your tea?"

"Just one spoonful of sugar, please."

Adeelah browsed the numerous personnel disclosures which hung on a bulletin board. When the receptionist returned with the tea, Adeelah walked over to her and smiled. "Thank you."

She sat down, put her briefcase on the floor beside her, and asked, "What's your name?"

"Henrietta Clay," she responded without making eye contact.

Henrietta, a young African American woman, was gracious, despite her excessive shyness. Adeelah chatted with her briefly, and Henrietta covered her mouth when she responded to hide her enigmatic smile.

Adeelah just finished her tea when Sarah came to get her. "The first thing I want to do is introduce you to the people who will be reporting to you and the other department heads in the city."

Adeelah put the teacup on a nearby table and picked up her briefcase as she stood. "Sounds good." With a shaky smile and lifted eyebrows which wrinkled her forehead, she inquired, "I want to confirm there will be no problem for me to take an extended lunch break on Fridays, as we discussed during our earlier interviews, so I may attend the weekly services at the mosque where I worship."

Sarah rolled her eyes, and her nearly imperceptible scowl revealed that Adeelah's question irritated her, and she replied with a subtle, scornful tone of disapproval, "That should be no problem for the most part. Can you be flexible on that if something urgent comes up?" What she didn't say was that she found it presumptuous to expect the city would have to accommodate Adeelah's desire to attend the weekly Friday prayer service at her mosque.

"Of course." Having experienced such negative vibes on other occasions, Adeelah ignored Sarah's non-verbal reaction, and asked, "Another question I wanted to ask you: Of the employees who will be under my supervision, are there any who aspired to become the finance director?"

"Only one. That would be Roger, the payroll clerk."

"Is he qualified?"

Sarah raised an eyebrow, and her mouth displayed a slight, close-lipped smile. "He expects to complete his bachelor's degree in accounting in June, and he's competent. Nevertheless, I don't think he has the level of broad experience which would qualify him to be the city's finance director. A good next step for him would be to accept a position as assistant finance director."

"That's good information for me to know. Thank you."

Adeelah anticipated the possibility that Roger might be resentful because he was not selected for the finance director position, and she wanted this information so she could effectively deal with this possible issue.

They first stopped at the City Manager's office. His door was open, and Sarah stuck her head in and asked, "Frank, do you have a minute? I want to introduce you to our new finance director."

Frank looked up from the laptop computer on his desk and stood as he responded, "Sure. Come on in."

Frank Washington, an African American, was about 6 feet 2 inches tall, and on the chubby side.

Sarah made the introductions, "Adeelah, you'll recall your previous interview with Frank Washington, our City Manager. Frank, this is Adeelah El-Sayed's first day as our new Finance Director."

Since he didn't remember Adeelah's name, Frank was grateful that Sarah said her name when she reminded him about their previous meeting. He shook hands with her and smiled. "Welcome to the City of Waynesboro, Adeelah. You certainly impressed me during the interview you and I had earlier, and Sarah speaks highly of you. Let me say, I look forward to the active role you'll play as a member of our management team, and I'm happy to have you on board. Please don't hesitate to let me know if there's anything I can help you with."

The sound of a car horn startled Adeelah. She felt her jaw tighten, and she fiddled with her hijab. "Thank you. It's a pleasure to see you again. I look forward to getting started."

As they walked out the door, Sarah drew close to Adeelah and whispered, "Frank is rather serious and formal, reserved, calm, and somewhat quiet. He values tradition and hard work. He's a patient man, but occasionally, he asks a lot of questions, and you may not always know exactly where he's coming from."

Adeelah wasn't sure what Sarah meant by her last comment, but she made a mental note to remember it and to be ready to see how she might recognize this trait in Frank.

The next stop was the City Clerk's office. The door was open, and they walked in. "Clara, I want you to meet Adeelah El-Sayed, our new Finance Director. Adeelah, this is Clara Carney."

Clara smiled warmly with kind eyes, stood up, shook hands with Adeelah, and replied, "Welcome. I'm sure you'll quickly learn you and I will work together on many city issues."

Grateful for Clara's pleasant disposition, Adeelah felt the tension in her jaw begin to subside, and she responded with a relaxed smile, "I'll look forward to working with you, and I'm glad to meet you, Clara."

As they walked out of Clara's office, Sarah commented, "Clara has been with the city longer than anybody. She's a good person to know, especially when you want to know something about the city's history or culture."

"I'll remember that."

Afterward, they walked down a short hallway to Adeelah's office in the finance department, where she met the accounts payable clerk, the accounts receivable clerk, the payroll clerk, and the utility billing clerks (for water and gas)–the five subordinates who would be working for Adeelah.

When Adeelah and Sarah entered, all five employees looked up from their desks and stared with astonishment at Adeelah's attire, which clearly revealed she was a Muslim. Worried about her first impression, Adeelah reached for her hijab and noted with consternation how everybody crossed their arms in unison. She also noted their obvious darting eyes and the gasps they tried and failed to hide.

Sarah noted their reaction as well. This concerned her. Her voice quivered as she announced, "This is Adeelah El-Sayed, the city's new finance director."

For an awkward moment, breathing was the only sound in the room.

As a Muslim, Adeelah was accustomed to the initial hesitation which non-Muslims typically exhibited when they met her. But generally, once people got past this naive bias, they quickly found they liked her. Always ready to see the humor in life, she laughed freely. And once people got to know her better, they frequently described her as approachable and full of zest.

Adeelah took a deep breath, and, with brave frankness, cool confidence, and a gentle smile; she nodded her head, took charge, and addressed them. "I want you to know the perplexity I clearly see on your faces doesn't surprise me. As a Muslim woman, I've experienced such perplexity many times." She pointed her forefinger upward and assured them, "I promise, as we begin working together, you'll come to see us have a productive, professional, and harmonious relationship in which we will work together effectively. I encourage you to count on that."

Her words immediately reduced the tension in the room. Adeelah and Sarah observed how everybody uncrossed their arms and took a deep breath, and they noted that their tenseness subsided with the air which they exhaled.

As they walked out of the finance department, Sarah complimented Adeelah. "I'm amazed at how well you handled the hostile reception we just encountered."

With a gleam in her eye and a subtle smile, Adeelah replied with inner satisfaction, "Thank you."

After meeting all the department heads in City Hall, Sarah said, "I'd like to take you to lunch before we go to meet the police chief and the fire chief."

"That would be great. Thank you."

They walked around the block to the Good Day Café, and Sarah explained, "This is the only restaurant within walking distance of City Hall. It has great ambiance, and it's popular with the locals, which would not be the case if they didn't serve really good food."

As they entered the restaurant, all eyes focused on Adeelah, as she sat down at a table with Sarah. Adeelah noticed that conversations came to an abrupt halt. The restaurant's clientele varied widely with respect to race and economic status. But it was clear to Adeelah, she was the only Muslim. Soon conversations among staff and customers resumed, and their chatter became animated, filled the room, and reminded Adeelah of the sounds of a flock of cackling geese.

Adeelah hoped she could count on future opportunities to eat lunch with Sarah, so she commented, "I assume you come here with some frequency."

"Actually, most of us at City Hall bring our lunch from home and eat at our desks, but I do come here on occasions."

Adeelah found it amusing that one of the items on the menu was *Yesterday's Soup*, with the comment, *Because it's always better the next day.* When she learned it was potato soup, that is what she ordered, along with a Good Day Caesar salad. Sarah ordered a cup of Vidalia French onion soup and a spinach salad.

When the waitress brought the food, Adeelah raised her hands just above the table, and, with palms facing upward, she raised her eyes upward and prayed silently, *Oh Allah, the most gracious, the most merciful, bless the food You have provided for us and save us from the punishment of Hell.*

Sarah followed her example, bowed her head, and also prayed silently, *Dear God, thank you for this food which you have blessed us with. In Jesus' name. Amen.*

The meal was good, but Adeelah found it somewhat challenging to get Sarah to engage in casual conversation. Sarah responded to Adeelah's efforts to make conversation with short answers and made minimal effort to keep the conversation going. She was friendly enough but seemed uninterested in making conversation. After the meal was over, Adeelah again prayed silently, *Praise be to Allah Who has fed us, given us drink, and made us Muslims.*

They now returned to City Hall, got into a city car, and drove to the fire station so Adeelah could meet the fire chief. As they arrived, Sarah commented, "This is quite a guy you're about to meet. If anybody ever had the stereotypical image of a fireman, Martin Webster is that guy."

Adeelah left her briefcase in the car, and they entered the fire station, which was immaculately clean. The two highly polished fire trucks parked inside glistened impeccably. They walked to the fire chief's office, but he wasn't there. Sarah said, "I'll bet I know where he is."

They walked around the corner and went into a small but well-equipped gym. The typical funky stink of a gym hit them in the face, and both of their heads turned to the side as they winced their noses. Two bare-chested men, dressed in exercise shorts, were inside. One was doing bench presses, finishing his final repetitions. The other served as a spotter to help place the barbell in the rack attached to the bench. John, the spotter, counted out the final repetitions: "Eight . . . nine . . . . . ten."

Sweating heavily, his face contorted, his teeth clenched, Martin grunted. With veins bulging in his neck, he arched his lower back up. His arms trembled as he struggled to finish the last repetition. Not quite able to complete it, John grabbed the barbell to assist him, and they dropped the barbell into the rack's three-inch wide brackets with a reverberating metallic thud.

Sarah pointed at the man on the bench and said, "That's Martin Webster, the fire chief."

Martin breathed heavily as he stood up and wiped the sweat from his brow. He was surprised to see the pretty Muslim woman who stood before him. He admired her attractive maroon colored skirt, buttoned down the front with large white buttons. The skirt reached to her mid-calf. Her rose-colored blouse coordinated well with the skirt. And the hijab (headscarf) she wore covered her hair and nicely framed her attractive, light olive-colored face. The hijab was the same color as her skirt. Martin thought, *I wonder what she would look like without her hijab.*

Adeelah took a step backward, and her religious eyes almost popped out of her head. As a Muslim woman, this was the most provocative male nudity she had ever seen close up and in person, and a hot blush painted a reddish hue on her face, which erased her olive-colored complexion.

She guessed Martin to be about 30 years old, and she was captivated by his chiseled face and his deep blue eyes, which matched the bluest blue of the ocean. His broad shoulders and thick chest tapered down like the letter V to a slender, muscular, six-pack waist. Wondering if his waist might be smaller than her petite waist, it was all Adeelah could do to keep her jaw from dropping, and she quickly tried to look away. But her eyes kept coming back to this Hercules, who attracted her like steel to a magnet.

Sarah, entertained by Adeelah's shock and awe, brought her back from this mesmerizing vision, and said, "Adeelah El-Sayed meet Martin Webster, the Fire Chief. Martin, this is Adeelah El-Sayed, our new finance director."

Adeelah did her best to conceal how amazing she found him and was tempted to pull her hijab down over her eyes, as she shyly replied with a coy smile, "It's good to meet you."

Martin also smiled and replied, "It's good to meet you too, but I'd much rather have you meet me when I'm not so badly in need of a shower. Is there any chance you two can come back again a little later?"

Sarah responded, "Adeelah still needs to meet the police chief. We'll come back after that."

Before they walked out the door, Sarah, Martin, and John watched with amusement as Adeelah walked over to the exercise bench, placed her hand on the barbell, and tried to move it within the three-inch brackets. She couldn't. She glanced over her shoulder, tilted her head, and looked at Martin. "How much does this weigh?"

Tickled that she couldn't move it, Martin's chest expanded as he grinned. "350 pounds."

She straightened her head, and her eyes reflected astonishment. "Wow! You pushed this barbell up and down like it was a pound of butter!"

Martin blushed, ran his fingers through his dark blonde hair, and grinned with pride.

Sarah again intervened to tear Adeelah away.

~.~

Sarah introduced Adeelah to the police chief, and then they returned and found Martin in his office. As they entered, Martin stood up, and a delightful scent emanated from this freshly bathed man, which serenaded Adeelah's nose. He wore dark-colored trousers and a white, tight-fitting polo shirt with embroidered words which read *Martin Webster, Fire Chief, City of Waynesboro.*

Martin gazed into Adeelah's eyes with an intensity which again resurrected a hot blush on her face. He smiled warmly and said, "I'm glad to be more presentable now, and I'm pleased to meet you, Adeelah. I like unique names, and yours is certainly that. Where does the name come from? And is there some meaning attached to it?"

It surprised her that Martin remembered her name. With her eyes hypnotically fixed on his penetrating gaze, she smiled and responded, "My parents are from Morocco in North Africa, and they came to the United States thirty years ago. Adeelah is a popular name in Morocco. The name means: just, honest, and equal."

"Equal, you say. What a contemporary name in times like these, when so many women are asserting their equality. What part of Morocco does your family come from?"

"Marrakech. Are you familiar with the city?"

"As a matter of fact, I've been there. When I was in the military, the Air Force sent me with other Air Force firefighters to an air force base located about an hour from Marrakech. We trained some Moroccan Air Force personnel on fire rescue for some new aircraft they purchased. We stayed at the Al Fassia Aguedal Hotel in Marrakech, and I had a great time." He then asked, "Were you born in Morocco?"

She raised her eyebrows, and her eyes reflected surprise that Martin had visited Marrakech. This revelation eased the pain of her shyness, and she replied with a pleased smile, "No. I'm an American citizen. I was born in Augusta."

"Well, Adeelah, I hope you'll find your work rewarding here. If there's anything I can do for you, just let me know."

Her eyes inadvertently flirted with him, and she replied, "Thank you so much."

Oblivious to the world, they remained standing, smiling, and gazing into each other's eyes until Sarah intervened. "We better get going."

As they drove back to City Hall, Sarah asked, "So, what did you think of Martin?"

Her lips formed a girlish smile, and she rolled her eyes. "I must say, I find him amazingly attractive–both dressed and undressed. And he was the most cordial of the people you introduced me to today. Is he married?"

Adeelah surprised herself that she would ask such a question–not a question a Muslim woman should be asking about a non-Muslim man. In her mind, she pondered, *What was I thinking*?

Sarah responded to the question she heard–not the question in Adeelah's mind, "Nope, he's very single. And I think every single woman in City Hall has her eye on him, as you might imagine. The way you two stood gazing at each other, I'm wondering if you'll be among them."

"Probably not an option for me. It's just not compatible with our Muslim culture for me to be interested in a non-Muslim man. Not only that, my father is negotiating a wedding proposal with a friend of the family in Rabat, Morocco. So, my future is kind of laid out for me."

"Do you know this guy from Morocco?"

"No. His name is Fahim Bakkari. I know he's a physician, we've exchanged some emails, but I've never met him."

Sarah tilted her head in contemplation. "I don't know if I could handle that. How do you feel about it?"

"The truth is, I'm very reluctant about marrying a man before I have the opportunity to know him thoroughly, which is not likely to occur."

"Will your family force you to marry him?"

"No. Islamic law doesn't permit forced marriages. But they will probably put a lot of pressure on me to make the commitment to marry him."

In her mind, Sarah was concerned Adeelah might not be the long-term manager which the city hoped for, so she asked, "If you were to marry this guy, would you move to Morocco?"

"That would be a real possibility, which is another reason why I'm reluctant about marrying him. I have no intention of leaving the United States."

Adeelah's response alleviated Sarah's concern.

When they arrived back at City Hall, it was close to quitting time.

"I guess I'll look forward to getting started tomorrow. Thanks for taking me around to meet people."

"You're welcome, Adeelah. I'll see you tomorrow. Take care."

As Adeelah drove home, she found she couldn't get her brief encounter with Martin out of her head. Of the people she met during the day, he was by far the one who most impressed her. She recalled his blue eyes which gazed so intently into hers, and passion stirred within her which breathlessly aroused her, a passion she savored. This sensual attraction caused her some distress, however, because she knew this attraction to a non-Muslim man was unacceptable for a Muslim woman.

Martin also found himself thinking about his encounter with Adeelah on his drive home to Augusta. Her enticing exotic smile, her gracious shyness, and the gaze of her deep, mysterious coal-black eyes warmly touched his soul. While he had many friends, he always enjoyed meeting people who did not fit a cookie-cutter mold, and this Moroccan woman was certainly not a cookie-cutter person.

Martin had no idea that much of the shyness he perceived in Adeelah was actually a manifestation of her inner struggle about being attracted to a non-Muslim man.

# Adeelah Struggles to Fit In

Adeelah, who lived with her parents in south Augusta, prudently left home at 7:00 AM–one hour before the normal 8:00 AM arrival time. Because of a car accident, traffic was unusually heavy. Consequently, the normal thirty-minute commute time stretched to about fifty minutes. So, she still managed to arrive ten minutes early at her office for her first actual workday.

She took a good look at her office to evaluate where she would now be spending a significant amount of her time. There was a nice window which overlooked the employee parking lot, where there was at least an abundance of trees to give some semblance of a view. She appreciated that the window let enough natural light come into the office to provide adequate illumination, so she would not have to use the overhead fluorescent lights all the time. She liked this because the natural light coming through the window was much more pleasant than that coming from the fluorescent lights. The position of the window with respect to her desk was also optimum because the sunlight would not produce excessive glare for her as she worked.

Her desk was configured in an L-shape, so part of the desk was against a solid wall. On this part of the desk, she had the benefit of four computer monitors, which pleased her. She knew she would be able to make full use of the four monitors. Her desk chair was positioned to allow her to sit with her back to another wall, and the other part of the desk faced toward the entry door. A table extended out from this part of the desk, which would allow her and her five employees to sit comfortably in her office for meetings.

On her desk was a desktop calculator with the typical roll of calculator tape. Most accountants feel they can't live without a desktop calculator. She, however, disconnected the calculator with the intention of removing it from her office. Given current computer technology and the convenience of computerized spreadsheets, she viewed desktop calculators as a relic of the past and had no use for them.

As she waited for her employees to arrive, she began thinking about what she would do to personalize her office. She planned to bring a lovely lamp, and she saw places for pictures and plants.

~.~

When the five employees, who were now under her supervision, arrived, Adeelah called a meeting with them. They sat at the table in her office, all of them with arms crossed, heads tilted, looking up at her with a wary stare.

She stood, leaned forward, rested her hands on her desk, and made direct eye contact with each of them. She found the tension in the room somewhat intimidating, as she said, "I look forward to working with all of you, and I hope we can enjoy a professional, productive, and happy working environment. There are two principles I want to emphasize as we start working together. I believe they will not only enhance your productivity but will also help you enjoy some satisfaction from your work life. First, I encourage you to exceed standards. I'll do my best to set standards which can be exceeded. Second, I encourage you to complete your work to the point where you can be proud of your performance. My experience tells me if you exceed standards and are proud of your work, you'll not only enjoy a satisfying working environment, but you can expect I'll be very satisfied with your performance as well. Moreover, it will be easy for me to rate your performance as excellent to outstanding. Any questions?"

Impressed with what she said, the five reluctant clerks unfolded their arms. Roger asked, "What shall we call you?"

"Please call me Adeelah."

Miriam rubbed her chin with some apprehension, which all five experienced, and asked, "Do you anticipate making any changes to our department?"

Adeelah directed her gaze at Miriam, smiled, raised her hand in a friendly gesture, and complimented her. "Good question, Miriam. I currently have no intentions of changing anything. I have no way of knowing at this point if anything needs to be changed. As we work together, it may become apparent to me that some changes will be necessary. The need for some changes may already be apparent to some of you. If this is the case, I'll welcome the opportunity to hear your views about needed changes. But for now, I don't want to change anything until I have a much better understanding of how our department operates."

Surprised with this Muslim woman's professionalism, everybody liked her response to Miriam's question. They relaxed some more. Nobody else asked additional questions.

Adeelah nodded her head and observed, "It appears there are no other questions. This is certainly not your last opportunity to ask questions. Miriam's question leads me to say this: I want you to understand that initially, I expect to work with all of you very closely–maybe more closely than you might like. Don't let this bother you. My goal is not to criticize you or to see if you're doing something wrong. As a matter of fact, I'll concentrate more on seeing where you're doing things right."

The idea that Adeelah would be looking over their shoulders closely resurrected more uneasiness among the five clerks, despite her assurance they had no reason to worry about her increased scrutiny.

Adeelah continued. "It's one thing to be knowledgeable about finance and accounting. It's another thing to know how finance and accounting functions occur in a specific organization. I enjoyed some good success in my previous position with the City of Augusta. By working closely with you initially, I hope to develop the knowledge and competence which will allow me to be effective in this finance department. As I gain a greater understanding of our operations, you'll find I won't look over your shoulder so closely. So, please, don't be overly concerned. That concludes our meeting for now. So, let's get to work. Roger, I'd like to talk to you a little more."

When the clerks understood the increased scrutiny would only be temporary, the anxiety they experienced subsided. Roger's demeanor, however, reflected some reluctance about a one-on-one conversation with Adeelah. He slumped in his chair and struggled to make eye contact with her.

Adeelah did not perceive him to be lacking in self-confidence. So, she concluded that maybe he was not very happy to be working for her. After the others departed, she remarked, "Roger, I understand you applied for the position of finance director, and I also know you'll soon graduate with your bachelor's degree in accounting. Congratulations. It would please me to attend your graduation ceremony."

Her kind comments put him more at ease, and he relaxed some as he said, "Thank you."

"I asked the human resources director about your qualifications and potential to function as a finance director. Her response was: You certainly have the potential, but she was concerned you lack the necessary qualifications and experience. During our conversation, she suggested to me that a good next step for you would be to become an assistant finance director, and I concur with her opinion."

Roger's demeanor improved. He sat up in his chair and leaned forward.

"Given the size of our staff here, the need for an assistant finance director position will continue to be unlikely. Nevertheless, because I understand your aspirations for greater responsibility, I'll try to give you projects I believe will help prepare you for an assistant finance director position. Please take seriously the two principles I emphasized earlier. When you eventually identify a suitable assistant finance director position, exceeding standards here and achieving performance you can be proud of will make it easy for me to recommend you wholeheartedly for such a position, and I'll be happy to make such a recommendation. Will you cooperate with me on this endeavor?"

Adeelah's generous promise immediately brightened his countenance, and Roger beamed. "Yes, of course. And I thank you for taking the time to discuss this matter with me."

She rejoiced that she might be able to help him with his aspirations. She smiled, nodded her head, and assured him, "You're welcome."

Thus, Adeelah began her duties as finance director for the City of Waynesboro, Georgia. Whatever their initial impressions of Adeelah were, her subordinates were increasingly impressed with her and enjoyed working with her.

As she completed her first month with the city, she was pleased her subordinates turned out to be competent, and they took her counsel to heart. She was always quick to commend her people for good work. She knew, when the time came to correct performance, they would be much more receptive to her corrective actions, after having seen how she appreciated the good things they were doing.

As they continued to work together under Adeelah's supervision, finance department members' productivity improved, and they became a more cohesive team. They made several suggestions to improve the effectiveness and efficiency of the department. Adeelah was careful not to make quick changes in department operations. However, in addition to implementing many of her subordinates' suggestions, she also initiated some of her own changes, which the City Manager and other department heads welcomed.

Adeelah's only concern was that she did not enjoy the camaraderie she had in her former employment. People were cordial and respectful, but she worried that she was not wholeheartedly accepted as a team player among the other department heads. She felt like an outsider. She clearly understood it might take predominantly Christian co-workers some time to get used to the presence of a Muslim in their midst. Still, she was eager to demonstrate that her religion would be no impediment to close and satisfying working relationships.

The one person who had not treated her as an outsider and made her feel most welcome was Martin, the fire chief. But his office was located at the larger of the city's two fire stations. So, she rarely saw him, except during weekly staff meetings. During these meetings, they increasingly caught each other's glances with nearly imperceptible smiles on their faces–glances which shifted away quickly when their eyes met but subtly communicated their attraction to one another.

Since most of the city management staff ate lunch at their desks, opportunities for her to interact with them were infrequent and limited, for the most part, to these weekly staff meetings conducted by the city manager.

Adeelah asked her father, Omar El-Sayed, for his advice.

Omar's strong character could be very intimidating. He was a serious, formal, and prudent man, and he abided by traditions and old-school values, which uphold patience, hard work, honor, and social and cultural responsibility. Because of his strong character, even among the Muslim community, there was a tendency for him to be misunderstood. However, Adeelah loved him, respected him, and trusted his sage advice.

In response to her question, he counseled her. "Your hard work will ultimately earn you respect and the acceptance you seek. You must be patient, my daughter. I suggest you watch for opportunities outside of work to interact with your co-workers and take full advantage of such opportunities. You have the personality to win them over. So, it's just a question of time. Is there a lunchroom for employees?"

"No. Most employees eat at their desks."

"Instead of eating at your desk, maybe you should go out for lunch. Is there a restaurant close by?"

"There is a restaurant called The Good Day Café, which is only a block away from City Hall. On my first day, Sarah, the Human Resources Director, took me there for lunch. The food is good, and I liked the ambiance."

"Then I suggest you eat lunch there regularly. You may want to invite other department heads to join you. You have to be in places where you can interact, not only with your co-workers, but also with other people in the community."

Grateful for her dad's advice, she felt more optimistic and promised, "I'll do that, Dad. Thank you."

While she had not broken the ice with her fellow department heads, she quickly gained respect from her subordinates, and they spread the word among other city employees about how much better the finance department operated. All of them liked Adeelah. She soon established herself as a competent professional.

## MARTIN ENCOUNTERS ADEELAH DURING LUNCH

Adeelah followed her dad's advice and began eating lunch daily at the Good Day Café. Other customers' stares in her direction made it apparent they were talking about her. Adeelah's manner of dress, especially her headscarf or hijab, made it evident to them that she was a Muslim–that she was different. Self-conscious about this non-verbal reaction, Adeelah went out of her way to show herself friendly, especially with restaurant employees. For the last couple of weeks, she always ate alone. Today, that would change.

The waitress had just brought her a menu, when Martin, the fire chief, walked in. When he saw Adeelah, his face brightened up, he walked over to her table, and said, "Adeelah. *As-salāmu ʿalaykum.* (The peace of God be with you.) How are things going for you?"

Adeelah's face also brightened up, and she smiled from ear to ear. "Your greeting certainly surprises me. *Wa alaykumu s-salam.* (And the peace of God be with you as well.) Things are going well for the most part. How are you?"

"I'm doing well."

"So, you speak some Arabic?"

"Not really. I just learned a few words when I worked in Morocco. Do you mind if I join you?"

With a touch of shyness contrasted with her bright smile, which made the ambient light in the restaurant pale in comparison for Martin, Adeelah replied, "I'd be pleased if you would."

Martin sat down at the table with Adeelah and motioned to the waitress to bring him a menu. All eyes in the restaurant focused on this Muslim woman and their fire chief, as they now sat together. The café now boomed with chattering whispers.

Adeelah felt Martin's gaze as he looked into her eyes, a feeling which made her perceive he understood her thoughts. The usual bustle of activity in the café suddenly sounded far away. All she could hear was the throbbing beat of her heart. The intensity of the moment made her heart flutter. In her mind, she wondered, *Why does he affect me this way*?

Martin recalled how well-dressed Adeelah was when he met her at the fire station, and he was struck once again with how attractive she was. Her attractive, light olive-colored face was framed by a solid pink hijab. She wore a black blouse with a hot pink skirt which reached down to her mid-calf. She was not just attractive. Martin found her exotically attractive.

Martin wore the same quasi-uniform, which he wore when they first met. The waitress brought him a menu, and Martin reached out with one hand to accept the menu, while he also removed the Panama hat which he wore. From time to time, he would raise his hand to run his fingers through his dark blonde hair. Adeelah could not help but notice his bulging muscular arms, which more than filled up his polo shirt's short sleeves. His Herculean image captivated her, and she could not resist his deep blue eyes.

Adeelah looked at the menu and asked, "What do you like to eat here?"

"They make a great Reuben."

She looked up at him with a coy smile on her face, shook her head, and, without taking her eyes off of him, she replied with an innocent-sounding voice, "I don't think I've ever had a Reuben. What's it like?"

His eyes were locked on hers, and he was captivated by the radiance of Adeelah's face. "You've never had a Reuben! Do you like to try new foods?"

"Yes. I always like trying new things."

Martin showed her the menu. "As you can see in the menu, it's a sandwich piled high with corn beef, oozing with sauerkraut, thousand island dressing, and melted Swiss cheese served on toasted rye bread."

"Maybe I'll give it a try."

With a broad smile, he replied, "Well, since you've never had one, I'll treat you to a Reuben."

Martin's unexpected offer prompted Adeelah to look up from the menu. She made eye contact with him again and grinned. "No. You don't have to do that."

They hypnotically gazed at each other, and Martin's smile intensified as he lightheartedly complained. "You won't deny me the pleasure of buying you lunch, will you?"

"If you put it that way, I guess not," Adeelah replied with a smile which went from coy to enticing.

The waitress took the order for two Reubens and two Cokes.

Martin commented, "I hear good things about your finance department since you took over. I hope you're happy to be a part of the city."

His comment interrupted her euphoria. "I feel the department functions to my satisfaction. I like the people who work for me, and I'm pleased with their productivity. However, I must say I haven't had many opportunities to mingle with other department heads."

With an impish grin, Martin shrugged his shoulders and tilted his head to one side. "Well, I hope you'll be pleased to mingle with this one."

Her smile went from enticing to foxy, her euphoria resumed, and unconsciously her eyes flirted with him. "I'm glad you've joined me."

The waitress brought the food, and Adeelah and Martin each bowed in silent prayer to give thanks for the meal.

Martin paused and said, "I'm curious to know what a Muslim prays when a meal is served. I'll tell you what, you tell me what you prayed, and I'll tell you what I prayed."

Adeelah, surprised by Martin's curiosity, responded, "My prayer is, 'Oh Allah, the most gracious, the most merciful. Bless the food You have provided us and save us from the punishment of Hell.'"

Martin observed, "You and I could've prayed that prayer together. It's not so different from my prayer, which was, 'Dear God. Thank you for this food which you have blessed us with and help us to honor you in all we do. Amen.'"

"I like your prayer too. And, as you just said, we could've prayed the words of your prayer together as well. I assume you're a Christian."

"You assume correctly. I don't know about you, but I find it rather interesting that both of our separate prayers are prayers we could've prayed together." Then Martin leaned forward. "I perceive you take your faith in God seriously."

"I absolutely do. Do you?"

"Oh yes. As a matter of fact, I earned a degree in Christian theology. However, I must tell you, my experience working with Muslim friends I met in Morocco significantly affected my religious perspective."

She tilted her head and raised her eyebrows. "Really! How so?"

"Well, for one thing, it prompted me to read the Holy Quran. And I'd find it fascinating to talk to you someday to get your reaction about my experience in Morocco."

Adeelah was surprised to hear Martin had read the Quran. She had never read the entire Quran herself, and it impressed her that Martin, a Christian, would take the time to read it.

Martin put his elbows on the table, held his head up with his fists, and changed the subject. "I must confess I've never had a conversation with a Muslim woman before. What should I know about Muslim women?"

Adeelah took a sip of her coke, looked at Martin out of the corner of her eye, and responded, "You might be surprised to know there's nothing so different about Muslim women compared with women in general. Our families are important to us. We may dress more conservatively than many contemporary women, but we want to look good in our clothes, just like any other woman. I, like many educated women, am active professionally. And, like many women, Muslim women tend to be more chatty than men."

Martin listened with fascination as Adeelah painted the air with her words. He smiled and quipped, "Well, I guess you don't come from some other planet after all."

Adeelah's eyes showed she enjoyed their conversation. She laughed gleefully and asked, "Did you think I might come from Mars or something?"

"No. I'm just having fun with you." Adeelah's comments about Muslim women prompted Martin to say, "There's one thing I observe about you which makes you unique among most women in this area. You dress much more attractively than most women."

She touched her hijab to partially cover her face and blushed. "Thank you. While most Muslim women dress modestly, we, like many women, pay attention to what is fashionable."

As they finished their lunch, Martin asked, "So how did you like your Reuben?"

She cleaned her mouth with her napkin and laid it on the table. "I liked it. You've certainly made me a Reuben fan. There will undoubtedly be more Reubens in my life. Thank you for treating me to lunch."

"You're certainly welcome. You know, when I worked in Morocco, I recall that many Moroccan women didn't wear a hijab. Since you are of Moroccan descent, I'm interested to know why you choose to wear one. Now before you respond, let me say, you look very good with a hijab. I'm just curious."

She leaned forward, as if to reveal a secret, looked directly into Martin's eyes, and confessed, "Please don't think poorly of me, but I find men rarely hit on me when I wear a hijab. It isn't that I don't want men to be interested in me. I just don't care for the obnoxious way some men act toward women they don't know but find attractive."

"I get it. You're trying to avoid men who don't behave themselves very well." Martin then lightheartedly quipped, "Do I presume correctly you have hair under your hijab?"

Adeelah burst into laughter. "Of course!"

"What does your hair look like?"

She reached for her hijab again. "It's about shoulder-length, black, not totally straight, but not too curly either," she shyly replied.

Their joy-filled faces revealed they were enjoying themselves immensely, and Martin asked, "So, if I behave myself, is there some chance I may one day see what you look like without a hijab?"

Adeelah, desperately trying to resist the tempting attraction she was feeling for Martin, reminded herself, *A Muslim woman has no business enjoying the company of a non-Muslim man.* However, her efforts to resist temptation were not going well at all. She liked Martin, and she smiled playfully. "Do you suggest we should see each other again?"

"Since you asked, Adeelah, I'd very much like to see you again. How about you?"

Adeelah kicked herself for asking such a question. She opened her mouth to say no, but that word would not come out. What escaped from her mouth instead was, "Yes."

"Fantastic! Where do you live?"

She bit down on her lip, hesitated, and reluctantly replied, "South Augusta."

With a gleam in his eyes, Martin paid no attention to her reluctance. "Great! So do I. Shall I pick you up at your home?"

She rolled her eyes, frowned, and nodded. "That would definitely be a bad idea. My parents wouldn't understand at all if a man, especially a non-Muslim man, came to pick me up at our home."

Martin raised his eyebrows, tilted his head, and tried to read the expression on her face. "That complicates things. You won't chicken out, will you?"

"No. But I must tell you I'm asking for trouble by agreeing to go out with you."

Martin shrugged his shoulders. "So, we need to be discreet. How about a picnic at the Augusta Canal?"

"That sounds discreet."

"Okay. Let's meet at the Discovery Center at Enterprise Mill at the canal. Will ten o'clock, Saturday morning work for you?"

"Yeah. I think it will."

"Perfect! I'll look forward to it."

Martin paid the check. Adeelah returned to City Hall. Martin returned to the fire station.

## CONFIDING IN CLOSE FRIENDS

When Adeelah got in her car to go home, she called her friend, Taslima.

Taslima Abidar was not just any friend. She was Adeelah's best friend. Of Palestinian descent, Adeelah appreciated that she was lively, fun, and enjoyed being the center of attention. Much more liberal-minded than Adeelah, she was warm, generous, friendly, sympathetic, and always concerned for others' well-being. Adeelah valued her opinions and loved her vivacious personality. Her free spirit was contagious, and she continually urged Adeelah to be a little more adventurous.

"Hello, Adeelah! What's new?"

Adeelah was happy to hear her voice come through the car speakers, and she confessed, "I think I'm getting into trouble."

"Really! Serious trouble or fun trouble?"

She replied with a timid voice, "I'm afraid it might be both."

Taslima giggled, and with an eager, exuberant voice which expressed curiosity, she guessed, "You've met a guy!"

"You sure got that right!"

She giggled again. "So, tell me about him. I can hardly wait to hear!"

"His name is Martin. He's the fire chief for the City of Waynesboro. I met him, along with other department heads, on the first day when I started my new job there. Today I went to a nearby restaurant for lunch, and he came into the restaurant. When he spotted me, he walked over and said, '*As-salāmu ʿalaykum*,' and asked if he could join me for lunch. He ended up buying me lunch."

"So, he's Muslim?"

"No!" she hesitated. "That's the problem. He's a Christian, and he takes his faith seriously. He even earned a degree in Christian theology. Some time ago, he worked in Morocco. So, he knows a few Arabic words, which explains his greeting."

"Oh my goodness! Maybe you are asking for trouble. Don't tell me he's asked you out."

Adeelah hesitated again. "As a matter of fact, he has."

"And you accepted?"

With a tone of regret and distress in her voice, Adeelah tilted her head to the side. "Yes. I did."

"So, what's he like?"

With a measured voice which was invaded with a touch of exhilaration, Adeelah responded, "He's an impressive man! He's about six feet tall, with an incredible muscular body, dark blonde hair, and deep blue eyes. To make matters worse, he has the most charming personality. I felt so at ease with him during lunch, and I thoroughly enjoyed being with him."

"Will you mention anything to your parents?"

Her voice quivered. "Not a chance!"

"What are you going to do?"

"We're going on a picnic at the Augusta Canal on Saturday."

"Are you bringing the picnic lunch?"

"We didn't talk about that. He invited me. I'll see what he comes up with."

"That should be interesting. Do you think this will be the beginning of a relationship?"

Questions about her judgment invaded her mind, and Adeelah confided, "I could honestly see myself in a relationship with him, if it weren't for our religious differences. So, I'm not too optimistic about dating him on a regular basis. I just don't know if I can resist the temptation which draws me to him, even though I know a relationship with him would cause a small war with my family. But I really like him so far. What do you think I should do?"

In a more subdued tone, Taslima replied, "My liberal point of view suggests you give him a chance since you like him so much. On the other hand, the potential religious and family opposition may be more than you want to handle."

Adeelah hesitated. "Coming from you, that worries me a lot."

"Well, it's just one date. Go have fun. But you need to be prepared to walk away."

Conflicted, when she got off the phone, Adeelah prayed, "Oh Allah, the most gracious, the most merciful, please give me wisdom about this matter, and lead me in accordance with Your will."

When Adeelah arrived home, she changed into her running clothes and prepared for her daily three-mile run. As part of her routine, she removed the small holster from her purse, which contained a vial of pepper spray, and attached it to the belt on her exercise pants. Omar, her father, gave her the pepper spray to carry in her purse for self-defense purposes. Adeelah thought her father was overly protective of her. However, she felt she had good reason to carry the pepper spray with her when she ran because several people in the neighborhood also ran and took their large dogs with them. And some dogs occasionally showed themselves to be aggressive.

As she ran, she pondered her conversation with Taslima. She knew only too well her family would never tolerate her relationship with a Christian man. However, in her two brief encounters with him, there were so many things about Martin she found attractive, triggering sensations which produced a lovely euphoria in her which fueled her desire to be with him. She gave serious thought about canceling the date, but her desire to be with him quickly overpowered any thought of doing such an obviously prudent thing.

~.~

Just as Adeelah talked to her friend, Taslima, Martin also called his friend, James.

"Martin, how are things going?"

James Landers, a committed Christian, was very faithful to his church. Both he and Martin took seriously the traditions, doctrines, and conservative evangelical Christian values promoted by their church. James and Martin had been close friends for many years, and they frequently discussed doctrinal issues, especially in the Bible class they both attended at Friendship Community Church.

"Things are going well. However, I need to talk to you about something which concerns me. Do you have a minute?"

"Sure. What's on your mind?"

"Not long ago, I met a new city employee–a young woman. Her name is Adeelah. She's the new finance director for the city. Today I ran into her at the Good Day Café, and we had lunch together. I enjoyed her company, and she appeared to enjoy mine. So, I asked her out."

"That doesn't sound so bad. What's to be concerned about?"

Martin hesitated before he answered. "She's a Muslim."

"And you knew that when you asked her out?"

Martin hesitated again. "Yes. I did."

"You know you're asking for a bucket of worms, don't you?"

Martin responded with a voice which crescendoed and became spirited. "I understand that potential exists. However, not only is she a very attractive woman, there's an elusive facet about her which draws me to her. So, while I can't quite put my finger on what prompts this compelling attraction which I feel for her, I find I can't resist it. The fact is, I have no desire to resist it. I really look forward to taking her out."

"Well, you know, the biggest issue is, she worships a false god."

"I know that is a common view among evangelical Christians."

"And you believe otherwise?"

"You know, we both prayed separately before eating our meals, and I asked her what she prayed. In addition to asking God to bless her food, she also asked God to save her from the punishment of Hell. That, along with the experience I had with the Muslims I worked with in Morocco during my military days, leads me to believe Muslims do, in fact, worship the same God as we do. And Adeelah appears to take her faith in God every bit as seriously as you and I do."

With a voice which expressed concern for his friend, James replied, "I have to tell you, I don't think you'll get much support from our church if you start dating a Muslim woman."

Martin responded with firm resolve, "Well, I will see her on Saturday. I'm not sure where this is going–maybe nowhere. I do know I like this woman."

James promised, "I'll keep you in my prayers."

"Please do that."

Conflicted, when he got off the phone, he prayed, "Dear God. Please give me wisdom about this matter, and lead me in accordance with Your will. Amen."

# A Walk in the Park

On his way to the Augusta Canal, Martin stopped at Popeyes Louisiana Kitchen to get a bucket of chicken which included a side of rice and beans, a side of coleslaw, and some biscuits. Before leaving his apartment, he had also prepared a large thermos with sweetened iced tea.

He arrived at the Augusta Canal just before 10:00 AM and parked his yellow Ford Mustang at the Discovery Center at Enterprise Mill. This April spring day was superb for a picnic. The sun was shining with plenty of blue sky and white puffy cumulus clouds, which produced the shapes of puppies, kittens, lions, tigers, and bears–among other happy images, which no sculptor could possibly improve upon. There was a cool, pleasant breeze, birds were joyously singing, and the air was fragrant with the scent of new spring foliage.

Martin closed his driver-side window, and, as he got out of the car, a lime-green Kia Soul pulled into a parking place, and Adeelah stepped out. Adeelah had no trouble spotting Martin. His uniquely muscled body made him stand out easily among just about anybody. He wore a pair of khaki Levies, a maroon polo shirt, and his white Panama hat. She would quickly learn he always wore a white Panama hat.

Martin saw her walking toward him, but he wasn't sure who he was looking at–Adeelah arrived without her hijab. She wore blue jeans and a light blue long-sleeved blouse. As she got closer, there was no longer any doubt in his mind. Martin indeed found Adeelah attractive before, but now that he saw her with her shoulder-length black hair, he found her enchantingly beautiful.

As she arrived, Martin removed his hat and boyishly ran his fingers through his blond hair. The bright smile on his face and the clear sparkle in his blue eyes revealed how happy he was to see her, in a way which melted Adeelah's heart. With the inaudible sweet song his smiling face was singing to Adeelah, Martin exclaimed, "Good morning! So, you've deemed me worthy to look upon your beautiful face without your hijab."

In fact, Adeelah omitted the hijab, so it wouldn't be so obvious that a Muslim woman was meeting with a non-Muslim man. Nevertheless, she smiled gleefully with a spirited joy which blossomed on her Moroccan face, a smile which showed she was very pleased to be back in his presence. These non-verbal manifestations said so much more than her actual words, which simply said, "Good morning."

Martin put his hat back on, and they began their hike along the canal. "I know a very nice place for our picnic," Martin commented as he led the way. As they approached a place along the canal which required a steep step up, Martin placed his hand on the small of Adeelah's back to help her up. Adeelah's heart fluttered when he touched her for the first time, and she felt as if a surge of electricity made her body tingle. No man had ever touched her that way before. She very much liked the sensation of him touching her.

They arrived at the picnic location. It was secluded enough to give them some intimate privacy, but not so secluded to make Adeelah feel uncomfortable with this dream guy which she barely knew. It was only about 10:30 now–too early for lunch. They spread a blanket out on the ground and sat down facing each other.

Where they sat, the water in the canal was like a quiet pool. Just beyond them, the canal's current flowed over some nearby rocks to produce a pleasant melodic sound of rushing water which embellished their mutual enjoyment. The canopy of trees filtered the sun in a dazzling way, which produced a glimmering light show which sparkled and danced on the water. They were entertained by two blue jays, which repeatedly called to each other. Blue and yellow flowers decorated the varying hues of the green grassy knoll where they sat, like a tapestry which reminded Adeelah of the famous Moroccan rugs from her native land.

Martin commented, "I recall you told me you live with your parents. I suspect they don't know you're with me."

His words touched a nerve. The look on her face revealed her inner distress about what he said. Adeelah shook her head and confided, "They don't know. They think I went to visit my friend, Taslima. And if we decide to see each other with any frequency, I'm not sure if I know how to tell them about us. I don't know how you feel, but I'm concerned we shouldn't let this thing go any further than today."

Martin stared into the air and frowned. "I haven't said anything to my parents either. It's a little easier for me since I don't live with them. I do understand why your family would be reluctant to accept our relationship, which may be more serious than any concerns I have with my family. What would it take to win your parents over?"

"You underestimate my family. Here's the problem. I must tell you, my parents are negotiating with a family in Morocco to get me engaged to marry their son, Fahim Bakkari. He's a physician and lives in Rabat, the capital of Morocco. If I were to marry him, it's quite certain I would have to move to Rabat. Even more important, my parents would adamantly oppose any relationship I might have with a Christian man."

The disappointment on his face revealed his crestfallen countenance, "That is a problem! How do you feel about Fahim?"

She wrung her hands and lowered her head. "Although I'm sure he's an honorable man, I've never met him, and I really wouldn't like to leave the United States to live in Morocco."

"Can your parents force you to marry Fahim?"

"No. Islam forbids forced marriages. But they can put a lot of pressure on me, especially if they learn I'm seeing a Christian man."

Martin stroked his chin, pondered her words, and commented, "Between a potential marriage engagement and the fact I'm a Christian, I perceive the biggest problem is that I'm not a Muslim."

"No doubt about that. How will your parents react if they learn you're seeing a Muslim woman?"

Martin threw a flat stone, which skipped across the surface of the water. "They would also oppose our relationship, but I don't think their opposition would be so strong."

She gazed downward with a feeling of melancholy and reiterated with hesitancy in her voice, "Since we barely know each other, it's somewhat premature to be discussing these issues now. But the fact is, I think it's prudent we have this conversation now. As I said before, we might be better off not to let this thing go any further than today."

Martin took Adeelah's hand in his, which caught her by surprise. He gazed into her eyes, and countered, "That would certainly be a prudent course of action. The question is: What do you and I want? Let me tell you, even on the day Sarah introduced you to me, there was something about you which drew me to you. It was obvious we had eyes for each other during meetings with the city manager. I thoroughly enjoyed having lunch with you the other day, and I'm so happy to spend this time with you now. I, for one, would like to count on seeing more of you."

Martin continued to hold Adeelah's hand in his, which for her was a taboo, which she found to her liking. Knowing the difficulties they would experience if they continued to see each other, Adeelah was reluctant to admit it, but she also had no desire to stop this relationship, which was very much in its infancy. Martin could see in her face that she was struggling with this dilemma.

She affectionately squeezed Martin's hand. "I confess I feel the same way as you do."

Martin pointed out, "It's my understanding a Muslim is a person who worships God and has submitted his life to God. By that definition, I could define myself as a Muslim. I take my faith in God very seriously, and you tell me you do too. And I'll tell you, the fact we each take our faith in God seriously is very important to me."

Adeelah rolled her eyes. "That's all very good, but I doubt my parents, and the Muslim community in which I'm very involved, would accept your claim to be a Muslim, given you are what the Holy Quran calls one of the people of the book. How would your church react if you were to openly call yourself a Muslim?"

Martin pursed his lips and raised his eyebrows. "Without seeing how you and I just defined the word, they would certainly not react in a favorable way."

Adeelah shrugged her shoulders. "So, both of us face the same dilemma."

Still holding Adeelah's hand, Martin suggested, "So, we have a difficult decision to make, but let's not make this decision now. May I share with you the experience I had when I worked in Morocco?"

The change in subject made Adeelah sigh with relief. She leaned forward and made eye contact with Martin, which showed her eagerness to listen to him, and said, "I'd love to hear it."

Martin released Adeelah's hand, so he would be free to gesture with his hands as he responded. "You'll recall I told you about my friendship with some Muslim firefighters I worked with in Morocco. When I asked them what they prayed during their five daily prayer times, they quoted the first Surah in the Holy Quran, in which they asked Allah to guide them in the straight way. Their response had a profound impact on me."

"Really! How so?"

"Well, Christianity teaches one must accept Jesus Christ as Savior in order to go to Heaven. But as a Christian, I also believe if we pray and ask God for anything which is in agreement with His will, God will grant our petition. So, I concluded: Certainly, it is God's will that all of us should follow the straight way. So, God must be granting my Muslim friends' petitions, and He must, therefore, be guiding them in the straight way. And the straight way certainly wouldn't lead them to eternal punishment. So, it must lead them to eternal life in Heaven. Consequently, I believe this Muslim prayer is a prayer for salvation."

With a puzzled look on her face, Adeelah remarked, "I must say. I never looked at it that way."

"Well Adeelah, I, for one, rejoice to know that you, as a Muslim, and I, as a Christian, share a common faith in God, even though we have some things we understand and believe differently."

Amazed at the depth of what Martin shared with her, and that he found common ground between their two religions, Adeelah remarked, "You sure have given this a lot of thought, haven't you?"

With a happy voice, he proclaimed, "I have. And these thoughts lead me to believe that, just possibly, God may be pleased you and I have come to know each other. The fact is, when you shared with me the words you prayed when we ate lunch together, you strengthened my thoughts on this issue. Because, in your prayer, you specifically asked God to save you from the punishment of Hell. That is an even more explicit prayer to God for salvation. And Adeelah, I believe God hears your prayers and grants your petition for salvation."

That comment brought a tear to her eye. And, if she felt drawn to him before, she now felt a connection to him which was even stronger.

This serious conversation produced a different, peculiar, increasing intensity which invaded them–not unpleasant, but an intensity which prompted Adeelah to take a deep breath. So, she changed the subject and said, "Well, after such a thought-provoking conversation, I'm hungry. What's for lunch?"

The intensity promptly subsided. Martin raised happy eyebrows and smiled. "I hope you like chicken. I have a bucket of Popeye's chicken with beans and rice, coleslaw, and biscuits. And I brought a thermos of sweet iced tea."

"Sounds good. Let's eat."

Their joy of being together took over, and they conveniently put their serious conversations out of their minds. As they brought out the food, their hands inadvertently touched from time to time. Both found they craved this contact, and such contact became discreetly more intentional.

Martin asked, "May I ask God's blessing on our food?"

Adeelah happily replied, "Of course."

"Most merciful Allah, dear God Almighty, we thank you for providing us with this food and all the blessings of this life. We come to you as two people from different religions–I, a Christian, Adeelah, a Muslim. But we rejoice to see we both seek to worship you faithfully and in truth. Dear God, we like each other, and we like being together. Our prayer is that we can continue to enjoy this relationship, which is currently in its infancy. You know the challenges we'll face. We pray you will bless our relationship, help us to overcome these challenges, and lead us to take the right path. Help us to live our lives in accordance with your will and to honor you in all we do. Amen."

With a tear in her eye, Adeelah looked at this man she was with and agreed wholeheartedly with every word of his prayer. And so, she responded, "Inshallah." (As God wills.)

Their conversation, as they enjoyed their lunch, was not so deep now. And Martin, with a broad smile on his face and eyes filled with hopeful expectation, commented, "I was hoping we could meet for lunch this week."

Still reluctant about doing anything to encourage an ongoing relationship, Adeelah asked, "When?"

Still smiling, Martin nodded and responded, "Every day would be fine with me."

Adeelah was about to pick up another piece of chicken, but she stopped. "Every day?"

"Am I asking too much?"

"I guess not," she admitted, "But I can't have lunch with you on Friday. I take a late lunch every Friday, so I can attend the 1:30 prayer services at the Islamic Center of South Augusta."

Martin smiled again and shrugged his shoulders. "Then I guess we'll just have to make plans for next Saturday."

Adeelah tilted her head, looked at him out of the corner of her eye, and smiled with a touch of mischievousness. "We'll see. Let's talk about that during our lunches together."

After a splendid afternoon, they now reluctantly made their way back to the Discovery Center. As they walked, Adeelah and Martin paused, gazed into each other's eyes, and she slipped her hand into his–a hand which happily accepted hers. When they arrived at their cars, each went their separate ways. And there was only one thing on their minds. Lunch on Monday!

# SUNDAY'S SERMON

The church orchestra just finished playing their music selection while the plate was passed for the offering. Martin enjoyed playing his violin in the orchestra. The orchestra members now took their seats among the congregation, and Martin sat with his parents. A young, attractive female soloist stood to sing. She had long, shoulder-length, brunette hair and wore a long white dress which nicely enhanced her slender figure. She wore a corsage of tiny red and white roses which adorned her dress. A professionally produced soundtrack accompanied her as she sang the song, *I Sing the Mighty Power of God.* As he listened to the song, it occurred to Martin that Muslims would easily find the song's words compatible with their beliefs.

She finished her song, and Pastor Mark Sawyer stood to deliver his sermon. He became the pastor at Friendship Community Church about five years ago, and he was a gifted speaker. A well-educated man, he was in his mid-thirties, and today he was well-dressed in a dark, two-piece suit. He looked very much like a successful businessman. Martin enjoyed hearing him speak.

Today, however, he came to a place in his sermon where he was very critical of Muslims, calling Islam a religion of hate. He emphatically claimed Allah was a false god and not the God of the Bible. At one point, he shook an ominous finger in the air and warned, "Let me say this without any hesitation. Islam is a false religion, based on a false book, which was written by a false prophet." He went on to state that Islam promotes violence against all who will not become Muslims.

The pastor's words disturbed Martin, and he found it difficult to sit still in his seat. Having read the Quran, he knew the Quran did not permit the forced conversion of anyone, and those passages which allowed for violence against non-Muslims stipulated that such violence was only justified if non-Muslims initiated the violence. Moreover, he knew many passages in the Quran promote tolerance toward Christians and Jews, who are referred to in the Quran as people of the book.

He felt a sense of foreboding, and he could see how Adeelah and he would undoubtedly face some turbulent times if they continued their relationship–from both sides, Christian and Muslim.

After church, Martin, his parents, and his sister, Priscilla, had dinner at a local restaurant. As they viewed their menus, Martin asserted, "I don't agree with the pastor's criticism of Islam and Muslims."

Everybody lowered their menus and stared at Martin with bewildered looks on their faces. His mother, Ellen, responded, "Surely you know Muslims don't trust Jesus Christ as their Lord and Savior. How can you question the pastor's affirmation that Islam is a false religion when Muslims don't even believe Jesus is God?"

Martin's jaw tightened, and he leaned forward. "Muslims don't use that specific language about salvation, but they do recognize their need for salvation. And they specifically ask God to lead them down the right path, and they specifically ask God to save them from the punishment of Hell. These are prayers of salvation."

He went on to argue that Muslim's rejection of the deity of Christ does not mean they worship a false god.

As they enjoyed their meal, David, Martin's father, contemplated Martin's comments. He cleaned his mouth with his napkin and asked, "What about all the Muslim terrorists?"

Martin shot back. "There are Muslim terrorists. But they make up a very small number of the Muslim population. The Muslims I worked with in Morocco were good people who took their faith in God seriously. There was nothing violent about them. I count them as friends, and we got along very well."

Priscilla, Martin's sister, put her fork down and tilted her head, "Why do you feel so strongly about this?"

Not ready to reveal his nascent relationship with Adeelah, he vehemently replied, "Because my experience has taught me differently. And I find it sad that so many groups, which take their faith in God seriously, can't have fellowship with one another. This occurs not only between Christians and Muslims, but also between Christians and Jews, between Catholics and Protestants, and even among different Protestant groups."

Ellen put her coffee cup on the table and commented, "I don't see how Christians could possibly have fellowship with Muslims."

Martin folded his napkin and placed it on the table. "Well, I'll tell you what, the City of Waynesboro just hired a Muslim woman, and I have met her. She seems like a very nice person, I believe she takes her faith in God seriously, and I like her. I have to believe God is not pleased with the animosity which exists between Christians and Muslims. My experience is: Yes. We can have fellowship with Muslims."

Martin felt he stated his position well because nobody said much more. He hoped that maybe he had laid some groundwork for the day in which his family might meet Adeelah.

## A Precarious Love Blossoms

On Monday, the morning hours advanced ever so slowly. Both Adeelah and Martin could hardly wait to get to the Good Day Café to eat lunch together. Adeelah arrived first. When Martin arrived, their smiles could not hide their eager desire to be together. Without even thinking about how responsive Adeelah might be, Martin hugged her. Initially surprised, Adeelah was responsive. She hugged him right back. Their warm embrace was short and somewhat timid, and both craved a longer, more intimate embrace. Both felt their embrace was a natural and right thing to do–a very necessary thing to do. Their brief embrace satisfied a passionate longing in their souls–a satisfaction which was destined for the two of them alone.

Martin was dressed in the city's usual fire department uniform, with his dark-colored trousers and his white tight-fitting Polo shirt. He also wore his omnipresent Panama hat. Adeelah looked enchantingly exotic with an exquisite, multicolored, floor-length dress which featured large patterns of red, blue, yellow, and black, accented with well-placed patches of white. Her white hijab contributed amazingly to her image of loveliness. She took Martin's breath away.

Martin grinned, "The way you look, maybe we should take the afternoon off and go dancing."

While Adeelah's eyes showed she was pleased with his comment, she shyly covered her broad smile with her hand, which revealed the same subtle shyness which was starting to have a pleasant, addictive effect on

Martin. In response to his comment, she socked him on the shoulder and facetiously scolded, "Do you really think we should do such an impetuous thing when we need to get back to work?"

With an impish grin on his face, he gazed into her eyes, put his right elbow on the table, and leaned his head on his fist. "Probably not. But what bliss it would be!"

As they waited for their food to come, Martin asked, "So, how did you spend your Sunday?"

"It was a rather quiet day, except my family sat down for our customary Sunday afternoon family dinner."

Happy to listen to her speak, he asked, "What did you eat?"

"Our dinner typically begins with a series of hot and cold salads, followed by a tagine. We always have bread. We also had lamb with couscous topped with meat and vegetables."

"I remember eating couscous when I was in Morocco, but what is tagine?"

"Tagine is meat fried with fresh coriander, onions, hot spices, and a little garlic, and it typically includes sheep's tail. You must try it someday."

Martin wrinkled his nose and exclaimed in jest, "Sounds rather exotic, especially the sheep's tail. But I'll try anything at least once."

Amused, Adeelah touched her hijab to ensure it was properly covering her hair. "So, how was your Sunday?"

"Sunday is always a busy day for me. I don't think I mentioned it, but I play the violin in my church's orchestra, and . . ."

Adeelah interrupted, "You surprise me. So, you're a musician?"

"Yeah. Playing my violin is one of the most rewarding things I do. Our church has both a morning and evening service every Sunday, and our orchestra plays during the offering, and we accompany the church choir for both services. I arrive for a short practice at 8:30 AM. We have Sunday School, followed by the morning worship service. The orchestra comes back at 4:30 in the afternoon for a more extensive practice, and the evening service ends between 7:30 and 8:00 PM. Throw in dinner with my family around noon, and you can see my Sundays are very busy."

As he spoke, Martin remembered the pastor's sermon, and he decided not to mention his pastor's very critical comments against Muslims.

"I had no idea you spent so much time in church."

"You mentioned you attend a mosque service on Friday afternoons. What is that service like?"

"As you know, Muslims observe five daily prayer times. The Friday afternoon prayers are virtually the same as the prayers performed during the rest of the week, except on Fridays the imam or prayer leader delivers a two-part sermon known as the khutbah, with a pause between the two parts of the sermon to allow for a time of personal prayer called du'a. Whoever in the community is considered the most learned person in matters of religion can serve as the imam, since there exists no official clergy in Islam. Unlike the several services you have on Sundays, this Friday service typically only lasts about 30 to 45 minutes."

As they finished their lunch, Martin brought up the plan to go out together on Saturday, as they discussed briefly during their picnic at the Augusta Canal. "I'd like to take you to Albert's Restaurant this Saturday. Have you been there before?"

Adeelah put her coffee cup on the table. "I've been there once. Do you really want to go to such an expensive restaurant?"

With hopeful anticipation, Martin leaned forward, touched her hand, and responded, "Well, our picnic was kind of an informal date, although it was a very memorable occasion for me. For our first formal date, I'd love to treat you to something very special, which for me symbolically expresses how very special you are becoming for me and how much I hope to enjoy your company going forward. And Albert's is definitely special. Would you prefer dinner around noon or early evening?"

Martin's touch aroused a tingling sensation in her. Flattered by his comment, and with a mischievous smile on her face, Adeelah flirted with him. "I haven't said yes or no, yet."

Smiling right back at her, Martin leaned forward again. "I don't want to hear you say no, and that's why I gave you two options to choose from, which don't allow for a yes/no response."

Enjoying this little word game, Adeelah tilted her head to the side and cooed as she smiled. "I see. Okay, I'd love to have dinner with you on Saturday. I prefer the noon option."

"Wonderful. Since you don't want me to come to your parent's home to pick you up, we need to decide where we'll rendezvous. One option would be for you to come to my apartment, but I'm open to your suggestions."

"Give me your address, and I'll meet you at your apartment." Adeelah spontaneously responded before she had time to dwell on the prudence of such a decision.

They also firmed up their plans to eat lunch together on Tuesday through Thursday. After making these arrangements, they returned to their respective work locations.

They increasingly enjoyed each other's company. However, it was always on their mind that it was merely a matter of time before opposition due to their different religions would invade them like a cruel demon. But their growing insatiable desire to be together made the prudent option to end their relationship harder–no, virtually impossible.

On the way home from work, Adeelah called her friend, Taslima.

"So, how was your picnic on Saturday?" Taslima asked.

In her mind, she was conflicted by the threatening storm clouds which would inevitably darken her relationship with Martin. But her smiling face reflected the happiness which animated her response. "It was absolutely too good! Martin and I thoroughly enjoyed being together. Our picnic location was enchantingly romantic. At the same time, we had a lot of conversation about the challenges we'll face if we allow our relationship to continue. Martin is a wonderful man, and it became obvious very quickly that we both like each other, and it looks like we're willing to face whatever religious challenges may arise. We ate lunch together today. We plan to eat lunch together for the rest of this week, except for Friday. And he's taking me to Albert's for dinner on Saturday."

"Wow! May Allah be gracious to both of you. How religious is Martin?"

"As I mentioned earlier, he takes his Christian faith seriously, but he seems very open to the Islamic faith as well. His theology degree from a Christian college gives him interesting insight into those things our two religions have in common, and it still surprises me that he has read the Quran. When it was time to eat our picnic lunch, we prayed together to ask Allah's blessing on the food. And in his prayer, he asked Allah to help us face the coming challenges and to grant our desire to be together."

"*Alhamdulillah*! (Praise the Lord) So when am I going to meet this fantastic man?"

"I don't know. I'd like for you to meet him. I'm just about home now. I'll have to talk to you later."

"Okay. Goodbye."

~.~

On Saturday, Adeelah arrived at Martin's apartment a little early, just before 11:00 AM. Elegantly dressed, she again omitted her hijab.

Martin opened the door and admired the woman who stood before him. "Such a lovely woman you are! I'll certainly be proud to be seen with you today."

"Good morning." Adeelah blushed at his compliment, with eyes which looked lovingly at him. Martin invited her in, and she sat down on the sofa while he finished getting ready.

Martin's apartment was comfortably furnished. In the living room, in addition to the sofa, there were two comfortable chairs separated by a lamp table. Against one wall, there was a small, slightly cluttered desk, with a laptop computer on it, as well as a Holy Bible, and, to Adeelah's surprise, an English copy of the Holy Quran. She noticed a slight discoloration on the wood floor, which revealed that Martin had moved the desk recently to its current location. By the desk was a music stand with several sheets of music on it. A couple of sheets had fallen to the floor. Beside the music stand was Martin's violin.

The kitchen was small, and its neatness made it fairly evident Martin did very little cooking. There was a nice dining area, where a small dining room table also reflected very little use. It was very definitely a man's dwelling. The lack of a woman's touch was quite notable–only a few pictures on the wall, few knickknacks, and no plants. The apartment was clean, comfortable, and cozy. Adeelah liked it.

Martin was now ready, and they departed together in Martin's yellow Ford Mustang.

Adeelah commented, "My friend, Taslima, wants to meet you."

Surprised, Martin raised his eyebrows. "Will we be happy for her to meet me?"

"Taslima is a Palestinian Muslim, but she, like me, was born and has grown up here in Augusta. She has actually encouraged me regarding the possibility of our relationship, but she has also warned me about our impending religious battles. She's very outgoing and quite liberal in her opinions. So, I think, yes. We can be happy for her to meet you, and I think you'll like her."

"Well, then I'd certainly be happy to meet such a good friend of yours. Just let me know when that can happen."

Martin pondered as he changed the subject. "I've been trying to be sensitive about how our two cultures differ. Some differences are quite obvious. You're a Muslim. I'm a Christian. I find the way you dress is uniquely attractive. I find myself wanting to dress in a way which is consistent with your sense of fashion, which is somewhat inconsistent with the casual fashion of my culture. Other than that, I see us as a man and a woman who enjoy each other's company, and we like to be together. How would you define our cultural differences?"

Adeelah bit her lip. This topic reminded her about the difficulties which awaited them, and the blank stare on her face reflected worry and anxiety. "I must tell you, dating, as we're doing, is very inconsistent with Moroccan Muslim culture. However, I think there's more toleration for it for Muslims who live in the United States. One reason dating is not common in our culture is the fact that a young man and a young woman's parents usually negotiate with each other to arrange for a meeting between the man and the woman. From that point on, the man and woman develop a relationship with the understanding that the intended outcome is marriage. And I hope you fully understand. Any relationship between a Muslim woman and a Christian man is destined to be contentious."

Inner consternation made Martin purse his lips, and he confessed, "There will be some contention on my side as well. I expect it won't be so strong with my parents. The bigger source of opposition will come from my church."

"And we will also experience some serious opposition from my mosque."

"So, how will we deal with this opposition?"

With feelings of uncertainty, Adeelah shook her head with worry. "I honestly don't know."

They put this dark discussion behind them as they arrived at Albert's Restaurant. The hostess seated them at a cozy table in a quiet corner of the dining room. The ambiance was quaint but sophisticated. The waitress served them water, hard-crusted bread, and a plate of olive oil mixed with herbs. And she gave them menus.

Sensitive about ordering something too expensive, Adeelah looked up from the menu and asked, "What do you see that you like?"

"I'm going to have the grilled sea bass Charleston. As far as I'm concerned, sea bass is the most delicious fish you can eat. How about you?"

She took advantage of Martin's response to choose something which would be consistent with the price of his meal. "I've got my eye on the roasted rack of lamb. It's hard for a Moroccan to turn down a plate of lamb."

The waitress took their orders, and they also ordered raspberry iced tea. They took turns dipping bread in the olive oil with herbs as they casually chatted.

When the waitress brought the food, Martin asked, "Do you wanna ask God's blessing on the food?"

Martin's question caught her by surprise, and she raised her eyebrows. "You want me to pray?"

"Sure. Why not?"

"It's not customary for a Muslim woman to pray when a man is present."

"Well, it's not customary for Christians either. If you prefer, I'll pray. But I'd be happy to hear your prayer. What do you prefer?"

Not quite in her comfort zone, she looked at Martin, nodded, and declared, "I'll say the prayer."

"Good. While you pray, would you also ask God to give us wisdom and direction about you and me?"

"I will." Lifting her hands just above the table, with her palms facing upward, she looked up and prayed, "Oh Allah, the most gracious, the most merciful, we pray you would bless this food which you have provided for us, and save us from the punishment of Hell. We also pray you would grant us wisdom and direction about how our relationship should proceed. Our desire is that we will be able to overcome the inevitable opposition to our relationship which will surely occur, and we pray our relationship will proceed in accordance with your will. In the name of Allah."

"I couldn't have prayed any better than that."

Adeelah felt ironically pleased that Martin would ask her to say the prayer.

They shared their food. Martin tried the lamb, and Adeelah tried the fish. They thoroughly enjoyed their meal, their animated conversation, and the pleasure of each other's company. Each one's gazes found the eyes of the other, and frequent smiles brightened their faces. Like a red rosebud about to bloom, their love for each other, still unbeknownst to them, began to blossom.

When they got back to his apartment, Martin made some tea, and they sat and talked for a while.

As they talked, Adeelah revealed, with some apprehension, "Before I met you, I tended to view Christians as superficial about their religion–even hypocritical. So, it surprised me to see you take your faith in God seriously. Many describe the United States as a Christian nation, but this country only gives token recognition to God. What am I missing?"

"The idea this is a Christian nation is a misconception. I'm sure you understand one of our constitutional rights is freedom of religion, so you and I may freely practice our religions with no political repercussions. At least there should be no political repercussions."

"Your comment that there should be no repercussions is unfortunate but necessary."

Martin continued, "Absolutely true. The fact is, many don't practice any religion. And some people describe themselves as Christians, but they also describe themselves as not religious. I imagine there are Muslims like that as well. Like most Muslims, however, there are many Christians who take their faith in God just as seriously as you and I do. If you were to come to my church, you'd find many who view their faith in God as very important."

"I guess that makes sense."

"Now, let me ask you a question. Many non-Muslims believe Islam oppresses women. Do you feel like you're oppressed?"

"Of course not! Such oppression is usually due to local, non-Muslim customs and traditions in countries where Islam is the predominant religion. Muslim women have been presidents and prime ministers. Violence toward women and forcing them against their will is not permitted in Islam. Care for widows, orphans, and the poor is one of Islam's strongest teachings. So, such views are also an unfortunate misconception."

"I trust you understand I don't hold such views."

"Certainly! One of the things I most cherish about you is your enlightened views."

After a lull in the conversation, Adeelah looked at Martin's violin, and asked, "Will you play something for me on your violin?"

Martin put his teacup down on the coffee table. "Sure! Allow me a minute to find something I think you would enjoy."

Martin set up soundtracks to accompany him with the music he chose, and among the songs he played were the following: *You Raised Me Up* and *Can You Feel the Love Tonight.*

As he played, Adeelah perceived Martin played each song in a way which said to her, "I love you," especially the last song.

Before Adeelah left his apartment, Martin kissed her tenderly, and they embraced in a hug which ended too quickly. Adeelah did not resist Martin's affection in any way. In fact, she responded passionately.

On her way home, Adeelah called her friend Taslima. When she answered the phone, she asked, "How did it go?"

"We had a wonderful time, and we're getting to know each other better. After our meal, we went to his apartment, and . . ."

Taslima interrupted, "Adeelah! Shame on you!"

Adeelah deviously laughed. "Nothing like that happened. He made us some tea, we sat and talked for a while, and then he serenaded me with his violin."

"How romantic!"

Reminiscing momentarily, with a faint smile on her lips, and with her eyes semi-closed, she savored her memory of this intimate interlude, and purred, "Yes. It was romantic! Martin is the most amazing guy I've ever met." But then there was an immediate interruption in her mind which stole away her euphoria, and she sadly mumbled, "The daunting question is whether we should continue to see each other."

"I understand perfectly. I feel for you."

After Adeelah hung up, she prayed, "Oh Allah, the most gracious, the most merciful, please make this relationship possible and honorable to You."

~.~

Martin and Adeelah had now been seeing each other for some months. They ate lunch together every day, Monday through Thursday, and they discreetly went out every weekend. The time they spent together was never enough. Movies, picnics, dinners, walks in the park occupied their time, but what mattered most was that they were together, and they savored each precious moment.

Since her parents knew nothing about Martin, it was increasingly difficult for Adeelah to explain what she was doing and who she was doing it with. Consequently, they planned their weekend dates with a rendezvous at Taslima's apartment, per Taslima's suggestion, so Adeelah was able to tell her parents she was visiting Taslima.

On their first visit to Taslima's apartment, Adeelah introduced Martin to her. Martin commented, "Adeelah talks about you frequently. It's good to finally meet you, Taslima. I'm glad you are such an important friend for Adeelah."

"Thank you. Adeelah is my best friend."

"Adeelah tells me you're of Palestinian descent. Do you have family that you visit there?"

Taslima found Martin attractive, and she momentarily yielded to the sin of envy. Looking over at Adeelah, she repressed this feeling, stuttered initially, and replied, "Ah, yes. My family comes from Hebron in the West Bank. As is the case with Adeelah, my family and I live here in Augusta, but I go to Hebron every two years or so to visit family there."

"What should I know about Hebron?"

With a slight frown and eyes, which subtly reflected defiance, she replied, "Well if you read the book of Joshua in your Bible, you'll learn how the Israelites, under Joshua, attacked the Canaanites there and, '. . . destroyed all that breathed, as Yahweh, the God of Israel, commanded.' (Josh 10:40) Hebron is also where Abraham, Isaac, and Jacob are buried along with their wives. Today, Hebron is divided into two sections. The largest section is populated by Palestinians, the smaller section by Israelis. The city's name, Hebron, ironically means The City of Friendship. Unfortunately, it's a rather dangerous place to live."

Sensing the militancy in her voice, Martin raised his eyebrows, and he unconsciously backed away. "Ooh! I see I've touched a nerve. The fact that you can quote Joshua chapter 10 certainly underscores how serious the Palestinian/Israeli conflict is. If I could visit you in Hebron, what would you want me to experience?"

Slightly bowing her head in repentance, she responded more amiably, "Please forgive me. Hebron is a very sacred city in Islam. Certainly, you would be fascinated to visit the tombs of the patriarchs. If I were with you, I'd want to take you to the Hebron market, and I'd love to see how you might like camel steak."

With a single nod, reflecting curiosity, and pressing his lips together, he asked, "Hmm! Camel steak, you say. What's camel steak like?"

"Well, I can tell you it doesn't taste like chicken. It's most delicious when it comes from a younger camel. Most describe its flavor as a cross between beef and lamb."

Martin lightheartedly quipped, "Does it come with one hump or two?"

All laughing, Adeelah socked him on the shoulder, and Taslima responded, "Ha Ha! Very funny."

"I think I'd find the Hebron market and the camel steak dinner to be the highlight of my visit."

Smiling now, his comment prompted Taslima to say to Adeelah, "I can certainly see why you like this guy so much."

In the course of their conversation, Martin commented, "Given the opposition we will inevitably face, I'm sure Adeelah will be grateful for her intimate friendship with you."

Taslima responded, "I'm sure you know the coming opposition is only a question of time."

~.~

Their dates almost always ended with a stop at Martin's apartment, and things between them were becoming increasingly intimate. While they didn't live together, nevertheless, during the brief moments they spent in Martin's apartment, they pretended they were living together and that they alone were all that mattered in their own little world.

One evening, their passion reached the point where they began a slow migration to Martin's bedroom. With increasing desire, they hastily took turns removing each other's clothing, which fell randomly to the floor on the way to the bedroom. They both were becoming erotically aroused. However, there was also an inner struggle within both of them about whether they should continue.

While passion became the driving force at this moment, the struggle was especially troublesome for Adeelah. On the one hand, her heart was pounding with desire. On the other hand, her stomach was churning with guilt. She contemplated the remorse she knew she would experience, if they allowed themselves this moment of ecstasy–a moment of ecstasy which both desired. Now in bed, they were only moments away from the point when Martin was about to penetrate her, and Adeelah began to cry. And then she sobbed uncontrollably.

Concerned, Martin immediately pulled back, took a deep breath, and failed in his attempt to hide the frustration which his eyes revealed. "What's wrong? Did I hurt you?"

Between sobs, it was all Adeelah could do to reply, "No."

Martin said, "Calm down. Please talk to me."

Adeelah did calm down some. But with tears continuing to spill down her cheeks, she uttered, "I'm a virgin!"

"Okay." Martin still struggled to overcome his frustrated passion and desire, and he tried his best to say with a calm voice, "Your emotional outbreak tells me pretty clearly you want to remain a virgin."

The sorrow on her face revealed her shame and regret, and she uttered between sobs, "Martin, I'm so sorry I've enticed you this way. For most

Muslim women, remaining a virgin until marriage is extremely important. Just before a wedding, a groom's family may require that a physician examine the bride to confirm she's a virgin. If she's not a virgin, the consequences can be severe. At a minimum, it will be a shame and disgrace for the woman and her family. Frequently, the groom's family will call off the wedding. And, in some countries, the woman can be executed."

"Wow! That's pretty severe."

Adeelah continued, "The custom in most Muslim countries is for the groom's family to pay a dowry to the bride. Even if the family is willing to proceed with the wedding, the dowry for a non-virgin bride is half of what it is for a virgin bride. And many believe a woman who is guilty of fornication outside of marriage is condemned to Hell."

Seeing her deep remorse, Martin, now more composed, took Adeelah in his arms and confessed, "For me, what we almost did was supposed to be a manifestation of our love for each other, and I'm sure you looked at it that way too. However, after your emotional reaction, there's no way having sex could be a manifestation of our love. Instead, I would see it as insensitive and selfish on my part if I had proceeded. I love you, and I have no desire to hurt you in any way."

Still quite emotional, Adeelah implored, "I love you too. Please forgive me."

"If you feel a need for forgiveness, consider yourself forgiven, but I tell you, as far as I'm concerned, you have done nothing which requires forgiveness from me. Like the Holy Quran, the Holy Bible also deems fornication to be a sin. So, it appears to me, both you and I should ask God for forgiveness."

And then Martin prayed, "Dear God. We thank you we didn't reach the point of committing the sin of fornication, and we pray you would forgive us for our intentions to yield to this temptation. Amen."

Adeelah now calmed down. The tears which reflected shame and regret were now replaced with tears of emerging joy, and she looked into Martin's eyes and said again, "I love you, Martin."

They hugged each other for some time in silence, then Martin said, "Adeelah, I promise you, the only way you'll ever come into this bedroom again is if we should become husband and wife."

When he made that promise, both understood there was now a potential for them to eventually get married–a potential both began to contemplate with joyous expectation.

## THEIR LOVE DISCOVERED

Adeelah and her mother, Kareena, were having tea while talking at the kitchen table. Adeelah's cellular phone, which was lying on the table, flashed a text message from Martin which read, "I'll be fifteen minutes late for lunch at the Good Day Café tomorrow."

Adeelah tried to grab the phone before her mother could read the message, but it was too late.

Putting her teacup down, Kareena raised one eyebrow and looked at her daughter out of the corner of her eye. "Who's this Martin?"

"Oh, he's the fire chief in Waynesboro," Adeelah replied. She tried to be as nonchalant as possible and hoped Kareena would not ask any more questions.

Kareena tilted her head with a stern look on her face. "So, why are you seeing this man?"

Adeelah could feel tiny beads of sweat which formed on her forehead as she contemplated plausible responses. She lied. "I'll see him tomorrow, along with some other department managers." She knew her answer would not be satisfactory for Kareena, and she hoped she could come up with a better response before Kareena asked her next question.

"And you're meeting at this Good Day Café?"

She avoided eye contact, and a second lie suggested itself. "We're meeting at the Good Day Café to plan a surprise birthday party for Sarah, the human resources director."

Kareena searched Adeelah's face and wondered if her response was truthful, but she didn't press her.

Adeelah perceived her mother's scrutiny had come to an end. So, she breathed an imperceptible sigh of relief and changed the subject. "What's for supper?"

She didn't care what Kareena's response was, as long as she asked no further questions about Martin. She was also determined to be more careful with her cellular phone.

Martin and Adeelah grew accustomed to their stealth relationship. This was just one of a few close calls in their efforts to protect their love from discovery.

One fateful Saturday evening, however, they went back to Albert's Restaurant. After finishing their meal, the waitress took Martin's credit card to process payment, and they were waiting for her to return.

Suddenly, Adeelah's eyes reflected dismay, her face became flushed, and a feeling of impending doom invaded her.

"What's wrong?" Martin asked.

Adeelah raised her hand to cover her mouth and took a deep breath. "Two close friends of my family have just walked in and are headed in our direction. I'm in trouble!"

Visibly shaken, Martin cried out, "Oh God!"

Adeelah quickly pulled her compact out of her purse and pretended to touch up her makeup in an effort to hide her face, but it was too late.

Fatima spotted Adeelah, and she and her husband, Elfatmi, came over to say hello. Martin had his back to them, and his Panama hat initially kept them from recognizing that Adeelah was with a non-Muslim.

Fatima approached their table and cheerfully greeted Adeelah, "*As-salāmu ʿalaykum.*" (Peace be with you.)

Nervous, Adeelah replied, "*Wa alaykumu s-salam.* (And peace be with you as well.) How are you, Fatima?"

Elfatmi and Fatima now got a good look at Martin, and they didn't know quite how to react. The silence which followed quickly became very awkward.

Martin feigned a smile and greeted them cordially, "*As-salāmu ʿalaykum.* Good evening. My name is Martin. I hope you are well."

Elfatmi, with a look of disbelief on his face, mumbled almost inaudibly, "*Wa alaykumu s-salam.* I am well. Thank you." He spoke these words without thinking. His mind was only processing the disquieting sight, which his unbelieving eyes were absorbing. Fatima was speechless.

Elfatmi glared at Adeelah and asked in Arabic, "This man is not Muslim, is he?"

A foreboding look overshadowed her, and, with a feeling of gloom and a blank stare on her face, Adeelah spoke no words. She could only shake her head to say, "No."

Another very awkward silence demanded a response, and the hostess, sensing the very tense situation, smiled graciously and provided it. "May I show you to your table?"

Elfatmi lifted his head. And, with bulging eyes looking down at Adeelah with dismay, he mumbled again, "Yes. Please." And they proceeded to their table.

Martin and Adeelah hastily left the restaurant and headed to Martin's apartment. Martin could see and feel the deep distress which Adeelah was experiencing.

Adeelah trembled, fought back tears, and whimpered with a look of traumatic desperation on her troubled face. "What are we going to do?"

Martin pulled over to the side of the road, drew Adeelah close to him, hugged her, and consoled her, saying, "Adeelah, we certainly don't know what is going to happen now. But you and I have continually prayed for Allah's wisdom and guidance. And we have requested that this wonderful relationship, which is increasingly important to both of us, would bring us happiness together, in accordance with His will. There's a verse in the New Testament which promises, 'All things work together for good for those who love God.' (Romans 8;28) We must now put our faith and trust in Allah and watch to see how He resolves this dilemma. And I'm confident we'll see how all things, in fact, will work together for good for us."

Martin's words had an immediate calming effect on Adeelah, and she clung tightly to him. In his arms, she felt a profound sense of security and peace.

Through her tears, she uttered, "I admire your faith in Allah."

"Right now, we have no other option. Sometimes it's easiest to put our faith in Allah when we have no other choice. When we do have a choice, trusting in Allah is frequently the last thing we do."

"*Alhamdulillah*!" (Praise God!)

They now proceeded to Martin's apartment in virtual silence. Martin held Adeelah's hand, and she held on to his tightly. When they got to his apartment, Martin suggested, "Let's go inside and talk about our situation a little."

Adeelah followed him into his apartment. They sat together on the sofa, holding each other, lost in the warmth and security of their embrace, but knowing that this warmth and security was in serious jeopardy.

As they discussed Adeelah's impending confrontation with her father, Martin's eyes reflected somber trepidation. "Will Elfatmi and Fatima contact your parents right away?"

With a tone of resignation in her voice, she bemoaned, "More than likely, they will. Elfatmi has probably already talked to my dad."

"Why don't I follow you home, and we can go see your father together?"

Adeelah rolled her tearful eyes. "That would only make matters worse. My dad would most likely not even let you come in."

"Well, it occurs to me the best thing to do might be for me to meet your family as soon as possible. If your father is really upset, *as soon as possible* may mean after he's had a chance to calm down. I'll do my best to be available if you want to call me, but keep in mind I'll be actively involved in my church during a good part of the day tomorrow, which will limit my availability. But if you text me, I'll respond as soon as possible. At any rate, I expect we'll have some time to discuss our options when we meet for lunch during the coming week."

Her tears made her eyes puff up, and Adeelah whimpered, "I'm pretty sure my dad will forbid me from seeing you."

"Will he succeed in forbidding you?"

Despite her dismay and the tears in her eyes, Adeelah replied with defiance, "Not if I can help it."

"Do you want to stay here for a while?"

"No. I'm anxious to face my dad as soon as possible to get this confrontation over with."

"I understand."

They walked to the door. Adeelah hesitated for a moment and gazed into Martin's eyes. Martin tenderly kissed her and said. "Adeelah, my love for you grows deeper every day."

She sniffled and hugged him. "Me too."

~.~

On her way home, Adeelah stopped to dry her eyes, and she put her hijab back on. Her father, Omar El-Sayed, confronted her immediately when she walked into the house, "You and I need to have a very serious conversation." While he was angry, Omar did not fail to observe Adeelah's despondent countenance.

The words which came out of her mouth with dread were simply, "I know, Dad." Her sinking heart wounded her soul and produced in her inner being a foreboding apprehension. She felt overwhelmed, anticipating what was to be for her the coming unjust punishment for the innocent but forbidden love she and Martin had sweetly dared to share. Tears fell from her eyes again.

He stared at her, veins bulging in his neck, and he sneered, "Who is this guy, and how did you meet him?"

She dried her eyes with a handkerchief. With a voice of despair and downcast eyes, she uttered, "His name is Martin Webster, and he's the fire chief for the City of Waynesboro. I met him on my first day when I started my new job. When he learned that I'm of Moroccan descent, he told me he worked in Morocco during his military service with some Muslim air force personnel. In our conversation, it became apparent he was somewhat knowledgeable about Islam."

"So, I understand he's not Muslim."

"No. He's a Christian, but he takes his faith in Allah seriously."

"So, how did you happen to go out with him?"

Adeelah did not disclose that she and Martin were eating lunch together Monday through Thursday. "Martin told me he was very interested in discussing the experiences he had in Morocco and how his Muslim friends there significantly changed his perspective about his faith in Allah. So, I agreed to meet with him."

With vain hope, Omar raised his eyebrows and asked, "So you just talked about religion?"

Adeelah reached up to ensure her hijab properly covered her hair. "No, Dad. We talked a lot about religion, but we also talked about many other things as well."

"How serious is your relationship with him?"

Adeelah took a deep breath, and, with a pleading voice, she declared, "Dad, I'm in love with him, and he loves me too. We enjoy being together. We pray together, and we've asked Allah to give us wisdom and guidance about how our relationship should proceed, and we asked Allah to help us proceed in accordance with His will."

Crestfallen, Omar affirmed, "You understand in some Muslim countries, an intimate relationship between a Muslim woman and a non-Muslim man is grounds for execution!?"

"I do." She looked up at her dad, lifted her left shoulder, and nodded, "And I thank Allah we don't live in such a country!"

"You understand it's Allah's will for you to remain a Muslim and marry a Muslim?"

She looked him straight in the eye and spoke with firm resolve. "I have no intention of abandoning my faith in Allah. Martin and I have not discussed any plans to get married. However, I recognize there are challenges when interfaith people marry, but I also understand the Quran accepts marriage between Muslims and people of the book."

The words which Adeelah dreaded most now came out of Omar's mouth. He shook his finger in her face and spoke with a stern voice, "I am opposed to any possibility you would marry a non-Muslim man. So, I forbid you from seeing this man again."

Adeelah again fought back tears. "Martin says he'd like to meet you and Mom."

Omar adamantly responded with irritation in his voice, "I don't see that happening."

Sobbing now, with a torrent of tears flowing down her cheeks, she implored, "Why can't you just meet him? I think you'd really like him."

Omar now became even more irate. "I don't want to discuss this any further."

Adeelah's lower lip quivered, and she begged, "Please, Dad, I . . ."

Omar interrupted her, "That's all. We're done here!"

Sobbing heavily, Adeelah ran to her room and flung herself on the bed. She struggled to see through her tears as she texted Martin, "I talked with my dad. He forbids me from seeing you, and it doesn't look good."

This news devastated Martin, knocked every wisp of air from his lungs, and wrenched his inner being. However, he had no intention of ending his relationship with Adeelah. He bowed his head and silently cried out, *Dear God, please make it possible for Adeelah and me to remain together*.

After a moment to compose himself, he texted back, "Let's not give up hope yet. I firmly believe God is on our side. We both need to pray about this, and we need to trust God that all things will work out for us."

~.~

With an unreasonable impending sense of urgency, Omar discussed with Kareena the conversation he had with Adeelah. "I told Adeelah there's no way we can allow her to see this Christian man. We need to accelerate the plans for Adeelah to marry Fahim Bakkari as soon as possible."

Worried, Kareena looked out the window, and with a wrinkled brow, she asked, "How is Adeelah taking your ultimatum?"

"She's not taking it well. I've never seen her react so strongly before. It's obvious she is very much in love with this man."

Kareena turned her head to look at Omar and leaned forward with curiosity. "Who is he? How does she describe him?"

"His name is Martin, and apparently he's a Christian who takes his faith in Allah seriously. Adeelah says they pray together about their relationship. He has shown some interest in Islam. And he has commented about how his perspective regarding Islam changed as a result of conversations he had some years ago in Morocco with Muslim Air Force friends of his. She says he'd like to meet us."

"It impresses me that they pray together. Would it be so bad if we agreed to meet him?"

Kareena's suggestion stirred his anger. He tightened his lips and insisted, "I made it clear to Adeelah, I'm not interested in meeting him."

"Is there any chance he might become a Muslim?"

With a look of dismay in his eyes, his wrinkled forehead reflected the concern and the worry which afflicted him, and Omar replied, "I don't know."

Kareena responded, "I think we should pray about this."

"I agree. We should certainly pray about this difficult matter."

~.~

Adeelah called her friend, Taslima. Before Taslima could say a word, she stammered between sobs, with anguish in her voice. "My dad has forbidden me from seeing Martin."

Taslima responded with a voice which was full of compassion, "Well, I think we knew that was a real possibility, but it isn't necessarily the end of the story. You can find numerous websites which discuss Muslim and Christian interfaith relationships. And viewpoints are changing, especially in the United States."

"What do you think I should do?"

"First, you need to be patient and trust in Allah. Second, I recommend you start gathering some of the more liberal Muslim viewpoints I just referred to. Third, don't be too quick to give up."

"Martin said just about the same thing, and he also said we should look for an opportunity for him to meet with my parents. Although he's a Christian, he really has some positive and enlightened views about

Islam and the common ground which exists between Islam and Christianity."

"Martin is certainly a unique and impressive man."

Through her tears, Adeelah, with passion in her voice, responded, "He is. How could I not love such a man!"

As they were talking, there was a knock on Adeelah's door, and she said, "Taslima, I have to go now. Goodbye."

"Okay. I'll talk to you later."

She opened the door, and Kareena, with a worried look on her face, spoke with the unique compassion of a loving mother and asked, "Can I have a talk with you?"

Craving some encouraging word, Adeelah stood aside. "Of course, Mom, come on in."

Adeelah's tear-stained face made it abundantly clear to Kareena that she was devastated, and the sorrow in Kareena's eyes made it evident that she felt Adeelah's deep despair. They sat down on Adeelah's bed, and with heart-felt sympathy, Kareena said, "Your father and I have talked, and he's adamantly against any continued relationship between you and your friend, Martin."

With defiance tempered by respect, Adeelah declared, "I understand, but I'm not willing to terminate our relationship."

"How strong are your feelings for him?"

Between sobs, Adeelah stammered, "They're strong! We're very much in love. He's a wonderful man, and we thoroughly enjoy each other's company."

Suddenly, Kareena remembered Martin's name, and she looked at Adeelah out of the corner of her eye. "Is this the same man who I saw in a text on your telephone recently?"

"Yes."

Kareena's eyes of compassion now reflected anger. Whereas before her eyebrows arched upward in the center of her face, now they arched downward. "So, you lied to me about your meeting with him!"

Adeelah looked down as she confessed, "I did."

Kareena shrugged and folded her arms. "What should I think about that?"

Adeelah looked her mother in the eye. "Now that Dad has forbidden me from seeing him, I think it's obvious why I chose to lie to you. I hope you can forgive me."

Kareena looked at Adeelah and paused. Then, she hugged Adeelah, wrinkled her brow, and a single tear spilled from her eye and flowed down her cheek. "I do forgive you. But you know this family takes our faith in Allah very seriously, and the relationship of a Muslim, especially a Muslim woman with a non-Muslim man, is not well tolerated at all."

Adeelah's lower lip quivered, and bitterness emerged on her face. She retorted, "I understand. I take my faith in Allah every bit as seriously as the rest of our family, and Martin takes his faith in Allah just as seriously. Moreover, Muslim attitudes about interfaith relationships in this country are changing and are more liberal than ever."

"That's all well and good, but you know your dad. He holds very strongly to traditions and old-school values."

"Do you see any chance Dad might be willing to meet Martin?"

"I don't know. The probability of such a meeting appears unlikely. We'll just have to wait and see."

Desperate for any possible glimmer of hope, Adeelah asked, "So, will you help me with this?"

"I don't know if I can."

Adeelah found little encouragement in her mother's words, and she experienced no glimmer of hope from her. She felt even more downcast, and the despair she was experiencing was more than she could bear.

# Sunday after Church

During church on Sunday, it was apparent something was troubling Martin. During lunch after church, Martin's father, David, asked, "Why don't you talk to us about what's troubling you, Son."

Martin took a deep breath and replied, "I'm seeing a woman, and we're in love."

With a perplexed look on her face, Ellen, Martin's mother, asked, "And why is that troubling you?"

Fighting back tears, he responded, "Her name is Adeelah El-Sayed, she's a Muslim, her parents now know about us, and they've forbidden her from seeing me."

David, Ellen, and Priscilla, Martin's sister, paused, put their forks down, and all three stared at Martin in bewilderment.

Tilting her head to the side, Priscilla asked, "Why would you want to date a Muslim woman?"

"Well, I certainly didn't just decide one day I wanted to date a Muslim woman! We met, we were attracted to each other, and we fell in love."

Priscilla responded, "You remember Pastor Sawyer recently preached that Islam is a false religion which is based on a false book which was written by a false prophet. Islam is a religion of hate, which advocates violence against non-Muslims."

Martin tightened his jaw, pursed his lips, and declared with defiance in his voice, "And you'll recall I disagreed with him, and now you know why. My experience tells me the pastor is wrong, and I don't believe his critical assertions against Islam."

David sipped his coffee and remarked, "You certainly don't believe the Quran is equal to the Bible, and that it's the inspired word of God, do you?"

Martin's eyes glared with passion, and he gestured heavily, both with his hands and his head, as he spoke forcefully. "I have read the Quran, and I find much which is edifying in it. Regarding the issue of violence, I tell you again, as I told you before, those passages which suggest Islam advocates violence against non-Muslims are taken out of context. Such passages only allow for violence as an option when non-Muslims violently attack Muslims first."

David put his coffee cup down. "You still haven't answered my question."

"Dad, you'd be surprised to read how frequently the Quran refers to biblical characters, with extensive mention of Jesus and Mary. Moreover, the church decreed in the fourth century which Biblical books were inspired and should be included in the Bible. They also decreed the church would receive no additional divine revelations, but the Bible itself says nothing about such limitations. Who are we to say God would not provide any additional divine revelations?"

With a look of disbelief on David's face, he responded, "So, you do believe the Quran is the inspired word of God!?"

"I didn't say that, but I don't discard the possibility God might have provided additional divine revelation through Mohammad. Regarding the theological doctrine of divine inspiration, I confess I have serious questions about the idea that everything written in the Bible is the perfect revelation of God. There are passages in the Bible which allege that God directed the Hebrew nation to commit atrocities against other nations. I find it difficult to believe a just and loving God would direct such atrocious and horrendous violence against innocent people. And their atrocities were far worse than the atrocities committed by extremist Islamist groups today."

Martin's family was shocked at what he just said but could not criticize his reasoning.

Feeling Martin's despair, Ellen asked with a sad smile, "How did you meet this woman?"

"Adeelah is the new finance director for the City of Waynesboro. On her first day, the human resources director took her around to meet the city management staff. So, they came to see me at the fire station. And that is when I first met her. You may recall I mentioned meeting her when we discussed the sermon in which Pastor Sawyer made his critical remarks against Islam. Then one day, I saw her at the Good Day Café during lunch. She was sitting by herself. So, I asked if I could join her, and she said yes. I learned her family is originally from Marrakech, Morocco, which is where I stayed when the Air Force sent me to work with Moroccan Air Force personnel. So, this common connection prompted some animated conversation between us. We enjoyed our conversation, and I asked her out."

Leaning forward, Ellen followed up, "What's Adeelah like?"

"She's a remarkable woman. We both take our faith in God seriously, we pray together, we have much in common, and we enjoy each other's company. And we have fallen in love. We knew her parents would be very opposed to their daughter's relationship with a non-Muslim man. So, we couldn't bring ourselves to tell them about us. Yesterday we ate dinner at Albert's Restaurant, and while we were there, some friends of Adeelah's family came into the restaurant and saw us together. By the time Adeelah got home, they had already told Adeelah's father about us. Now her father forbids her from seeing me."

David asked, "So, what are you going to do?"

Martin looked down and vowed, "We're going to try to win her family over." Then he looked at his dad with lifted eyebrows and a sorrowful face. And he asked with a pleading voice, "Will we have to win you over too?"

While he lamented his son's anguish, David replied, "The fact is, she's not a Christian, and the Apostle Paul clearly teaches in his second letter to the Corinthians that believers should not be linked together with unbelievers. You know, our church directs us to live as the Bible teaches. Is there any chance Adeelah will become a Christian?"

Seeing the hopelessness of his dilemma, Martin replied, "I honestly don't see that happening. I would argue, however, she is, in fact, a believer."

David paused. "I certainly don't think Pastor Sawyer will agree she's a believer, so it will be difficult for us to accept that as well."

"When she finally has the opportunity to meet you, will you please at least make her feel welcome?"

David sighed and looked down to avoid eye contact with Martin. "That's a good question. I honestly don't know. We'll have to see. Let me make it clear, however, I'm adamantly opposed to this relationship. I think you should find yourself a good Christian woman, and I think you are just asking for trouble with this Muslim woman."

His father's comments contributed even more to Martin's despair. He sent a text to Adeelah to share his parents' reaction. "I have told my parents about us, and we now know both of our parents are adamantly opposed to our relationship."

# Clandestine Dates

Martin and Adeelah continued to eat lunch together on Mondays through Thursdays. Since Adeelah took extended lunch breaks on Fridays to attend the prayer services at the Islamic Center of South Augusta, Martin and Adeelah also met for dinner after work on Fridays. And they took advantage of limited opportunities to rendezvous at Taslima's apartment. They cherished these precious moments, but such clandestine meetings were woefully inadequate–they rarely had time to be alone.

In early May, City Hall planned an employee picnic at the Pendleton Park in Augusta. May was a good time of year because the weather was very pleasant–not too hot, not too cold.

Adeelah wore a pair of blue jeans and a multicolored, patterned, light-weight sweater, mostly green in color, with yellow, diamond shaped designs. Because of the cool temperatures, she included a white shawl with tassels along its border. And she chose a ruby red hijab, also with tassels along its border. Martin wore bluejeans as well, and a green heavy-knit sweater with yellow diamond shaped designs, which unintentionally came close to the pattern in Adeelah's sweater. Instead of his usual Panama hat, he also wore a green felt, broad-brimmed, fedora which resembled a cowboy hat. They looked like they very much belonged together.

It was about an hour before lunch. Martin and Adeelah wandered off, hand in hand, to explore the park. Martin complimented Adeelah. "You look very casually fashionable today, my love."

She looked up at him with adoring eyes. "Thank you. You look pretty good yourself."

They came upon a quiet pond which featured a statue of a nude boy in the pond's center. Water emanated from the statue's male organ to function as a provocative fountain. It was a replica of an Italian statue. They paused there for a short while and enjoyed the pleasant splash of water falling into the pond, which was like sweet music which serenaded them. A small flock of quacking ducks swam in the pond and happily entertained them as well. They laughed as they remembered fond moments together which occurred before their innocent, happy-go-lucky love was forbidden.

Martin recalled the first time they met. "I was amused when you tried to move my barbell, but couldn't. And you looked over your shoulder with an enticing smile and a surprised look on your face to ask how much it weighed. As you stood beside the barbell, you looked like a precocious young school girl. For me, that was a pivotal moment in which you began to steal my heart."

With a sad smile, Adeelah's eyes teared up. "And I remember the first time you touched me when you put your hand on the small of my back to help me up the steep step on our way to our picnic location at the Augusta Canal. Your touch was magic for me."

They slowly meandered to a wooded area, which treated them to an abundance of red wildflowers. A chattering squirrel frantically jumped from branch to branch among the trees, as if to scold them for invading its space. A bicyclist rode by, but Martin and Adeelah otherwise found themselves to be alone together for the first time in a long time. Massive boulders provided them with a secluded grove, where they sneaked a passionate kiss. They lingered there, embracing each other.

The subtle scent of Adeelah's perfume enticed Martin with naughty fantasies. This rare opportunity for an intimate embrace made Adeelah tremble with emotion. Erotic thoughts played out in their minds–thoughts which would be a musical duet in perfect harmony if their twin thoughts were audible–twin thoughts which were troubling temptations for them as a Christian and Muslim but reckless rapture for them as lovers. No conversation occurred. Conversation would have rudely intruded on the romantic ecstasy of this rare, precious interlude.

Time for lunch now, they tore themselves away from this momentary, private Garden of Eden. Many watched as they returned to the picnic area. Again, they walked hand-in-hand. It was very clear to everybody that Martin and Adeelah were in love.

They waited in line to arrive at the serving tables, where servers dished out the food. When she arrived at the table, Adeelah picked up an empty paper plate, and the server asked her, "Would you prefer a hot dog or a hamburger?"

Adeelah smiled graciously and replied, "I'll take a hamburger, please. As a Muslim, there can be no pork on my fork."

The server laughed and commented as she gave her a hamburger, "That's a funny way to put it."

Although Martin liked hot dogs, he too asked for a hamburger.

During the picnic meal, they were inseparable. Afterward, they held hands, they laughed, and they cherished this rare, priceless time which they enjoyed together. For the moment, they forgot the challenges of their forbidden love.

Sarah, the human resources director, came up with Clara, the city clerk, to say hello. Sarah said, "Look at you two! Adeelah, it looks like your family's plans for your future are going up in passionate flames."

Adeelah blushed and grinned, but her eyes manifested a subtle melancholy. Nodding her head, she replied with a sad smile, "I hope you're right."

Sarah could see their apparent passionate paradise was not perfect.

In addition to the happy occasion for Martin and Adeelah to be together, the picnic also produced another benefit for Adeelah. She was performing well as finance director, but still, she felt she was not readily accepted among management staff. Since he was so well-liked throughout City Hall, seeing Martin and Adeelah together helped break the ice for Adeelah. From this point forward, she found that people were now warming up to her. However, looking around, Adeelah could see the hints of jealousy and envy on the faces of other single women, who also had fantasies of a relationship with Martin.

The picnic ended, but the challenges which threatened their struggling love persisted.

~.~

Their Friday nights together, while highly treasured, gave them very little quality time. They simply had dinner at various restaurants in Waynesboro, and then each went home. During one of their Thursday luncheons, as Martin handed the waitress his credit card, he asked Adeelah, "Have you made any progress with your father?"

Adeelah, with a blank stare, hesitated and replied, "Not much if any. I've tried to talk to him on several occasions, but I'm afraid to talk to him because he becomes angry every time I bring up the subject."

The weary sorrow in Martin's eyes was evident. "Things can't go on like this. This little bit of time we spend together is simply not enough."

Looking down, Adeelah struggled to say, "My father wants to have Fahim Bakkari come visit us from Morocco to discuss the possibility of an engagement for me and him to get married."

Martin leaned forward and glared with disbelief. "Certainly, you wouldn't want to go along with that!"

Adeelah hesitated. "I don't like the idea at all. But given the opposition we're facing, I'm questioning whether it's Allah's will for us to be together."

"Have we been patient enough to know what Allah's will is?"

Adeelah shrugged, gestured with her hands, and lifted her eyebrows. "Well, we certainly don't have a path before us which is favorable for our relationship."

Martin noted Adeelah's marked hesitation, and he asked, "Are you suggesting we should break up?"

Again she hesitated and struggled to express herself. A single tear filled her eye, spilled over, and ran down her cheek. She looked down and spoke almost inaudibly, "I love you, Martin, and I want us to be together. But certainly, you, as well as I know, Allah's will is more important than our relationship."

As he contemplated the possibility Adeelah might marry this Muslim man, Martin's face paled, a blank stare reflected the forlorn emptiness which invaded his soul, and he spoke with a voice which reflected both anger and despair, "So you are breaking up with me!"

She noted how her words wounded her Martin, and she now sobbed and very reluctantly stammered between sobs. "For the moment, I think it would be better if we don't see each other."

The full impact of what was happening pierced Martin's heart like an arrow. He did his best to fight back tears, but the tears which now bathed his face showed he lost this fight. His voice quivered as he responded, "I can see this is as difficult for you, as it certainly is for me. If you think this is best, I won't oppose you. But I want you to know my love for you grows increasingly deeper, and surely, you must know you're breaking my heart."

Sobbing uncontrollably now, and with a quivering voice which harmonized with Martin's quivering voice, Adeelah responded, "I know, Martin. My heart is broken too."

Neither had any appetite to finish their lunch, so Martin took Adeelah back to City Hall. The short drive seemed to last an eternity, and the silence as they rode together was excruciating.

When they arrived at City Hall, they both reached out to each other for a bittersweet hug, which marked the end of their relationship.

Adeelah got out of the car, and still sobbing, she said, "Goodbye, Martin."

Martin, weeping as well, could not bring himself to say goodbye, and he could not bear to watch as Adeelah walked away.

Later, sobbing as she drove home, Adeelah called Taslima. When she answered, Adeelah blurted out between sobs, "My relationship with Martin is over."

Taslima responded with sorrow which sympathetically shared Adeelah's despair, and she tried to find words of encouragement, but couldn't. "I'm so sorry to hear that. Are you sure there's no hope?"

"I don't see any hope. Both of our parents are adamantly opposed to our relationship. My father is trying to arrange for Fahim to visit us from Morocco to discuss a possible wedding. I understand Fahim is a good man, but I have no interest in even contemplating marriage with a man I don't even know. Why is Allah allowing this to happen?"

Taslima hesitated and then replied, "I wish I had a good answer for you, Adeelah."

## FAHIM BAKKARI COMES TO MEET ADEELAH

Several weeks had passed since they broke up, and Martin and Adeelah only saw each other on those occasions when Martin had to come to City Hall. Adeelah continued to have lunch at the Good Day Café, and on occasions, she enjoyed the company of other management personnel with whom she had now become friends. When Martin and Adeelah did inadvertently encounter each other, neither could hide their longing and painful gaze–a pain of loneliness which caused them to fight back tears.

Adeelah overheard her parents discussing the plan for Fahim Bakkari's visit, and there was no doubt in her mind that the motive of his visit would be to arrange an engagement which would lead to her marriage with him. She had no idea how imminent his visit would be. The very next day, Omar El-Sayed, Adeelah's father, drove to the Hartsfield-Jackson Atlanta International Airport to pick up Fahim.

As they drove back, Fahim asked, "How receptive is Adeelah to our prospective marriage?"

Omar pressed his lips together. He felt embarrassed. Fahim's difficult question made him experience sudden regret that he invited Fahim to make this long journey, which could very well be in vain. He hesitated before proceeding to answer Fahim's question. "I wish I could tell you she's eagerly awaiting your visit. The fact is, she doesn't even know about your arrival today. Not long ago, I discovered she was seeing a Christian man, and of course, I opposed their relationship and told Adeelah she could not continue to see him. She doesn't talk about it, but I suspect she still has very strong feelings for him."

Twisting the ring on his finger, Fahim looked out the car window and asked, "Have you met him?"

"I haven't. Since he's not a Muslim, I don't see much point in meeting him."

Trying to hide the rising displeasure he experienced, now that he learned he was possibly wasting his time with this visit, Fahim looked over at Omar. "Do you think my visit will be worthwhile?"

Omar tilted his head to the side in a nod. "I'm hoping it will be, but I must confess I really don't know."

When Adeelah returned home from work, it wasn't necessary for her father to make any introductions. Adeelah was surprised to see Fahim, but she knew exactly who he was. Omar nevertheless made the introductions.

Fahim said in Arabic, "*As-salāmu ʿalaykum.* It's good to finally meet you, Adeelah." (He was not fluent in English.)

This was an extremely awkward moment for Adeelah. She avoided eye contact with him when she responded. "*Wa alaykumu s-salam.*" She had no other words to say. Her countenance was as one who felt compelled to resign herself to a foreboding fate.

Fahim Bakkari was a good-looking man. A physician, he expressed himself well, and it was clear he was highly intelligent and open-minded. Consistent with Moroccan culture, he was very respectful toward Omar and Kareena and presented gifts to each family member. His gift for Adeelah was an ornate gold bracelet.

Adeelah could see why her parents would choose him as a potential husband for her. He had many admirable qualities. She liked Fahim. But, while she didn't consciously make the comparison, he simply was not Martin.

Kareena, Adeelah's mother, prepared a special meal for dinner, and they all sat down to eat. Everybody joined in the conversation, but Adeelah was both a shy and reluctant participant.

After dinner, everybody gathered in the living room for additional conversation. Kareena left to clear the dining room table, and the conversation continued. After a short while, Omar and Habib, Adeelah's brother, strategically excused themselves as well, with the hope Fahim and Adeelah would begin the process of getting to know one another.

Adeelah's silent reluctance was clearly apparent to Fahim. Her expressionless face and her somber demeanor reminded Fahim of a patient who knowingly waited to hear a grave medical diagnosis. After some polite conversation, Fahim commented, "Your father has told me about a relationship you had with a Christian man. I perceive your father may have been a little too hasty to bring me here to meet you and to talk about a potential marriage. What are your thoughts?"

Despondent and, feeling the pressure of everybody's expectations, Adeelah looked Fahim in the eye and responded in Arabic, "My first impression of you is that you're a good man and an intelligent man. I can easily see why my parents would conclude that you would be a good marriage choice for me. Regarding the Christian man I was seeing, his name is Martin. We had strong feelings for each other. Both of our families opposed our relationship due to our different religions. Because of that opposition, I made the decision to end the relationship–a decision which was very painful and difficult for both of us. The lingering affection I still feel for Martin makes it difficult for me to consider the possibility of a relationship with you or anybody else at this time. I've resigned myself to the fact that our relationship is over. And, with time, I expect I will once again be interested in pursuing a new relationship. I just can't bring myself to do that now, and I'm sorry you came all this way at this time to meet me."

Disappointed, Fahim attempted a smile and responded, choosing his words carefully, "I appreciate your honesty. Under different circumstances, I'd be pleased to pursue a relationship with you. But I certainly will not pressure you in any way, since it's obvious you are not ready for such a relationship now. My interest remains strong, but it's important to me that you also should have a strong interest. I suggest we leave our options open for the moment."

The building pressure within her now began to subside. And, breathing easier now, Adeelah nodded in agreement. "Thank you for your understanding. I agree with your suggestion to keep our options open. Let's see where Allah leads us."

"So be it."

As she reflected on her conversation with Fahim, Adeelah couldn't help but compare this business-like conversation about a potential marriage with the more passionate romantic experience she had with Martin. Right now, she missed Martin more than anything.

Omar was not happy with this outcome, but he too didn't want to pressure Adeelah to make a commitment which all might one day regret. Fahim stayed for a week, established a close friendship with Habib, Adeelah's brother, and returned to Rabat, Morocco.

# Rosalyn Bartlett Comes Home

Martin was putting his violin away after the Sunday morning church service when Rosalyn Bartlett came up and said, "Hello, Martin. How have you been?"

Martin looked up and was pleasantly surprised to see Rosalyn. He smiled his most happy smile in some time, stood up, and replied, "I've been well. It's good to see you. I presume you've come home with your MBA."

Rosalyn's sparkling eyes and coy smile had a reviving effect on Martin, and she bragged, "Yes, I graduated summa cum laude, and I've accepted a position in the marketing department at Morris Communications."

"Well, good for you. I'm happy for you."

Rosalyn, a very attractive blonde, came from a respected family who knew Martin's family well. Both families had been active members of Friendship Community Church for many years. She was outgoing, full of energy, and was the stereotypical image of a southern Georgia girl, to include her sweet Georgia southern accent. For the past two years, she was a student in the MBA program at the University of Georgia in Athens. There was a long line of men who dreamed of dating her, but she always had eyes for Martin. She and Martin dated rather extensively before she left to study in Athens. Now that she was home, she had her heart set on resuming her relationship with Martin.

Rosalyn moved closer to Martin, and he got a whiff of her enticing perfume. "Some of my friends are getting together at our home this afternoon. I'm hoping I can count on your presence as well."

Martin savored this ray of sunshine which lifted his spirits, and he replied, "I can't think of any place I'd rather be than at a party to welcome you home, Rosalyn!"

Her eyes fluttered, and, with a bright, enticing, flirtatious smile, she replied, "Well good! I'll look forward to having you over!"

After so much time dwelling on his failed relationship with Adeelah, Martin experienced a welcome sense of happiness and exuberance. In his thoughts, he pondered, *Just maybe I could renew my relationship with Rosalyn and forget the feelings I have for Adeelah.*

When he arrived at the Bartlett home, Rosalyn enthusiastically greeted him with a hug and a kiss on the cheek. "I'm so glad you came!" She looked up at him, linked her arm with his, smiled, and led him into the living room.

"It's really good to see you again, Rosalyn."

"I have to help Mother with the food. Please make yourself comfortable."

James Landers, Martin's friend, came over to say hello. "I haven't talked to you for some time outside of church. Are you still dating that Muslim woman?"

With a touch of pensive sadness in his voice, he sighed and shook his head. "No. We just couldn't handle the opposition from our families. So, we broke up."

"I know you had strong feelings for her, but I think you'll be better off in the long run. Maybe Rosalyn's return will do you some good. I know you two were dating quite a bit before she went off to college."

He looked at James, frowned, and pursed his lips. "I confess it has been hard for me to get Adeelah out of my mind. I was so in love with her, and I still love her now. However, it did my heart good to see Rosalyn today. I'm hoping maybe we can pick up where we left off."

The party was a joyous occasion. The room bubbled with happy chatter. Everybody had a great time. And Martin and Rosalyn went out of their way to be close to each other.

As people started to leave, Martin's eyes brightened with expectation as he took Rosalyn by the hand. "I'd very much enjoy having dinner with you. Would Friday or Saturday work best for you?"

With a bright smile on her face, Rosalyn replied, "Let's do Friday and see what we can do on Saturday as well."

"I like that idea. I'll pick you up at six o'clock."

Rosalyn kissed Martin on the cheek, hugged him, and whispered in his ear, "I'll look forward to it."

As he returned to his apartment, Martin began experiencing guilt, as if he were betraying Adeelah. He knew that didn't make sense since they were not seeing each other. But the guilt was there nevertheless.

On the way to work on Monday, Martin told himself he should be looking forward to going out with Rosalyn. They knew each other well, their previous relationship bordered on being intimate, and she was attractive and intelligent. There were good reasons to think they could develop a truly intimate relationship. However, as much as he tried to convince himself, the fact was, Martin's heart was just not in it.

On Wednesday, Martin was at City Hall, and sure enough, he encountered Adeelah in the hallway.

Relishing in the image of her loveliness, Martin looked at her with longing eyes and said, "Hello Adeelah. I hope you're well."

Adeelah arched her eyebrows with a look of sorrow on her face. "I'm okay. I hope the same for you."

In this very brief exchange, they experienced an undeniable, mutual longing to be together–a longing both failed to effectively suppress and hide.

~.~

Martin picked up Rosalyn on Friday, and they went to the Texas Roadhouse restaurant for dinner. They enjoyed each other's company and talked about the good times they had before she went to the university in Athens to study.

Rosalyn noted his subtle downcast countenance and asked, "Martin, you appear to be somewhat preoccupied. What's on your mind?"

Martin's hesitation and his face reflected the conflicting feelings which weighed on his heart, feelings he tried and failed to hide, and he confessed, "I must tell you I'm recovering from a broken relationship." And he proceeded to tell Rosalyn about Adeelah. He concluded by declaring, "I'm thrilled to see you again, Rosalyn. But I'm still dealing with a broken heart. Can you be patient with me?"

She paused in reflection before answering. Her eyes reflected both sympathy and uncertainty. She touched Martin's hand, shrugged, and her voice quivered as she asked, "Do you want to see where you and I can go with our relationship?"

Martin nodded slowly and replied, "I'd like to see us have a relationship. If anybody can make me forget Adeelah, that would be you."

Encouraged by his response, her eyes brightened. She grinned, put her hands on her hips, and declared with enthusiasm, "Then let's see where we go!"

Martin spoke truthfully when he said he would like to see him and Rosalyn have a relationship. At the same time, there was a genuine desire on his part to have Adeelah back in his life.

Rosalyn and Martin started seeing each other regularly. They attended Friendship Community Church and sat together. And their families were pleased to see them together, especially David and Ellen, Martin's parents, who were pleased that he seemed to be forgetting about Adeelah. Priscilla, Martin's sister, and Rosalyn were close friends, so she was also happy to see her brother with Rosalyn as well.

Martin still saw Adeelah at City Hall on occasions, and it was apparent such encounters were awkward and painful for both of them.

On one occasion, Martin and Rosalyn were together and walked hand in hand at the Augusta Mall. They went there to buy a birthday present for Priscilla. As they walked out of Macy's, Martin spotted Adeelah with her family. Adeelah saw Martin too. It was clear this encounter was very traumatic for both of them.

Adeelah had no idea Martin was in another relationship, and she almost collapsed when she saw Martin holding hands with Rosalyn. Her mother, Kareena, put her arm around Adeelah to keep her from falling, and Adeelah clung to her mother. The expression on her face screamed with the despair which she was experiencing. Omar, Adeelah's father, who saw Martin for the first time, was shocked to see how his daughter reacted when she saw him, and how she suffered physically when she saw Martin was with another woman.

It was all Martin could do to resist the urge to run to Adeelah's aid. Guilt afflicted his heart with a penetrating pain. Rosalyn could see the grief on his face.

As they went their separate ways, both Martin with Rosalyn and Adeelah with her family, they were speechless.

As they drove away in Martin's yellow Ford Mustang, Rosalyn broke the silence, saying, "Now that I've seen Adeelah and your reaction, which this encounter just produced, I need to know. Where do I stand with you?"

Martin pulled over to the side of the road, put his arm around Rosalyn, and drew her close to him. "My relationship with you is important to me, and you've helped me deal with the deep disillusion I experienced after my relationship with Adeelah ended. It was opposition from both of our families which caused us to part–opposition because she's a Muslim, and I'm a Christian. As you just saw, both she and I are dealing with a separation which neither of us wanted. I don't see any hope for Adeelah and me to get back together, and I desperately need to get over this. All I can promise is that I'm trying to get over it, and my desire is that you and I will find our relationship deepening with time. I know this is risky for you, and I will leave it up to you to decide whether you want to run this risk."

Rosalyn's voice quivered as she said, "I'm falling in love with you, Martin. So, I feel compelled to accept this risk."

Martin tenderly kissed her. Rosalyn responded with tears in her eyes. Martin responded with guilt.

# A Desperate Encounter

On Monday, Adeelah was glad to get back to work. Over the weekend, she could not fully recover from the shock of seeing her Martin with another woman. She understood it was only reasonable for Martin to seek another relationship after she broke up with him. But the reality of seeing Martin with this other woman deepened the wound in her heart, which showed no signs of healing. Now, back at work, she was only too glad for the work issues which diverted her attention from the deep despondency and despair she was experiencing.

Martin also had a tough weekend. He could not get Adeelah's reaction at the Augusta Mall out of his mind. It was clear to him that she still had feelings for him, which confirmed she never wanted their relationship to end. And he felt exactly the same way.

He knew he could probably find her at the Good Day Café during lunch, and he yearned to see her. He held back on Monday. On Tuesday, he started for the café but turned back. Wednesday came, and he couldn't stand it anymore. He just had to see her.

He walked into the café and, sure enough, he saw Adeelah seated in a booth by herself with her back to him. As he approached, he noticed she had ordered a Reuben and commented, "It looks like you did indeed become a Reuben fan."

A painful joy flooded her soul, and Adeelah turned to see Martin standing at her side.

"May I join you?" Martin asked with an almost imperceptible quiver in his voice.

She looked up at him with moist, longing eyes. "You know I should say no, but I just can't bring myself to turn you away. Please do join me!"

As Martin sat down, both felt so much more at ease than they had during their weeks of separation. Both sat gazing at each other during a momentary silence in which they mutually savored the joy of their presence together.

Adeelah looked away from this man she loved so much and asked, "What's her name?"

Martin paused before responding, "Rosalyn."

She shrugged her shoulders. "How long have you known her?"

"For many years. Our families have been friends for a long time. We go to the same church. She and I have known each other since grade school. I dated her for a while before she went to study at the University of Georgia in Athens, well before I met you. She recently returned after finishing her MBA, and we started seeing each other again."

Adeelah desperately fought back tears and asked, "Can you be happy with her?"

"I was thinking that, with time, I might be happy with her, until I saw the tortured look on your face the other night at the shopping mall when you saw us together. And your torture was my torture as well."

"You know, we haven't known each other so long. It seems almost unreasonable for our strong feelings for each other to persist as they have."

Martin leaned forward and took Adeelah's hand in his. "So, you admit you still have strong feelings for me! What is unreasonable is for us to deny our feelings–our love for each other."

Adeelah could no longer hold back her tears as she reacted to the truth of Martin's words and felt his tender touch. "I don't deny the love we have for each other. There are simply other factors which deny us the joy of loving each other."

Still holding her hand, Martin replied, "Ironically, it's religion which denies us such joy–not Allah. Allah could not be so cruel that He would bring you and me together to love each other the way we do, and then tear us apart from each other. I believe Allah looks at our love with a divine wink of approval."

Softly sobbing now, Adeelah released Martin's hand. "Don't you see, our situation is hopeless. You described our encounter the other night as torture, and it was. But our encounter right now is torture as well. I think you should seek your happiness with Rosalyn, and maybe I will have some hope of happiness with Fahim. Please. Let's not do this again."

Martin cried out, "God! How I love you, Adeelah!"

"I know. I love you too." With unbearable anguish, Adeelah got up without finishing her lunch, paid her bill, and walked out. Martin never experienced such despairing despondency in his life.

And so, their separation continued. Martin continued to see Rosalyn with the hope and honest intent to fall in love with her and to forget Adeelah.

# A New Strategy

Despite his best efforts to develop his relationship with Rosalyn, Martin became obsessed with efforts to find a solution which would make his relationship with Adeelah at least tolerable for both of their families. He started collecting articles and other documents from the Internet about the challenges, feasibility, and viability of interfaith relationships which could potentially lead to an acceptable marriage between a Christian man and a Muslim woman.

He learned that in Islam, it was traditionally much more readily acceptable for a Muslim man to have a relationship with a Christian woman than it was for a Christian man to have a relationship with a Muslim woman. However, he also found that in many countries, including the United States, this inequality was steadily disappearing within Islam. So, relationships between Christian men and Muslim women were becoming more readily accepted as well. It occurred to him how ironic it was that Adeelah's name means equal, and it was this lack of equality which was keeping Martin and her from being together. He also compared the essential teachings of Christianity and Islam, with the goal of finding additional common ground between the two faiths.

He found one article which he sent via email to Adeelah entitled, "What happens when you fall in love across the religious divide?" In the article, an interfaith couple discussed the struggles and successes they had experienced. The one thing which impressed Martin the most was their affirmation that both the husband and wife found their faith in God deepened as a result of their interfaith marriage. While Adeelah read the article with interest, she did not respond to Martin's email.

Martin also found another article which he read with great interest, entitled, *I am Muslim and Christian.* It was about the Reverend Paul Reynolds, a Methodist minister, who professed to be both Muslim and Christian. On the subject of incompatibilities between the two religions, Reverend Reynolds acknowledged there are some, but he emphasized, "With respect to the essentials, I find the two religions are compatible. For me, that's sufficient." Martin also sent this article to Adeelah.

Adeelah did not respond to this email either. But talking to her father, she asked him, "Dad, can I share something with you about Martin?"

Omar took off his glasses and gestured with them. "I've told you many times, I don't want to discuss this matter any further."

"Please hear me out, Dad. You know how difficult this is for me."

Recalling how traumatic Adeelah's reaction was when she saw Martin with another woman in the shopping mall, Omar replied, "Okay. Tell me what's on your mind."

Adeelah proceeded, "Would you agree the only reason you oppose my relationship with Martin is the fact he's not a Muslim?"

"I don't know the man, so I have nothing else against him. You know how important it is for me, for our family to remain Muslim."

Adeelah showed Omar the article she received from Martin and asked, "If Martin were to follow this minister's example and profess to be both Christian and Muslim, would that make a difference for you?"

Omar hesitated and gestured again with his glasses. "That would be a very controversial thing. I don't know. The other major issue would be the matter of your children's faith if you were to marry Martin."

"I agree. But I understand other interfaith couples have dealt with this issue and have found satisfactory solutions."

"Let me read the article."

Meanwhile, Martin scheduled an appointment with Javed Rajput, the Imam at the Islamic Center of South Augusta, the Mosque which Adeelah attended.

Javed was known to be a man of unrelenting logic. He had a keen eye for picking up on discrepancies and a keen ability to read people. When presented with an issue, there was no limit to the time and energy he would expend in developing an insightful and unbiased understanding which would lead to a satisfactory resolution. He was very intelligent and highly respected. Martin would come to appreciate these qualities and this man's character.

When Martin arrived for their appointment, Javed welcomed him. Javed appeared to be in his thirties and wore a white salwar, a garment which resembled a doctor's coat and extended down below his knees. The garment featured patterned ornate, red and white, one-and-a-half-inch wide stripes which adorned his shoulders and extended down the length of the garment on both sides where it zipped together. His trousers were also white. His face was graced with a well-trimmed beard and mustache, and on his head, he wore a taqiyah, which is a white cap with no brim.

Javed instructed Martin to remove his shoes and asked, "May I offer you a cup of tea?"

Martin removed his shoes and placed them in one of the cubbyholes located in the mosque's entryway as he replied, "Thank you. I would enjoy a cup of tea."

Still in the entryway, Martin took a seat. Javed brought the tea, sat down, and asked, "Is this your first visit to a mosque?"

"It is. The building is very impressive. It looks like a glistening white palace. What's the tower for?"

Javed was pleased with Martin's kind words and explained, "That's the minaret, and it's used to call people to prayer."

After they finished their tea, Martin asked, "Would you show me around?"

"Of course. Here, where you came in, you've already noticed the purpose of the several cubbyholes along the walls. All worshipers use these cubbyholes to store their shoes when they enter the mosque, as you just did. You will also notice the basins which are available for ablutions, or ritual cleansings, which are required before prayer."

Martin also noted a ceramic decoration placed on a large table in the entryway, which was quite ornate and looked like an enormous pitcher. "What's this for?"

"It's only a decoration, but it symbolically emphasizes the importance of the ablutions which precede prayer." Then Javed took Martin into the prayer room, and explained, "You will note the mihrab, which is a niche in the wall which indicates the direction of Mecca, toward which all Muslims must pray. And you can see that the carpet is designed with decorative areas where individual worshipers can position themselves during our prayer meetings. Notice also the large dome which rises above the prayer room, which is a symbolic representation of the vault of Heaven. The interior decorations within the dome emphasize this symbolism with intricate geometric, stellate, or vegetal motifs to create breathtaking patterns meant to awe and inspire. Around the dome's base, you can see calligraphic Arabic inscriptions, which are quotations from the Holy Quran."

Martin noted the enormous chandelier which hovered over the prayer room and commented, "I've never seen a chandelier so large in my life! It's stunningly beautiful."

Javed's smile indicated his pleasure with Martin's compliment. "Thank you. Over here, you can see the courtyard. This is an area used for fellowship."

Martin admired the enormous fountain in the courtyard, and Javed explained, "This fountain is mostly decorative. In many mosques, however, it's used for the ablutions or ritual cleansings, which I told you about earlier. In this mosque, we only use the basins which you saw in the entryway."

Javed led Martin into a well-stocked library, where the two men sat down together, and Javed asked, "What did you want to talk to me about?"

Martin began by explaining how he and Adeelah had met, and that his initial interest when they met was to share the experience he had when he worked with Muslim friends in Morocco. He explained, "However, during these first meetings, Adeelah and I enjoyed being together. So, we began seeing each other regularly, and we fell in love. When her father discovered our relationship, he forbade Adeelah from seeing me, which devastated both of us. Both of our families oppose our relationship, which very reluctantly led us to stop seeing each other."

As he spoke, tears filled his eyes, spilled onto his cheeks, and flowed down his face to the corners of his mouth. Martin could taste their saltiness, and his lower lip quivered as he continued. "Javed, the truth is, both of us long to be together."

Touched by Martin's grief, but knowing there was no way he could approve of a relationship between Martin, a Christian, and Adeelah, a Muslim, Javed observed, "You certainly understand such opposition is common among both Muslim and Christian families."

"Adeelah and I both take our faith in God seriously. We know there are significant differences between our respective religions. So yes, we certainly understand the opposition from both of our families is quite common."

Martin brought with him a copy of the article, entitled, *I am Muslim and Christian*. He went over the article with Javed, which explained how the Reverend Paul Reynolds, a Methodist minister, had come to profess to be both Christian and Muslim. Martin continued, "I am eager to explore the possibility of doing the same thing, with the hope that my profession of faith as a Muslim would eliminate the opposition from Adeelah's parents."

Javed looked at Martin with a skeptical gaze and replied, "Surely you can see that becoming a Muslim, just for the purpose of having a relationship with a Muslim woman, will most likely be viewed as hypocritical. This will especially be the case if you propose to practice both the Christian faith and the Muslim faith, which is very unusual, as you must certainly know. And what about the opposition from your parents?"

Martin leaned forward. "I do understand what you say about perceived hypocrisy, which is one reason I wanted to meet with you. I have two goals: One, to demonstrate that my interest in Islam has roots which predate my relationship with Adeelah. And two, to make sure I understand the ramifications of becoming a Muslim. Regarding my parents' opposition, I don't see my proposed course of action as such an insurmountable obstacle."

"I think you need to be prepared to learn your parents' opposition may be more of an obstacle than you think. At any rate, please continue."

"First, I want to confirm my perception that Muslims who are members of your congregation are predominantly Sunni Muslims. Is that correct?"

"That is true."

"That appeals to me because it's my understanding that Sunni Muslims don't recognize the more formal organizational hierarchy, which is a characteristic of Shia Muslims. It's also my understanding that, unlike Shia Muslims, Sunni Muslims don't recognize any authoritative source of doctrinal interpretation, like the Catholic Church does, for example. So, I understand that, among Sunnis, anyone can interpret the Holy Quran and other religious scriptures with freedom and greater acceptance. Are my observations accurate?"

Javed stroked his chin as he listened to Martin. "What you say is true."

"That's important to me for two reasons. One, it's more compatible with my independent evangelical Christian background, which also doesn't recognize any organizational hierarchy. And two, such freedom of interpretation would make it easier for me to adapt to theological issues, which have been a traditional source of division between Muslims and Christians. I view this freedom of interpretation to be especially important in a scenario where I profess to be both Muslim and Christian."

Javed paused to ponder what Martin said and then replied. "Nevertheless, there are some significant differences between Muslim and Christian theology."

"I happen to have a degree in Christian theology, and I have read the Holy Quran. So, I probably understand such differences better than most. I'm hoping you and I can discuss such differences in a frank and open way, without offending each other."

Javed sat back in his chair. "I'd find that interesting."

"Good. So would I. Let me begin by sharing my first significant encounter with Muslims, which occurred in Morocco."

Lifting his hand with a welcoming gesture, Javed encouraged Martin, "Please, go ahead."

"Some years ago, the Air Force sent me to Morocco, where I worked with a small number of Muslims during Ramadan, and we came to view each other as friends. One day, I asked them what they prayed during their five daily prayer times. Their response included what I've come to know as the first Surah in the Holy Quran, which I've memorized, 'In the name of Allah Most Gracious Most Merciful. Praise be to Allah, the Cherisher and Sustainer of the Worlds. Most Gracious Most Merciful Master of the Day of Judgment, Thee do we worship and Thine aid we seek. Guide us in the straight way. The way of those on whom Thou hast bestowed Thy Grace, to those whose portion is not wrath and who go not astray.'"

Javed interrupted, "I'm impressed you've memorized the Surah. Please proceed."

"Thank you. This is a prayer that I, as a Christian, also pray. When my Moroccan friends shared this Surah with me, it was somewhat of an epiphany for me. There's a similar prayer in the Old Testament book of Psalms, which both Jews and Christians sometimes pray, which goes like this: 'Search me, God, and know my heart. Try me, and know my thoughts. See if there is any wicked way in me, and lead me in the everlasting way.'" (Psalm 139:23 24)

"I'm familiar with this prayer, and you're right. It's very similar to the Surah."

Martin stood and faced Javed. "As an evangelical Christian, I was taught we must put our faith in Jesus Christ, who taught us that by God's grace we are saved and have the assurance we'll one day go to Heaven. But Christians also believe, as I expect Muslims believe as well, that if we pray and ask God for anything which is in agreement with His will, God will grant our petition."

Javed commented, "We certainly do believe Allah grants our petitions when they are in agreement with His will."

Martin continued. "In my experience with my Moroccan friends, it occurred to me that Muslims, who pray the prayer found in this first Surah of the Holy Quran, are essentially asking God for salvation so that they will go to Heaven after their life on earth ends. There's an even more explicit prayer in the Holy Quran which reads, 'Our Lord, avert from us the punishment of Hell, for the punishment thereof is a lasting torment.' (25:65) Both of these prayers and the prayer found in the book of Psalms are clearly prayers for salvation."

"Since God not only gave us the first Surah in the Holy Quran and expects us to use it as our prayer, I must believe He must also desire that we all find the straight path which leads us to eternal life, which is the request we make in this prayer. So, certainly finding the straight path which leads us to eternal life must be in agreement with God's will. So, I had to conclude then, and I believe now, that God grants the requests of those who pray these prayers. And I see in these prayers the essentials which reflect common ground between the three monotheistic religions–Judaism, Islam, and Christianity."

"That's very insightful."

Martin sat down, leaned forward, and continued with animated gestures. "But we remain divided! Javed, the ironic thing is that someplace right now there is, most likely, a group of Jews meeting in a Synagogue who are rejoicing that they alone possess the full truth of God. And there is also right now, most likely, a group of Muslims meeting in a Mosque, who are also rejoicing that they alone possess the full truth of God. You, sir, may have participated in such conversations. And there is also right now, most likely, a group of Christians meeting in a Church, who are also rejoicing that they alone possess the full truth of God. I confess that I, as a Christian, have been a part of such conversations on occasions."

Javed replied, "I must also confess, I too have participated in such conversations."

"Obviously, none of these three groups fully agree about what the full truth of God is. Consequently, there are only two possible outcomes. The first is, only one of these groups can truly be right and possess the full truth of God. The second possibility, which is more probable, is that all three of these groups understand something of the truth of God. But, as humans, we're incapable of perfectly understanding all of the mind of God. So, the understanding which each group has independently attained is simply imperfect. Consequently, it occurs to me that Jews, Muslims, and Christians all understand God's truth adequately, but not perfectly."

"Very interesting. You give me something to contemplate."

Martin continued, "There have been many attempts to reduce our differing views to a set of truths we can all agree on. In the seventeenth century, there was a philosopher known as Herbert of Cherbury, who saw the serious divisions among the various religions–Muslims, Jews, Roman Catholics, Eastern Orthodox Catholics, and Protestants. And he came up with five essential assertions which he believed were common to all monotheistic religions."

Martin pulled out his pocket notebook and said to Javed, "Here they are:"

> *1. There is a God;*
> *2. This God ought to be worshiped;*
> *3. The connection of virtue with piety is and always has been the most important part of religious practice;*
> *4. While people are aware of their evils, they can and must expiate them by repentance; and*
> *5. People face reward or punishment after this life.*

"Well, I see no reason to dispute his assertions."

"Neither do I. Javed, I believe if Judaism, Islam, and Christianity isolate these, and possibly other, essential truths, we will also find that such essential truths can bring us into acceptable agreement. The question is, how do we identify these essentials?"

"Do you propose that Herbert's assertions are adequate to bring us together?"

"I like Herbert's list of five commonly held truths. However, it occurs to me that, when we explain to a new convert what it means to be a Muslim or what it means to be a Christian, we, of necessity, limit ourselves to a set of essentials which we teach these new converts. That's because new converts are simply not capable of grasping anything deeper than such basic essentials. So, these essentials, which we explain to new converts, are also the essentials which may make it possible for our two religions, as well as Judaism, to find sufficient common ground."

Javed listened with intense interest to Martin's words and commented, "That's a very fascinating approach to this issue."

Martin's face brightened, and he continued with conviction. "Yes, sir. Let me illustrate. It's my understanding that to become a Muslim, one must acknowledge two things. One, there is only one God. And two, Muhammad is His messenger. These are the absolute essentials to become a Muslim, and I understand these two assertions are known as the *Shahada*. Anything else a new Muslim learns will be edifying and very important, but such additional instruction goes beyond these absolutely essential requirements to become a Muslim."

"I agree. What do you see as the absolute essentials then for Christianity?"

"Allow me to share with you what, I believe, is a Christian version of the *Shahada*. In the Gospel of John, chapter 17, Jesus prays for His disciples. As He prays to God in verse 3, Jesus says, 'This is eternal life, that they should know you, the only true God, and him whom you sent, Jesus Christ.' (John 17:3) This verse, like the *Shahada*, tells us that we must know the only true God. Since Jesus lived before Muhammad was born, the Christian *Shahada* tells us that we must know Jesus Christ, whom God sent. So, both *Shahadas* are the same, except they name different messengers. Consequently, I see that the absolute essentials for both Islam and Christianity are virtually the same."

Javed reached out and shook Martin's hand. "I really like how you developed your idea of the two *Shahadas*."

"Now Jesus tells us that knowing the only true God is eternal life. Elsewhere, Jesus says, 'Most certainly I tell you, he who hears my word and believes him who sent me has eternal life, and doesn't come into judgment, but has passed out of death into life.' (John 5:24) So, Jesus tells us twice, and Christians understand that, by faith, we have eternal life–that is by believing in God, who sent Jesus Christ to us."

Javed leaned forward and interrupted. "What you just said is, in fact, a significant difference between Muslim and Christian theology. Christians say that by faith alone we have eternal life. Do you really believe people can go to Heaven without doing any good works so that they can then live any way they choose?"

"No, I don't believe that. Christians believe that saving faith moves us to do good works. The Apostle Paul puts it this way, 'For by grace you have been saved through faith, and that not of yourselves; it is the gift of God, not of works, that no one would boast. For we are his workmanship, created in Christ Jesus for good works, which God prepared before that we would walk in them.'" (Ephesians 2:8-10)

"So, while good works aren't necessary for our salvation, Paul tells us, 'we are his workmanship, created in Christ Jesus for good works.' What this says is: God's grace not only saves us; it also changes us. We become his workmanship so that we will do good works. So, good works are the evidence of true saving faith."

Very moved by Martin's words, Javed responded, "Your views are very insightful. They bring to my mind an illustration made by Ibn Taimiyyah, one of our Islamic scholars. He compared faith and good works to a tree. The tree's roots represent faith. The tree's branches and fruit represent good works. Without the roots, there will be no fruit. Indeed, there will be no tree. In fact, Ibn Taimiyyah stated, 'Faith's root is what is in the heart, and the outer deeds are inevitable due to that.' This illustration is very consistent with your comments about the role of good works and faith with respect to our salvation–that good works are the evidence of saving faith."

Martin was greatly encouraged by Javed's words. "Wow! Javed, you just made my point. That is a remarkable illustration which underscores this important common ground between Islam and Christianity. This Islamic scholar could not have supported my assertions more effectively! In the book of James, we read, 'Yes, a man will say, "You have faith, and I have works." Show me your faith without works, and I will show you my faith by my works. You believe that God is one. You do well. The demons also believe, and shudder. But do you need to know, you fool, that faith apart from works is dead?' (James 2:18-20) Javed, both Ibn Taimiyyah and James are saying the same thing! On a conceptual basis, I contend there is no significant difference between the Christian and Muslim views of salvation."

"I appreciate what you say. You've made your point well."

"Let me get back to my point about the absolute essentials. When you tell a prospective believer how to become a Muslim, and when I tell a prospective believer how to become a Christian, we only explain these essential truths. Afterward, when the new believer is ready to understand more about his faith in God, you teach him about Muhammad and the importance of the Holy Quran. And Christians start learning about the Trinity, the Holy Bible, and the death, burial, and resurrection of Jesus Christ. These teachings are very important to our respective religions. But, as I just illustrated, they are not the absolute essentials."

Javed interrupted. "But Christian belief in the Trinity and the deity of Christ is blasphemous for Muslims."

"I understand that very well, but I reiterate these teachings go beyond the absolute essentials. I would respond to your comment as follows: In the daily life of a Christian, he rarely thinks about the Trinity, or the deity of Christ, or any other theological doctrine for that matter. When he prays, he's praying to God, just as Muslims are praying to God. You say, Allah. I say, God. But we both understand there is only one God, and we both are praying to Him."

"I'm very impressed with your insight into these issues. But nothing separates Muslims from Christians more than the issue of the deity of Christ."

"Thank you for your kind words. I know the issue of Christ's nature, in the earliest days of Christianity, was a significant controversy. And it was not just whether he was God or not, but also whether he was a physical being or not, and there were Christians who believed Jesus was a separate god. There were many other efforts to identify who Christ was as well. But believers who held these different views nevertheless took their faith in God seriously, just like you, a Muslim, and I, a Christian, take our faith in God seriously. And it took the church four centuries to agree on the doctrine of the Trinity and the deity of Christ."

"Interesting! So, the question of the deity of Christ was controversial, even among Christians during the early centuries of the Church."

"Exactly! So, Javed, I see the rationale in the Holy Bible for both sides of this question of whether Jesus is God or not, and therefore I can confidently have fellowship with both Christians and Muslims despite these conflicting views. That is why I believe I can profess to be both Muslim and Christian. And while I don't include belief in the deity of Christ among that which is absolutely essential, I do understand why Christians see this doctrine as very important. And I see that, while the Holy Quran disputes the Christian doctrine of the deity of Christ, nevertheless, the Quran does assert that God-fearing Christians and Jews are people of the book, and consequently, the Quran views them as believers."

Javed replied, "You've made some interesting points. How is it you never became a Christian pastor?"

"That was my intention when I studied theology, but God did not open the door for me to go into the Christian ministry, and I conclude that it was not His will."

"So, you think you're capable of embracing both Christianity and Islam?"

"I certainly have no problem acknowledging there is only one God, which is the first part of the *Shahada*. The only other essential is my acceptance that Muhammad is God's messenger. I've already taken up enough of your time today. The next subject I feel we need to discuss is what does it mean to accept Muhammad as God's messenger. When can we meet again?"

"That should be a fascinating conversation. Why don't we meet next week at the same time?"

"That will work for me. I'll look forward to our meeting. I'm enjoying our conversation, and I thank you for taking the time to meet with me."

## THE SECOND MEETING WITH IMAM JAVED RAJPUT

A week passed, and Martin arrived for his second appointment with Javed. Both men were eagerly awaiting their conversation today. Both men found it edifying that they could discuss Martin's questions at a higher conceptual level due to their respective levels of academic theological education.

After Javed served the tea, Martin began, "First, I want to reiterate. I'm seeking a way to have a relationship with Adeelah which is acceptable to her family and my family as well. The possibility of my conversion to Islam may be an option to achieve that goal, but only if, as we discussed, I can do so in a non-hypocritical way which is consistent with my faith and my relationship with God. During our conversation last week, it was clear I've already acknowledged there is no god other than Allah. The second part of the *Shahada*, however, requires I also acknowledge that Muhammad is the messenger of Allah. For me to do that, I see it as necessary for me to understand what it means to recognize Muhammad as the messenger of Allah, which is the subject I want to explore with you today."

Javed took a sip of his tea and asked, "What does it mean to you?"

Martin leaned forward. "I'm glad you asked that question because, as I observed earlier, it's my understanding that Sunni Muslims in Islam recognize no authoritative source of doctrinal interpretation, like the Pope in the Catholic Church, for example. And every Muslim is, therefore, free to interpret the Holy Quran for themselves. That tells me nobody has a right to impose upon me his or her interpretation of the Quran. So, nobody can coerce me into a course of action, and nobody can ask me to endorse an interpretation of the Quran with which I don't agree. So, if I can profess the complete *Shahada* with that understanding, then I have no problem doing that. Is my understanding correct?"

Javed pressed his lips together with a slight frown. "That's essentially true. However, there are many very important expectations which are commonly accepted among Muslims as core practices in Islam–the other four pillars of the faith, of which the *Shahada* is the first pillar, is a primary example."

"I understand. However, I would reiterate that the additional four pillars of Islam go beyond the absolute essential which is necessary for a person to become a Muslim, which is the *Shahada*, or the first pillar, as you just clarified. Moreover, it's my observation that, like Christianity, the level of seriousness with which Muslims practice their faith varies widely, to include people who profess to be Muslims, but describe themselves as 'not religious.' Therefore, it appears to me that, in this country at least, Muslims have the liberty to practice their faith as they deem to be appropriate. So again, as we discussed extensively in our last meeting, I understand that the absolute essential starting point for every Muslim is the *Shahada*."

Javed bit his lip and objected. "What you say is true, but most Muslims don't practice their faith in such a superficial manner."

Martin stood and gestured with his hands. "Granted. I would hasten to say, and I'm sure you have observed, that the way I currently practice my faith is in no way superficial, neither from the standpoint of Christianity nor Islam. But if I'm to profess to be both Christian and Muslim, I need to know I have the freedom and discretion to interpret both the Muslim and the Christian scriptures in a non-conflicting way."

"And you think that's possible?"

Martin sat down, looked directly at Javed, and spoke with conviction. "I think it's very possible, as long as I recognize and concentrate on the absolute essentials. Because again, I believe the essentials of both faiths are compatible with one another. Our earlier discussion of the Trinity is a good example of what I deem to be a non-essential. When a prospective convert wants to learn what they must do to become a Christian, we, as Christians, concentrate on the essentials. So, the complex subject of the Trinity is not a part of the instruction provided to such an individual. And for that reason, I, as a Christian, deem the Trinity to be very important, but non-essential."

Javed objected and emphasized, "However, there are many issues which may not be essential, but they are, nevertheless, very important."

Martin leaned forward. "You've just re-stated my point. So, I agree, the judgment of what is very important obviously varies widely, both within and between Islam and Christianity. However, the judgment of what is essential is more easily agreed upon. And I feel it's imperative that we must recognize and observe this important distinction between what is absolutely essential and what is very important. Not only does this distinction make it feasible for me to profess to be both Christian and Muslim, it also opens the door for Muslims and Christians to enjoy fellowship together, knowing that both Muslims and Christians take our faith in the only true God seriously."

Martin thanked Javed for his time. Both men enjoyed their meetings together and came to view each other as friends. Martin came away from these meetings, encouraged with the feasibility that he could indeed profess to be both Christian and Muslim, but undecided about whether he would make this important and provocative decision.

~.~

Right after Martin departed, Javed called Omar, Adeelah's father, "Omar, *As-salāmu ʿalaykum.*"

Omar responded, "*Wa alaykumu s-salam*. How are you?"

"I'm fine. I want you to know I've been meeting with a Christian man by the name of Martin Webster. I presume you know who he is."

Raising his eyebrows, Omar was surprised to hear this revelation. "I do know who he is. What did this man come to talk to you about?"

"He certainly is very fond of your daughter, Adeelah. He wanted to know what he should expect if he converted to Islam."

"What was your impression of him?"

"He's a good man. He takes his faith in Allah seriously, although he is currently a Christian. It's interesting that he has a college degree in Christian theology. Additionally, he has read the Holy Quran, and I was impressed by the fact that we could discuss his questions on a deeper conceptual level because of his theological education."

"It surprises me to hear he has read the entire Quran. As far as I know, he has only known Adeelah for a little over a year."

"The fact is, his interest in Islam started well before he met Adeelah. During his time in the Air Force, he was sent to Morocco to work with some Moroccan Air Force personnel, and that was his first significant encounter with Muslims and the Islamic faith."

That information was no surprise to Omar because Adeelah had told him the same thing. However, now hearing this again, he commented, "So, maybe there is more to his interest in becoming a Muslim than just his interest in Adeelah."

"I believe that's true. His main focus before meeting Adeelah was to reconcile the differences between Islam and Christianity. I'll tell you, he has some fascinating views about areas where Islam and Christianity are in agreement. Regarding Adeelah, I'd say his desire to have an acceptable relationship with her has certainly been an additional motivating factor for his interest in Islam."

With some hope in his voice, Omar asked, "Do you think he would convert?"

"Based on my conversation with him and his positive views about the Quran, I'd say he's virtually converted already. He just hasn't converted formally. He's very active in his church. So, even if he does convert, I don't see him abandoning his Christian roots."

"Is it possible for him to do that?"

"It's unusual, but I think it is conceivable."

Seeing some hope for a better outcome regarding Martin and his daughter, Omar confessed, "I know Adeelah is in love with this man. As you know, I've forbidden her from seeing him, and she is begrudgingly obeying me. We were at the shopping mall one day, and she saw him there with another woman. She became so emotionally distraught that she almost collapsed. Do you think I'm being too hard on her?"

"I think you made the right decision, given what you knew about the situation at the time. If Adeelah loves him so much, it might be worthwhile to meet Martin and see what he has to say."

"I'll certainly give that some thought, but I must say I'm reluctant to see her in a relationship with a Christian man."

"I certainly understand, but I do believe you would like the man."

## Disillusionment and Indecision

When he arrived home, Martin sent an email to Adeelah in which he wrote, "I just had my second meeting with Imam Javed Rajput, and I came away from our meeting, encouraged that there's hope for you and me to renew our loving relationship. I love you and long to be with you, and I look forward to the moment in which we can freely express our love for each other again. I firmly believe Allah's will is for us to be together. Love, Martin."

Adeelah read Martin's email several times. And, with tears in her eyes, she resisted the temptation to respond to his email. While she desperately wanted to share Martin's optimism and belief that Allah's will was for them to be together, her family's opposition made her believe Allah had other plans for their lives. With a broken heart, she still resigned herself to accept what she believed to be Allah's will, but she also begged Allah, "Please show me I'm wrong."

Martin's email left Adeelah feeling despondent and deeply disillusioned, so she called Taslima. She felt a strong need to talk to somebody who would be sympathetic to her merciless emotional volatility. Taslima answered the phone, and, sobbing, Adeelah began pouring out her heart, "Taslima, I feel so lost. Martin just sent me an email to tell me his conversation with Imam Rajput was encouraging and to tell me he loves me. Moreover, he believes it's Allah's will for us to be together."

Taslima asked, "Did you respond?"

"No. I just can't. There's no way my dad is going to let me see him. So, I don't want to give him any false hope."

"Do you love him?"

Adeelah hopelessly dried her tears with a tissue. "I love him with all my heart!"

"So, what if it is the will of Allah for you and Martin to be together?"

There was a long hesitation. Taslima could hear Adeelah's sobs as she waited for her response. Finally, she said, "Then I believe my dad will somehow change his mind. Until that happens, I refuse to see Martin, and I don't see us getting back together."

"The problem with this is, I see nothing to bring this matter to your dad's mind. So, what would prompt him to change his mind?"

"I don't know. I do know very well, however, my dad is totally unwilling to talk with me about Martin."

"What about your mom?"

"I think she would potentially like Martin and accept our relationship together. But, with her old-school ways, there's no way she's going to bring up the subject with my dad."

"And you're not seeing Martin at all right now?"

"No. I've made it clear to Martin I won't see him, he respects that, and it's killing me!"

"Well, I must tell you, other than keeping you in my prayers, I don't know what I can do for you."

"Please do keep me in your prayers. Other than that, there's nothing you can do. I'm just grateful I can talk to somebody who listens to me with a sympathetic ear. Thank you."

~.~

When Adeelah didn't respond to Martin's email, he also felt dreadfully disillusioned. While he seriously contemplated the possibility of converting to Islam, he began to wonder if even that would make a difference with Omar, Adeelah's father. *And even if I were to convert to Islam and win Omar's approval*, Martin pondered, *What about my own family's opposition to my decision to convert to Islam*? Suddenly, he felt very overwhelmed.

On Friday, he had a date with Rosalyn. He thought seriously about canceling the date. He was not in the mood to see her. But he reluctantly decided to proceed with their plan to go to the Clear Mug Drive-In for a casual dinner, followed by roller skating at the Royal Way Roller Way.

As he went over to pick Rosalyn up, he reasoned within himself, *Rosalyn is attractive, intelligent, very well-liked by everybody at church, including my parents*. He liked her a lot. He was close to falling in love with her before she went off to get her master's degree, and before he met Adeelah. She liked him too. There was absolutely no controversy for them to be together. The potential for a relationship, which would lead to marriage, made sense. By the time he got to her house, he was beginning to look forward to their date.

He knocked on the door at 6:30, and when Rosalyn opened it, Martin was awestruck by the woman who stood before him. With her long blonde hair and her very feminine figure, she looked sensational in her blue jeans and the red plaid blouse she wore. She greeted him with all smiles, a kiss, and blue eyes which were only too happy to be seeing Martin. Martin felt pretty good to be seeing her as well.

At the Clear Mug Drive-In, they both ordered the restaurant's cheeseburgers, French fries, and their famous root beer. No place had better root beer than the Clear Mug Drive-In. It had an almost creamy flavor, with only a touch of the tartness typical of root beer–but not so strong as that of most root beers.

The ambiance at the Clear Mug Drive-In was that of the bobby socks era of the 1950s and 60s, making it very popular with a wide range of clientele. Attractive young female waitresses came to each car on roller skates to take customers' orders and returned with trays of food, which they hung on the cars' driver-side windows. The windows had to be opened halfway, so the trays could be attached to the windows. Music from the 50s and the 60s added to the nostalgic ambiance.

Martin and Rosalyn's conversation was animated. They talked about their many friends, upcoming events at church, and what was going on with their families.

Afterward, they headed for the Royal Way Roller Way. While not great skaters, they could get around the skating rink as well as most. The rink was adorned with gaudy colored lights, and the music was loud and continuous. Some skaters were very talented. Some couples danced on their skates, doing underarm turns and other spectacular moves. Others formed trains, where long lines of skaters made their way around the rink. And some did remarkable and sensational acrobatics. Martin and Rosalyn skated hand-in-hand, enjoyed the music, watched the other talented skaters, and had an overall good time.

They arrived at Rosalyn's home just after 10:30, and they sat for a while on the porch swing in front of the house–one of the few remaining elegant older homes which had a porch swing. The evening breeze was pleasant, and the temperature was in the low 70s. They chatted for about fifteen minutes. As they said their goodbyes, Martin tenderly kissed her, and they hugged just before Rosalyn went into the house. Everything went well up to this point, but the kiss and embrace made Martin feel that he once again betrayed his love for Adeelah.

~.~

On Saturday evening, Martin called his friend James. "Do you mind if I come over to see you?" He asked.

"Of course not! Come on over."

When he arrived, James could clearly see on Martin's face that he was having a tough time. After making some coffee, they sat down at the kitchen table, and he asked, "How are things going with Rosalyn?"

Martin bit his lip, raised his eyebrows, and nodded. "Everything with Rosalyn is outstanding, except for one thing: I'm still in love with Adeelah."

"It's been a good while now, and you still haven't gotten over her?"

"Not at all. I went out with Rosalyn last night, and we had a great time. When I got her home, we kissed and hugged each other, and immediately I felt like I was betraying Adeelah."

"Hopefully time will resolve that problem for you. You know, a relationship with Adeelah is pretty hopeless."

Martin paused in reflection. "In fact, I'm not so sure," Martin declared, and he began telling James about his two meetings with Imam Javed Rajput.

With a surprised look on his face, James leaned forward. "So, you actually went to a mosque to talk with this guy! What's he like?"

Martin crossed his legs and nodded. "I found him to be a great guy, and we hit it off pretty well. The fact that I have a theology degree made it possible for us to discuss our respective faiths frankly and intelligently."

"What did he say about your chances with Adeelah?"

"Initially, he was very doubtful about us. However, when I made the case that the essential parts of our two religions are fairly compatible, I felt like he began to at least see some viability for our relationship, especially when I emphasized that the more conflicting issues, while very important to both Christians and Muslims, were not essential issues."

With a confused look on his face, James asked, "What do you mean by that?"

"Well, in my mind, the essential issue for both religions is the question of salvation. That is, what do we believe is necessary to go to Heaven when we die. I can tell you, if you examine some of the things they pray about, you'd find they explicitly ask God to save them, as we Christians do."

"But they don't trust Jesus Christ as their Savior!"

"On the surface, that's true because they believe they must earn their salvation by doing good works."

"Then how can you say the two religions agree about salvation?"

Martin leaned forward in his chair. "Well, they believe Jesus is the Christ, that He was born of the Virgin Mary, that He is a prophet, and that He will one day return. The Apostle John wrote in 1 John 5:13 about believers who did not know they had eternal life, and he said, 'These things I have written to you who believe in the name of the Son of God, that you may know that you have eternal life.' It occurs to me that Muslims are believers who don't know they have eternal life."

James interrupted, "I don't know if I can buy that."

"Well, listen to what Jesus said in John chapter 5. 'Most certainly I tell you, he who hears my word and believes him who sent me has eternal life, and doesn't come into judgment, but has passed out of death into life.' (John 5:24) As I just said, Muslims recognize Jesus Christ as both the Messiah and as a prophet, which can't be the case if they don't hear His word, and they certainly believe in Him who sent Jesus into this world. So, Jesus Himself says they have eternal life."

"I'll bet you'll have a hard time convincing Pastor Sawyer about that. So, how will this improve your chances with Adeelah?"

Martin sat back in his chair and pointed with his finger as he affirmed, "One option is this: Since I'm convinced our beliefs about the essentials are virtually compatible, I might be able to consider myself to be a Muslim as well as a Christian. By professing to be a Muslim, I may be able to eliminate the one objection which compels Adeelah's father to forbid our relationship."

Laughing and rolling his eyes in a way that irritated Martin, he scoffed, "That sounds pretty far out!"

Martin's jaw tightened, and he shot back, "The definition of the Arabic word *Muslim* means one who submits to God. I think both you and I can honestly say we've submitted ourselves to God, so by this definition, you and I are both Muslims."

Noting Martin's irritation, James insisted firmly but with a more conciliatory tone, "Again, you understand, Pastor Sawyer will never see your point of view."

Arching his eyebrows with a determined and defiant stare, he vowed, "I understand that very well. So, I fully anticipate he and I will have a very intense conversation about these issues when Adeelah and I win our battle to be together. But I'll do whatever it takes to ensure our religions don't keep us apart."

Having said that, Martin thanked James for hearing him out, said goodnight, and departed. He suddenly felt emboldened, with greater confidence, and renewed resolve to win the battle for Adeelah's heart and their love.

# A Providential Accident

Adeelah departed City Hall to attend the Friday 1:30 PM service at the Islamic Center of South Augusta. She was stopped at a traffic light. When she got the green light, she entered the intersection, just as a car in the cross street on the left accelerated through the red light and, with screeching brakes, struck her car on the driver's side with an ominous, ear-splitting crash. Broken glass and bursting metal parts went flying in all directions. The impact completely collapsed the left side of her Kia Soul, deployed the car's side airbag, and hurled Adeelah and the driver's seat into the front passenger seat. The smell of gasoline quickly permeated the air. A woman, who witnessed the crash, screamed. The thunderous collision set off several car alarms in the immediate area.

A bystander immediately called 911 for an ambulance, which also alerted Fire Chief Martin Webster. A police car, an ambulance, and a firetruck, with sirens blaring, sped to the scene of the accident. Martin arrived first.

When he saw the lime-green Kia, he was horrified, knowing almost immediately that it was Adeelah's car. When he got out of his car, the smell of gasoline prompted him to grab his fire extinguisher as well as his first aid kit.

As he approached the car, he could see a stream of gasoline which was slowly flowing toward a small fire which erupted in the engine compartment. He sprang into action and quickly extinguished the fire. When he got to Adeelah's contorted body, he could see that she was severely injured, bleeding, and unconscious. Martin cried out, "Oh God! No!! Please don't let me lose her. I love her. I need her in my life."

It was difficult to reach her because of the extensive damage to her car. The width of the car was reduced to about one-half of its original width. Debris from the accident was everywhere. Adeelah was shrouded with shards of glass from the windshield and was pinned underneath the steering wheel. Martin frantically cleared as much glass and debris as possible so he could reach her. He did his best to stop the extensive bleeding, both from her head and from her chest area, all the while crying out, "Oh God! Oh God!!"

Adeelah opened her eyes briefly and saw Martin. Her eyes reflected the fear and tormenting pain she was experiencing. But despite this trauma, when she saw Martin, there was a sense of relief which clearly showed in her eyes and on her face, and she mumbled his name, "Martin," and immediately passed out again.

The ambulance, police, and a firetruck had now arrived, and they immediately went to work, using their jaws-of-life tool to tear open the vehicle's roof so they could extract Adeelah from the car. It took about twenty minutes to get her out. Four first responders carefully lifted her up and placed her on a stretcher. Now that she was out of the vehicle, they discovered more extensive injuries. Ambulance personnel took over to provide additional critical first aid. Martin called for a helicopter to transport Adeelah to University Hospital in Augusta.

Meanwhile, a crowd had gathered. Many were praying. Police had to hold many of them back, so first responders could do their job.

The other vehicle which hit Adeelah's car had extensive front end damage. Fortunately for that vehicle's driver, the seatbelt and deployed airbag saved him from serious injury. He was stunned, however, and the police discovered he had been texting when he went through the red light.

The twerp, twerp, twerp of the helicopter could now be heard. As the helicopter landed, the blast of air from the whirling overhead propeller immediately sent Martin's Panama hat flying. He shouted to be heard over the roar of the helicopter's engine and directed one of the firefighters to drive his fire department sedan to University Hospital and explained, "I'm going with Adeelah in the helicopter to the hospital."

They placed Adeelah into the helicopter, and onboard emergency medical personnel went to work immediately to try to further stabilize her. She remained unconscious, and her pulse was very weak. She had lost a significant amount of blood. They asked Martin who applied the measures to stop the bleeding. Martin replied that he did. They commented, "While she's in very critical condition, your quick action kept her from bleeding to death."

Martin held Adeelah's unresponsive hand in his and prayed again, "Oh God, please spare her life and restore her so she can live a normal life."

The helicopter arrived at University Hospital in just under fifteen minutes, and they rushed her into the emergency room. Martin entered the emergency room with her, and a nurse asked Martin, "Why are you here?"

One of the onboard medics responded, "He's the fire chief. He stopped her bleeding and kept her from bleeding to death."

Frantic, Martin added, "She and I are in love. Please let me stay."

Because Martin was the fire chief, she responded, "Okay. But you need to understand, you may not like to see what we have to do for her. Do you have contact information for her family?"

"No. I do not. Because she's a Muslim, her family opposes our relationship. So, I've never met them. I know where I can get their contact information though."

As she started an IV for Adeelah, she said, "Please get it. We need to contact her family immediately."

Other medical personnel addressed her wounds, attached a heart monitor, and other monitors to check her blood pressure, pulse, and body temperature. Adeelah's face was ashen in color, and she remained unconscious.

Martin called Sarah Jefferson, Human Resources Director at the City of Waynesboro. His lower lip quivered as he spoke. With a sense of urgency, he said, "Sarah, this is Martin. Adeelah has been involved in a serious automobile accident. I'm with her here at University Hospital, and I need the contact information for her family, so we can let them know about the accident."

As soon as Sarah gave him the information, Martin hung up and dialed the phone number. When Omar El-Sayed answered, Martin said, "Mr. El-Sayed, my name is Martin Webster. I'm the fire chief for the City of Waynesboro. I need to urge you to come to the University Hospital emergency room as soon as possible. Your daughter, Adeelah, has been involved in a very serious car accident."

Omar cried out, "*Ya Ilahi!* (Oh my God.) We'll get there as soon as possible."

As Martin got off the phone, Adeelah's heart monitor sounded off with a shrill beeping sound. The nurse rushed to her side and hollered at Martin, "Stand back! Her heart has stopped beating!"

Martin quickly backed away, and his face paled as he watched in horror as medical personnel immediately surrounded her and bared her chest. They moved a defibrillator up to her bedside and applied the defibrillator's paddles to her chest. The electric shock made her body violently arch upward, but nothing happened. Martin was hyperventilating. They hit her a second time, and her body arched upward again, but nothing. After the third shock, the heart monitor indicated that her heart started beating again. After stabilizing her, medical personnel moved away. Only the nurse remained.

Martin, wide-eyed, with hands on his face and a quivering voice, asked, "Will. . . Will she be all right?"

"We have her stabilized, but we'll monitor her more closely now. You know, there's nothing you can do here, and your presence hinders us. Please go to the waiting room."

Trembling, Martin obeyed.

Omar and his wife, Kareena, arrived in about 30 minutes. Martin recognized them as soon as they walked in the door because Kareena wore a hijab. He introduced himself, "*As-salāmu ʿalaykum*. Mr. and Mrs. El-Sayed, my name is Martin Webster. I'm the fire chief for the City of Waynesboro."

Omar and Kareena were surprised to hear Martin greet them in Arabic. As they approached the nurses' station, Omar asked, "You are also the man who was seeing my daughter. Is that correct?"

Martin responded, "Yes, sir."

"And why are you here now?" Omar demanded to know.

Hearing this, a nurse responded, "The fire chief took quick action which saved Adeelah's life. Had it not been for him, she would've bled to death. He came with your daughter in the helicopter which brought her here."

Omar now softened his tone somewhat. "I'm grateful for your efforts to save Adeelah's life, but I request that you leave now. It is only important for her family to be here."

Martin, with a grief stricken-face, implored, "I understand how you feel, Mr. El-Sayed. But I beg you, sir. Please let me stay. I'm just as desperate as you must be to know that Adeelah will be all right."

Waving his hand with a defiant gesture, Omar snarled, "No! I will not permit it."

Kareena noted Martin's white polo shirt, stained with her daughter's blood, and begged him with a soft voice, "Omar. I don't see what harm will occur if Mr. Webster stays here with us. Please, let him stay."

Omar hesitated with conflicting concerns about his opposition to Martin's presence, his worry about his daughter, and his wife's plea. But, reluctantly, he agreed. "Okay. He can stay."

Martin gratefully responded, "Thank you, sir. Thank you, Mrs. El-Sayed."

Omar was now curious and asked, "How did you know that Adeelah was involved in this accident?"

"I didn't know. I responded as I would for any emergency. It wasn't until I saw her green Kia Soul that I knew it was Adeelah who was in the wrecked vehicle."

They all began to agonize because they weren't getting any news.

The firefighter now arrived with Martin's city sedan. Martin said to Omar, "Mr. El-Sayed, I need to drive back to Waynesboro to get my personal vehicle, and I'll return as soon as possible."

Omar coldly replied, "Do whatever you need to do."

Rush hour traffic was heavy. So, it took Martin about an hour and a half to get back to the hospital. His agonizing worry about Adeelah made the trip back seem like an eternity, and he continuously prayed for her. He stopped at a Chinese restaurant and picked up some chicken fried rice and some hot tea. When he arrived, he learned that Adeelah was in surgery.

Omar's tearful eyes were red with raised eyebrows and a wrinkled forehead, and he was wringing his hands. He explained, "Adeelah has several broken bones with some internal bleeding. They're afraid she might have some brain injury as well. The surgeon says she'll be in surgery for a few hours."

As with Omar and Kareena, there was a desperate look on Martin's face. "Thank you for the update." Martin then said, "I brought enough chicken fried rice and tea to share with you. Would you care for some?"

With a distressed look on her face and a handkerchief in her hand to dry the tears in her eyes, Kareena responded, "Thank you, Martin. With all that's going on, we're not very hungry. But we'll have a little something to eat. Again, thank you for your thoughtfulness. Thank you, especially for the tea."

"You're welcome. Mr. El-Sayed, would you care to pray for Adeelah and give thanks for the food?"

Bewildered, Omar was surprised and pleased that Martin would ask him to pray. "Oh Allah, the most gracious, the most merciful, my daughter here is clinging onto life. She is precious to us, and we don't want to lose her. Please guide the surgeons to use their skills effectively to save her life and restore her back to normal. We thank you for this food. In the name of Allah." His fervent, heartfelt prayer was moving for both Kareena and Martin.

Martin asked, "May I also pray?"

With tears flowing more heavily now, Kareena replied, "Please do."

With a broken, weeping voice and tears in his eyes, Martin prayed, "Dear God almighty. We're always grateful for your many blessings. I pray for Mr. and Mrs. El-Sayed that their faith in You may be strong in this desperate time. Help me with my faith as well. You know what our desire is for Adeelah, even before we make our requests known to You. We put our trust in You, and we thank You for what you will do. But we look forward to the moment when we can rejoice and thank You for what You've done. Help us to honor You in all we do. Amen."

Resisting the fondness for Martin which began to invade his heart, Omar fought back tears after hearing his prayer but failed. Tears streamed down his face. They sat down together to eat, and both Omar and Kareena found they were, in fact, quite hungry.

As they waited for the surgeon to come out, Omar commented, "I understand you went to visit Imam Javed Rajput."

"Yes, sir. I did."

"What prompted you to do that?"

"I'm sure it's no surprise to you that Adeelah and I are in love. I understand and respect that you oppose our relationship because I'm a Christian, and I met with Imam Rajput with the hope there might be a way to win your blessing. All of us. You, Mrs. El-Sayed, Adeelah, and I, we all worship the same God. I can assure you I take my faith in God seriously. Adeelah is such a wonderful woman, and I'm sure you as parents are very proud of your daughter. She and I have prayed together, and our prayer is that God will make a way for us to be together."

Omar responded, "As far as I'm concerned, the only satisfactory solution is for you to become a Muslim."

"As you most likely understand, my Christian parents would not be happy to see me convert to Islam."

"Then what hope is there? We're wasting our time!"

Martin leaned forward, took a deep breath, and told Omar what he had shared with Imam Rajput. "There's a Methodist minister by the name of Reverend Paul Reynolds, who has professed to be both Christian and Muslim. I am . . ."

Omar interrupted, "Adeelah showed me the article you sent her about this minister."

"Mr. El-Sayed, I'm contemplating the possibility of doing the same thing. I enjoy being around people who take their faith in God seriously, and I have certainly found that to be the case with Adeelah, and now with you as well. I understand such a course of action would be controversial–probably more controversial for the evangelical church where I'm currently a member. However, I think being a member of both religions would make it more acceptable to my parents and hopefully acceptable for you and Mrs. El-Sayed as well. Would that work for you?"

"If you and Adeelah were to get married, what would happen with your children?"

"Since Adeelah and I haven't discussed marriage at all, this issue has not been a subject of our conversations either. However, I'd be happy to see them become Muslims. That would not be a problem for me because I see many things which both religions have in common. I'd bring them up to appreciate both religions. Ultimately, as it is with anybody else, their choice of religion would be theirs to make."

Omar looked down and hesitated. Then he looked Martin in the eye. "Kareena and I will have to give this idea of yours some serious thought, and I assure you, we'll do that."

Now that Omar and Kareena had met Martin, they found they liked him.

Since it was Friday when Adeelah's accident occurred, Martin was supposed to take Rosalyn out. He called her and told her about Adeelah's car accident and broke their date.

With notable anger in her voice, Rosalyn asked, "Why do you have to be with her? And why do you have to break our date?"

Martin replied, "I'm sorry, Rosalyn. You know, I'm still getting over Adeelah. And, now that she has had this terrible accident, I just have to know she'll be all right."

"I'm not sure if I want to continue to see you. I need to know there's a future for us, and I just don't see that."

"I'm sorry you feel that way. I do understand. Maybe we can talk about this later."

"Don't count on it."

"Again, I'm sorry. I'll call you later."

The surgeon finally came out and reported, "We've done all we can do for the moment. We've addressed the internal bleeding and broken bones satisfactorily. She has casts on her left leg and left arm. The remaining question is her brain injury. She's currently in a coma. In the next two to three days we should know more as, hopefully, she begins to come out of the coma. I'm afraid, if the coma persists for more than three days, the probability for her survival will become increasingly questionable."

This was not the news Omar, Kareena, and Martin wanted to hear.

Kareena commented through her sobs, "Omar, I want one of us to be by her side until we see her come out of this coma."

Martin responded, "I understand your desire that Adeelah not be alone, and I certainly feel the same way. Please let me be a part of your vigil. My participation will make both of your efforts easier."

Omar, with reluctance, and Kareena agreed to let Martin participate. Kareena began the shifts. Martin would follow, and then Omar.

Martin's shift started at midnight and ended at 8:00 AM. When he got home, he called his parents, and when Ellen, his mother, answered, she asked, "Martin! What's up?"

"Mom, I'm calling to tell you that Adeelah was in a terrible car accident and almost died."

"Oh my God! How is she now?"

"She came out of surgery yesterday. Her left leg and left arm are in casts. She lost a lot of blood, and she's now in a coma. Her parents and I have organized a vigil. So, one of us will be at her bedside when she wakes up. If she doesn't wake up in the next three days, we have to face the possible reality that we may lose her. Would you please ask the church to pray for her and her family?"

"Of course. I'll do that right away. Did I hear you say you're taking part in a vigil with her parents?"

"That's right. As it turns out, I was the first to respond to the accident scene, and the first aid I provided for Adeelah kept her from bleeding to death and saved her life. Her parents are obviously grateful. So, they have agreed to let me take part in this vigil. I don't know what will happen after she wakes up. I'm hoping they'll agree to let us restore our relationship."

"Well, I'll call the church right away. Please keep me posted."

~.~

The first two days saw no improvement in Adeelah. At each shift change, they prayed for her. Martin was completing his vigil on day three, and Omar came in to start his vigil. Suddenly, they saw Adeelah begin to stir. As Martin and Omar watched with anxious hope, Adeelah opened her eyes and began looking around. She then called out, "Martin! Martin!"

Martin approached her bed and said, "Adeelah, I'm here."

She looked up at him with tears in her eyes and stretched out her free arm. Martin bent over, hugged her, and said, "I love you, and your parents and I are praying for you."

Adeelah responded, "I love you too. I'm so happy you are here with me."

Omar, moved to tears, approached her bed. "We all want to see you get well as soon as possible, my daughter."

Adeelah asked her father, "Can Martin stay here with me?"

"For the moment, yes. Afterward, we'll see."

As he drove home, Martin got back with his mother and said, "Adeelah has now come out of her coma, she is alert, and we're optimistic she'll eventually be all right."

Ellen replied, "I'm so glad to hear that. I'll let the church know about answered prayer."

"Thank you, Mom. I've been up all night. I'm on my way home now to get some sleep."

Two weeks passed, and Adeelah improved to the point that her doctor said she could go home. However, she would be confined to a wheelchair for the next few months and would require a significant amount of physical therapy during the coming months. Martin began stopping by every day to visit with her.

Adeelah called her friend, Taslima, to tell her about the car accident.

Alarmed to hear this news, Taslima asked, "What happened?"

Adeelah explained, "As I understand it, a car went through a red light and broadsided my car. They tell me I had severe injuries and nearly died due to loss of blood. Since Martin is the fire chief for the City of Waynesboro, he was among the first responders to be alerted about the accident. And he was the first responder to arrive at the scene of the accident. Martin took action to stop my extensive bleeding and saved my life. He went with me in the helicopter which took me to the hospital, and, consequently, he and my parents met and got to know each other."

"How amazing!"

Adeelah responded, "But that's not the most amazing thing. While Martin was working to stop my bleeding, I opened my eyes briefly. Despite the pain and the fear I was experiencing, and knowing I was severely injured, when I looked up and saw it was Martin who was caring for me, I felt this overwhelming inner strength which gave me a compelling desire to fight for survival. I believe Martin's presence in that precarious moment did more to save my life than his efforts to stop my bleeding. Because seeing him made me want to live for the day when we would be back together."

"That is astounding! *Alhamdulillah*! (Praise God!) So, how are you doing now?"

"I'm recovering from the accident, and I'm in a lot of pain. I'm confined to a wheelchair, I have both my arm and leg on the left side in large casts, and I'm facing a lot of physical therapy in the next several months. The wonderful thing is, my parents are now allowing Martin to visit me virtually every day."

"Wow! I'll tell you, I hesitate to assert that Allah has used your accident to change your parents' minds about Martin, but it does appear rather providential they are now letting you two see each other. And during our last conversation, you had no hope for such a thing to occur! Isn't it marvelous how Allah works in our lives?"

"It truly is. I'm so thankful I can see Martin so frequently. I just hope we'll be able to see each other going forward into the future."

~.~

The first time Martin saw where Adeelah lived with her parents, he was awestruck with their home. It never occurred to Martin that Adeelah's family was wealthy. To say her family lived in a luxurious home was an understatement. They lived in a mansion. A security gate opened to a cobblestone driveway, which gave him the impression he had been transported to some exotic place in Morocco. The attractive landscaping was immaculate and extensive.

Once inside the home, Martin was amazed at how elegant the interior of the home was. The home was so neat, tidy, and clean, it looked more like a model home which nobody lived in. Standing in the spacious foyer, he could see a large chandelier which hung from the vaulted ceiling in the living room. A very elegant staircase formed a wide semicircle down from the second floor to the living room. There was a beautiful large Moroccan carpet on the living room floor, and ornate and colorful mosaics adorned the walls. In one adjacent room, Martin noticed a pool table. In another adjoining room, Martin could see that it was dedicated to daily prayer, with prayer rugs for each member of the family. There was also a large dining room with a dining room table which seated twenty-four people. Another large chandelier added to the elegance of the dining room. Through the glass sliding doors in the living room, he could see a large screened-in swimming pool. And there were servants. During his first and subsequent visits, a servant ensured that Martin removed his shoes as he entered the home, and she was quick to bring Martin a cup of Moroccan tea.

During his first visit to Adeelah's home, Martin commented to Adeelah, "You never revealed you come from a wealthy family."

With a broad smile on her face, Adeelah responded, "I hope that doesn't bother you. As far as I'm concerned, I'm glad you didn't know because it leaves no doubt in my mind that you truly love me, and that you're not just interested in winning the heart of a rich girl."

"Then I'm glad too. I don't want you to ever have any doubt about my love for you."

## MARTIN AND ADEELAH TOGETHER AGAIN

Adeelah eventually got to the point where she could return to work but was unable to drive. Martin was only too happy to pick her up daily, take her to work, and bring her home in the afternoon. Omar and Kareena were increasingly getting used to Martin's visits. However, Adeelah's brother, Habib, was not at all happy with his visits. While Habib, age 19, was idealistic and zealous about his faith, he showed no signs of being radicalized or associated with extremist Islamist fundamentalists. He strongly felt, however, that his Muslim sister should not be seeing a Christian man.

Martin and Adeelah were also now eating lunch together daily at the Good Day Café, except for Fridays, when Martin took Adeelah to the Islamic Center of South Augusta for the afternoon prayer services. Both participated in these services, although not together, as is the custom in Islam.

Both were very happy to be seeing each other again. The challenge now was to help Adeelah get around in her wheelchair, which was especially challenging because of the unusually large casts she had on both her arm and leg on the left side. Although she was recovering well, she still experienced some significant pain.

Omar, by his silence, appeared to accept that they were seeing each other so frequently. However, both Martin and Adeelah were reluctant to confirm his acceptance because they were concerned they may not want to hear his answer. In fact, Martin's attentiveness to Adeelah's needs and his undeniable love for her made it difficult for Omar to be so adamantly opposed to their relationship.

On Wednesday, during lunch at the Good Day Café, Martin said to Adeelah, "I'd like to take you to a concert performed by the Symphony Orchestra Augusta Saturday night. Would you want to do that, or is there something else you would prefer to do?"

Adeelah responded, "That sounds like fun. I'd love to go."

"Great! It's a date."

This would be their first real date after more than a year of separation, and both were eagerly awaiting it with enthusiasm. Neither was aware that her brother, Habib, had been watching them for several days.

On Thursday, Habib spotted Martin and Adeelah leaving City Hall together, and he followed them to the Good Day Café. He went into the restaurant, found where they were sitting, and said in a loud voice, "Adeelah!"

Startled, Adeelah looked up and asked, "Habib! What are you doing here?"

He glared at her, with veins pulsing in his temples, and demanded, "The question is, what are you doing here? Nobody said you could be seeing this guy for anything other than transportation to and from work. You're done here, and you're coming with me."

Sitting in her wheelchair, Adeelah grabbed the wheelchair's arms. Despite the fear which appeared in her eyes, she responded adamantly, "No! I'm not leaving with you."

Habib went after the wheelchair. And, when Adeelah tried to stop him, he grabbed her by the arm, and she jerked her arm away to get free.

Martin shook his finger at him and warned, "Habib, do not touch her again!"

Habib glared at Martin with disdain and defiance. "You stay out of this!"

Restaurant customers were all watching. The manager called the police.

"I will not stay out of this." Martin's muscles tightened as he prepared to defend Adeelah. His muscular arms bulged and stretched his polo shirt's short sleeves, which were already tight. He nodded his head, and with a growling, angry voice, he showed his teeth and warned, "I think you should leave now!"

Habib grabbed for Adeelah again. Martin stood up, and, with his highly muscled body that towered over Habib, he pulled him away and wrestled him to the floor.

"I can't believe your father would approve of the way you're treating your sister here, especially with the injuries she's recovering from after her car accident. You tell your father, Adeelah will not come home until he agrees to have a conversation with us. You got that?"

Unable to move, with his head turned to the side and pressed against the floor, Habib gritted his teeth in anger and responded, "I'll tell him all right."

"Good! You do that." Martin looked at Adeelah, who was quite afraid now, and asked, "Are you all right with what I just said?"

With tears in her eyes, she responded, "I am."

A policeman now arrived, and Martin let Habib stand up.

The police officer asked, "Martin, what's going on here?"

"Charlie, this is Habib, Adeelah's brother. Their father has been very reluctant about Adeelah's relationship with me, and Habib came here today to force Adeelah to leave. Adeelah refused to go, and Habib got a little out of hand. Nobody got hurt, and I believe Habib knows it's time for him to leave. Can we just let him go?"

Charlie replied, "Yes. We can. But I must file a report about this incident." He filled out a police report which included Habib's name, address, and phone number, and, with Martin's assistance, he described the incident which occurred. Turning to Habib, he shook his angry finger in his face and sternly warned him, "Do not let this happen again! Do you understand me?"

Habib, now understanding the potential trouble he was in, looked up at the police officer, raised his eyebrows in fear, and replied submissively, "Yes sir."

Charlie then said, "Okay. You can go now."

Charlie then asked Adeelah, "Are you sure you're all right?"

"Yeah. I'm okay."

After Charlie departed, Adeelah, frightened, with tears in her eyes, turned to Martin and asked, "Now what do we do?"

"I think we have three options. I'm wondering if your friend, Taslima, can provide you with a place to stay while we find an apartment for you. If that doesn't work, I'll talk to my parents to see if they are willing to help. If neither of those options is feasible, you can come stay with me until we find a better arrangement. What do you think?"

She picked up her phone and replied, "I'll call Taslima right now."

Taslima answered, saying, "What's new?"

Adeelah's voice quivered as she explained, "As you know, Martin and I are back together again. However, the issue with my family got out of hand today." She told her about the incident with Habib, and then she said, "Martin told Habib to tell my father I would not go home until my father agreed to meet with us. I'm not sure how that will work out. I'm very upset and concerned."

"What are you going to do?"

"Well, Taslima, I was hoping you might be willing for me to come stay with you for a short period of time while I look for an apartment."

"As a matter of fact, I've been contemplating the possibility of getting somebody to move in with me to help me with the rent. Would that work out for you?"

Taslima's words immediately raised Adeelah's spirits, "That would be just perfect."

Adeelah called her father and explained what Habib did, and told him, "Martin will bring me by after work. I'm going to get my things, and I will move in with Taslima."

Omar replied, "Why would you do such a thing?"

The insecurity in her eyes contradicted the firm voice with which she replied, "It grieves me to do this. Martin and I love each other, and I'm not willing to be coerced by my family anymore about this matter. I want your acceptance. But I'm a grown woman, and I have a right to decide for myself who I want to have a relationship with, whether you accept it or not."

After she hung up, she turned to Martin with tears in her eyes and said, "This is such a difficult thing for me."

Martin hugged her and replied, "I love you, and I'm convinced more than ever that Allah wants us to be together. We find ourselves once again in a situation where we have no other choice but to trust in Allah and seek His guidance."

They arrived at the home of Adeelah's parents so she could get her things. While she struggled to pack a suitcase, Omar asked Martin, "Why does this have to happen?"

Martin hesitated and scratched his eyebrow with his thumb. With gestures which showed his concern and frustration, he said, "I must tell you, Mr. El-Sayed, Habib came into the café where we were having lunch and demanded that Adeelah leave with him. When she refused, Habib tried to manhandle her. You know she's still recovering from her car accident, and physical abuse is the last thing she needs. Even without the accident, physical abuse is simply intolerable. And this decision for Adeelah to move out is a direct result of that incident. Believe me. She doesn't want this. I know you don't want it, and I don't want it either. I've perceived, and I've hoped, there might be some acceptance on your family's part for our relationship, and I'd like to count on that."

Omar's face reflected disappointment. He raised his eyebrows, and with sorrowful eyes, he responded, "I too am not happy with what Habib did, and I want you and Adeelah to know I didn't ask Habib to do such a thing. He acted on his own initiative. That said, I think you do know that interfaith relationships, especially between a Muslim woman and a non-Muslim man, are not well tolerated in Islam."

"Believe me, I've researched this issue extensively ever since I met Adeelah. So, I do know that has been the case. But I also know such intolerance has been decreasing."

"Nevertheless, it's difficult for me to be tolerant about such matters."

"Let me say this to you. You know, Adeelah and I both take our faith in God seriously. Mr. El-Sayed, I promise you, if Adeelah and I can have your approval for our relationship, I'll do my best to ensure we'll always be faithful in our relationship with God."

Omar put his hand on Martin's shoulder and looked directly into his eyes. "I appreciate what you say, and I recognize your devotion to God. But can you become a Muslim?"

Martin paused, pursed his lips, and replied, "As you and I discussed before, I'm contemplating the option of professing to be both Christian and Muslim. If I decide to do that, I'll face some strong opposition from my family and my church, which is very conservative. With respect to Islam, at least Christians and Jews are viewed as people of the book. My church doesn't view Muslims that way."

With his hand still on Martin's shoulder, and still looking directly into his eyes, Omar nodded. "Well, Martin, if you become a Muslim, I will support your relationship with Adeelah."

Overjoyed and surprised, Martin's eyes brightened up. "Mr. El-Sayed, that is very encouraging for me. Can we share your decision with Adeelah?"

"Of course." Omar told a servant to have Adeelah come join them.

When she appeared, Omar said, "I've just told Martin, if he becomes a Muslim, I'll support your rclationship with him."

Tears came to Adeelah's eyes as Martin took her by the hand, and she responded ecstatically, "*Alhamdulillah*!" (Praise the Lord)

Martin followed up, "Thank you, Mr. El-Sayed. I must now ask for you to be patient with me as I meet the coming opposition from my family and my church. Additionally, I ask that you have a conversation with Habib to see if you can convince him to be more accepting of our relationship. I'd very much like to have a good relationship with Habib."

Omar replied, "I'll have that conversation with Habib." Then he asked, "Is there still some reason why Adeelah must move out?"

Adeelah replied, "Now that we've had this conversation, I see no reason to move out."

All three were happy with the result of their conversation. After Martin departed, Adeelah called Taslima to let her know it would not be necessary for her to move out of her family's home.

On his way home, Martin called his mother, and when she answered, he said, "Mom, I'm so happy to tell you, Adeelah's parents have agreed to let Adeelah and I see each other, so we're truly back together."

While Ellen was uneasy that her son would once again be in a relationship with a Muslim woman, she replied, "I'm very happy for you. I look forward to meeting Adeelah."

A tear flooded Martin's eye. "Thanks, Mom. I'm so glad to hear you say that."

Later that evening, Omar began to experience some uncertainty about his decision to approve Adeelah's relationship with Martin–a decision that wasn't easy for him to make. While he liked Martin, and even though Martin said he would become a Muslim, there was still some reluctance on Omar's part to allow Adeelah to have a relationship with this Christian man. His innate bias against non-Muslims made it difficult for him to fully put his faith in Martin's integrity. So, he called for Adeelah to come see him, and he said, "I make one additional condition, which I insist upon, if you and Martin are going to see each other."

Surprised, Adeelah replied, "Okay, Dad. And what is it?"

Arching one eyebrow, Omar pointed his finger at Adeelah and asserted, "If you two decide to get married, I will require a medical certification to confirm you are a virgin. And I'll tell you here and now, if you fail that examination, I will not consent to your marriage with Martin."

This really surprised and disappointed Adeelah, and she didn't understand why her father would make such a demand. Typically, it is the groom's family who requires such a certificate for a Muslim marriage. She pressed her lips together and looked down, unwilling to make eye contact with her father, and she muttered, "Dad, it saddens me that you would not trust my integrity in this matter, but I will consent to get such a medical certificate."

When she departed in her wheelchair, she recalled the moment in which she and Martin almost made love, and she mused, *I sure am glad Martin and I didn't yield to that temptation.*

~.~

Now confident that, not only was there a future for his love relationship with Adeelah, but also that God would bless their love, Martin now faced the need to have a difficult conversation with Rosalyn. Later Thursday evening, after a telephone call to arrange for him to visit Rosalyn, he arrived at her home to see her.

The frown on Martin's face reflected regret, and he struggled to make eye contact with Rosalyn. He began by saying to her, "It grieves me deeply that my relationship with you has been precarious at best. I hope you recognize that I've been honest with you about my broken relationship with Adeelah, and that neither Adeelah nor I wanted our relationship to end. Our separation was imposed on us by Adeelah's parents. And I hope you understand I made a sincere attempt to re-establish my relationship with you. However, I must tell you now. Adeelah and I have won our hard-fought battle to gain approval and acceptance from her parents, and she and I are now back together."

This revelation brought immediate tears to Rosalyn's eyes. Staring at the floor, she wept bitterly and did not say a word.

Martin continued, "I hope you'll find it in your heart to forgive me. And I want you to know, I'll always be fond of you, and I cherish the part you've had in my life. I hope you and I can continue to view each other as friends."

Still silent, Rosalyn could not bring herself to say anything. She was devastated. Martin departed with a heavy heart, but he knew he had done what he had to do.

Rosalyn would eventually fall in love with James, Martin's friend, and they would one day find happiness together as husband and wife.

# JAMES THROWS A PARTY

On Friday, as Martin and Adeelah left work for the day, Martin took a call from his friend, James.

When he answered, James said, "I'm going to have a few friends over tonight, and I'd like to see if you can join us. Are you free?"

Listening via the speakers in his car, Martin replied, "I'd be happy to come. I don't know if you've heard, but Adeelah and I are back together. I'd love to have you meet her. You don't mind if she comes with me, do you?"

"I don't mind at all! Bring her."

Martin turned to Adeelah, "Will a get-together tonight work for you?"

Adeelah grinned. "I'd love to go."

Getting back to James, "What's the show time? 7:00 PM?"

"7:00 PM it is. I'll look forward to finally meeting Adeelah!"

After Martin dropped Adeelah off at her home, she and Kareena spent over an hour, dealing with the impediment of her wheelchair, while trying various clothing options. This would be her first encounter with Martin's friends, and Adeelah was determined to look her best. They ultimately settled on a pair of black slacks with vertical white stripes. Her blouse was a satin ruby red. She chose not to wear a hijab because she was concerned Martin's friends might not be ready to learn his girlfriend was a Muslim. This combination, with her very feminine figure and her exotic Moroccan face, made her stunningly beautiful and yet, casually attired for the party with Martin and his friends.

Kareena remarked, "You look very lovely, my daughter."

Even her father, Omar, commented, "Martin will certainly be proud to be seen with you."

Hearing these words from her parents touched her soul, and she bubbled over with joy, a happy tear in her eye, and contentment.

That evening, for the first time, Martin came to Adeelah's home to pick her up for a date. For Martin to be picking up Adeelah at her parent's home for a date was a major step forward, and both felt as if a huge burden was lifted from their shoulders.

When she appeared in the living room, Martin's eyes opened wide, and he exclaimed, "You look absolutely beautiful."

Adeelah's ear-to-ear smile revealed clearly how pleased she was to be admired by the man she so dearly loved–the hard-won love of her life.

Martin helped Adeelah into his yellow Ford Mustang and put her wheelchair in the trunk. They arrived at James' home just after 7:00 PM. James greeted them, and Martin made the introductions. As Martin guided her in with her wheelchair, friends gathered around to find out who this elegant woman was who came with Martin, and Martin was only too happy to introduce her, "I'd like for you all to meet Adeelah. She and I have been dating off and on for a while now."

One of the wise guys in the bunch said in jest, "So Martin, did you have to beat her up and put her in a wheelchair to get her to go out with you?"

Both Martin and Adeelah laughed, and Martin responded facetiously, "It's good to be among friends who hold me in such high esteem. No! Actually, Adeelah is recovering from a very serious car accident."

As they were speaking, Priscilla and Rosalyn came over. Martin felt uneasy with Rosalyn's presence, but he nevertheless introduced Adeelah to them.

Adeelah, who also felt uneasy at coming face to face with Rosalyn, graciously responded, "I'm happy to meet both of you."

Both Priscilla and Rosalyn were coldly cordial, and Priscilla jeered with a devious smile and an air of contempt. "Adeelah! Hello! So, you are the Muslim girl Martin is seeing."

The crowd now backed away, not so much because they learned Adeelah was a Muslim, but because Priscilla obviously erected a serious wall between her and Adeelah.

Adeelah, trying her best to ignore Priscilla's hostility, graciously smiled and replied, "I see Martin has spoken to you about me."

"He has done that," Priscilla again jeered rudely, and she and Rosalyn turned their backs on Adeelah and walked away.

The scowl on Martin's face betrayed his shock at their rudeness toward Adeelah, especially how Priscilla, his sister, treated her. And Martin said to Adeelah, "I apologize for my sister. I've never seen her act so disrespectfully before."

Adeelah raised her eyebrows and shrugged. "I guess we still have to deal with some more opposition."

James now came over after observing what happened, and said to Adeelah, "It troubles me to see how Martin's sister and Rosalyn treated you. I suspect you know, Martin and I have been friends for many years, and I thank you for coming to my home this evening. Martin has told me a lot about you and the struggles you two have faced in order to be together. I, for one, hope you can feel welcome here, despite what just happened. And let me say I'm pleased to hear that you and Martin are now able to see each other again."

Adeelah smiled graciously and replied, "Thank you so much. I know Martin values your friendship and that he has confided in you about the difficulties we have faced due to our religious differences."

"You're welcome. Please make yourself at home."

Martin excused himself to go to the restroom, and Adeelah immediately felt alone and vulnerable. She made her way over to the food table in her wheelchair to get some refreshments. When she turned to move away from the food table, she found herself face to face with Priscilla. For a Christian, she had a look in her eyes which made her appear almost diabolical.

She glared with disdain and arched the left side of her lip upward as she spewed her venom. "You know you're wasting your time with my brother."

Adeelah smiled as pleasantly as she could, shrugged her shoulders, and replied, "What makes you say that?"

"You and your false religion just don't belong here!"

Adeelah did her best to restrain the trembling and the rage which was trying to manifest itself. She snapped back at Priscilla. "You obviously don't know what you're talking about. Martin and I both take our faith in the one true God seriously, which appears not to be the case for you. I've met many Christians. I value many of them as friends, and I don't find them to be so hypocritical."

"Are you calling me a hypocrite, you bitch?!"

That comment turned Christian heads and raised eyebrows all over the room.

Adeelah deviously smiled and replied with a soft voice in a way which goaded Priscilla, "I don't have to call you a hypocrite. Your horrible, mean-spirited social skills tonight scream out the word hypocrite. I honestly hope you and I can have another opportunity in which you can display the virtues which are common among God-fearing people. I'd sincerely like for you and me to be friends."

Martin now returned, and Priscilla, with her nose in the air, stomped away. Some of the rage within Adeelah now released itself. She fumed with anger, which she tried her best to restrain. At the same time, there were tears in her eyes–all making it very obvious to Martin there had been a nasty exchange between Adeelah and his sister.

Martin commented facetiously, "I'm going to have a talk with my loving sister. I'll be right back."

When Priscilla saw Martin approach, she immediately became defensive, and Martin could see the fear in her eyes. He demanded, "What happened between you two?"

"Nothing," she snidely replied, "Adeelah and I were just getting to know each other better."

"I want you to know, your bitchy attitude is completely unacceptable."

Priscilla said nothing, stuck her nose in the air, which now was accustomed to being in the air, turned around, and immediately went over to join Rosalyn.

When he returned to Adeelah's side, he asked, "Are you okay?"

Tight-lipped, Adeelah could not bring herself to comment, and Martin took her by the hand, "Let's get out of here."

Jerking her hand away, she adamantly replied, "No! I will not let your sister intimidate me."

They stayed a while longer, and Martin finally convinced Adeelah to leave. On the way home, Martin said, "Please tell me what happened."

Adeelah went tight-lipped again, shook her head, and said nothing.

After a short while, she finally said, "I'm sorry. I just don't want to talk about it."

They were now arriving at Adeelah's home. Worried now, Martin asked, "Is everything all right between you and me?"

Adeelah looked at Martin with a tear in her eye, and nodded to say, "Yes."

Then she reached out to Martin. He took her in his arms, and both could feel the rage begin to leave her body. Before he left, Martin reminded Adeelah about Saturday evening's concert, and confirmed, "Are you still up to going out with me tomorrow evening?"

"I'll be all right. I want to go."

On Saturday afternoon, Taslima came to visit Adeelah, and Martin had it out with Priscilla.

"Why were you such a bitch last night with Adeelah? You thoroughly embarrassed me, and I'm ashamed of you."

Mocking him, she fumed, "And what about you? You have no business dating a Muslim woman–a person who believes in a false religion."

"Hey! The fact is, whoever I want to date is my business, and I completely reject the notion that Muslims believe in a false religion. You don't know Adeelah at all. If you did, you'd find she's a superbly gracious woman who takes her faith in God just as seriously as any Christian. In my heart and mind, she's the most wonderful woman I've ever met. Your attitude toward her was totally uncalled for, and you hurt me deeply. You were not the sister I know and love."

These words brought tears to Priscilla's eyes. Martin's approval was very important to her. So, his disapproval of her now was devastating for her.

Her tears moved Martin, and he implored her, saying, "Priscilla, please give Adeelah a chance. I love her deeply, and you have no idea how we've struggled, and still struggle, to win approval from both of our families for our relationship. Both you and Adeelah are important to me. So, I longingly desire to see you two become friends. But I warn you. If you two can't become friends, you'll lose any devotion I have for you because she has my heart and my full devotion."

These words were a stab wound to her heart. Sobbing now, she assured Martin, "I'm sorry. I will try to do better."

At the same time, Taslima's visit gave Adeelah a needed opportunity to vent. With rage in her eyes and a defiant voice, she complained, "I can't believe the hatred which Martin's sister unleashed on me, simply because I'm a Muslim. As much as Martin and I have fought to win approval from my parents, such opposition from his sister just knocked the wind right out of me. I felt as if she socked me in the stomach. I'm not so sure if I can take this anymore."

Taslima gestured with both hands and encouraged her. "Adeelah, you've made such astounding progress so far. It would be tragic for you to give up now. The love you and Martin share is simply precious, and you both are winning your fight for acceptance. Don't quit now!"

Adeelah hugged Taslima. Their embrace and Taslima's words were like a balmy breeze which soothed the soul of a soldier which just made it through a hard-fought battle. And, in fact, Martin and Adeelah's battle had been hard-fought.

# THE GREAT DIVIDE NARROWS

Saturday evening, Martin picked Adeelah up, and they headed for the Miller Theater to hear the Symphony Orchestra Augusta's concert.

After dressing casually the night before, tonight Adeelah especially wanted to be more fashionably formal. Again, Kareena helped her choose what to wear. They ultimately settled on a white pantsuit. The white jacket looked like the female version of a tuxedo, with elegant lapels and coattails which extended down below her knees in the back. Her cobalt blue blouse and matching hijab added a touch of contrast, which nicely accented her elegance.

Martin showed up with a dark charcoal gray suit, a white shirt, and a bright red bow tie. Adeelah had never seen him so elegantly dressed. Together, they looked like they belonged on the cover of a fashion magazine–even though Adeelah was confined to her wheelchair.

After a thirty-minute drive, they arrived at the Miller theater. Neither had been there before. Built in 1940, the Miller Theater is a beautiful modern art-style building which features an Italian marble terrazzo floor, black walnut mill work, and a performance stage framed by fluted columns and hand-painted panels.

Before the concert began, Martin read to Adeelah from the printed program, "The first performance to occur in 1940 was A Night at the Moulin Rouge. The theater seats over 1,600 patrons and once had the distinction of being the second-largest theater in Georgia, second only to Atlanta's Fox Theatre."

Adeelah turned in her wheelchair to admire the theater's grandeur. "It sure is a huge theater." She noted how elegantly everybody was dressed and continued, "This is certainly a place where people come to be seen."

Martin took her by the hand and declared, "That may be the case, but I only have eyes for you, my love."

Her silent response was one of inner bliss–a response which her eyes happily reflected as she gazed into Martin's adoring eyes. She leaned her head on Martin's shoulder.

The concert was especially moving, joyous, and melodically enhanced Martin and Adeelah's joy of being together–a joy which was especially sweet after Adeelah's disastrous encounter with Martin's sister the night before. After the concert, they stopped at a nearby restaurant for dessert and coffee. Martin chose pumpkin pie, Adeelah chose pecan pie, and each shared their pie with the other.

Among their topics of conversation, Martin assured Adeelah, "I had a good talk with Priscilla earlier today, and I'm confident you'll see a significant change in her attitude."

Adeelah put her coffee cup down. "I hope you're right. Even during our sharp exchange on Friday, I told her I wanted to have a good relationship with her."

"Don't worry. I truly believe you two will one day become very close."

Martin got Adeelah back to her parent's home by 11:30. Their passionate kiss and embrace, impeded somewhat by Adeelah's wheelchair, was still sweetly perfect.

~.~

On Sunday, as Martin attended church, he was surprised to hear Pastor Sawyer announce that a Muslim folkloric group would be doing a presentation at the church during the coming Sunday's service. The church became notably quiet; church members were visibly astonished at this announcement.

The pastor explained, "This folkloric group comes from Uzbekistan, a Central Asian nation and part of the former Soviet Union. It is known for its mosques, mausoleums, and other sites linked to the Silk Road, which is famous as the ancient trade route between China and the Mediterranean. Samarkand, a city in Uzbekistan, is the location of a noteworthy landmark of Islamic architecture called the Registan. It is a plaza bordered by three ornate, mosaic-covered religious schools dating to the 15th and 17th centuries."

Now church members wondered if their pastor had gone mad.

Then Pastor Sawyer explained, "They asked if they could make their presentation here as a gesture for promoting goodwill. I want the congregation to know that my only reason for approving their visit is to have the opportunity to preach the Christian gospel to them."

This put the congregation somewhat more at ease, but still, there was a spirit of disbelief that their pastor would allow Muslims to speak in their church. Martin, on the other hand, was thrilled!

After church, Martin and Adeelah spent a wonderful afternoon at the Augusta Canal. Their love was sweeter than ever, now that they knew they had the approval of Adeelah's parents. When Martin dropped Adeelah off at her parent's home, he took time to say hello to Omar and Kareena. Kareena asked, "Did you two have a good time."

Adeelah responded, "We did! The concert last night was great, and the Augusta Canal has become one of our favorite places."

Habib came into the room, and Martin greeted him, saying, "Habib. How's it going?"

Habib responded coldly, almost begrudgingly, "I'm doing all right." Then he immediately left the room, showing no interest in being friendly.

Martin and Adeelah saw in Habib another battle to be won.

Before he left, Martin mentioned to Adeelah, "A Muslim folkloric group from Uzbekistan will be making a presentation at our church next Sunday. I'd like you to come with me to our church."

With an uneasy look on her face, Adeelah responded, "Do you think that's a good idea?"

"I'm confident most members of our church have not ever had any contact with Muslims before, including my parents. And I hope this folkloric presentation will help reduce the prejudice which our pastor has ignorantly fomented about Muslims in the congregation. So, I can't think of a more timely event to set the stage for my parents to meet you and understand that, not only am I dating you again, but that I plan to become both Muslim and Christian. I'm pondering whether I should disclose my plan to become a Muslim to my parents next Sunday, or if it would be better to make such a disclosure after they have the opportunity to get to know you better."

Adeelah tilted her head to the side and pursed her lips. "Are you suggesting I should start attending your church on a regular basis?"

"I'm pondering that as a possible strategy. If my parents and the people in my church can get to know you over time, they may be less judgmental when I disclose you're a Muslim, in the case of my church, and, when I disclose to my parents the plan for me to become a Muslim. Will you help me with that?"

Adeelah shrugged her shoulders. "Well, you've been participating in the services at our mosque. I suppose I can participate in your church services as well."

"Have you ever been to a church before?"

"No. I haven't."

"You might find our services both enjoyable and edifying."

~.~

It was now Saturday. The week had passed by quickly. Martin and Adeelah spent another happy day together, and Martin said, "I'll pick you up tomorrow at eight o'clock."

"Eight o'clock! Why so early?"

"As you know, I'm very active in my church. We have an orchestra practice at 8:30, where we rehearse the music we'll do during the morning service. At nine o'clock, we meet for our Sunday School classes, and the morning worship service starts at ten o'clock, which is when we'll hear from the Muslim folkloric group. The morning worship service normally ends at about 11:30. Afterward, we can go have lunch someplace."

The concerned look on her face reflected the question in her mind, *What am I getting myself into*? Her actual comment was, "That's a lot of church!"

"Yes, it is. But I think you'll find it interesting."

After Martin left, he called his parents to let them know that Adeelah would be attending church with him in the morning.

Ellen, Martin's mother, commented, "I'm sure we'll look forward to meeting Adeelah."

"And I'm looking forward to introducing her to you."

Adeelah mentioned to her parents that she would be going out with Martin early Sunday morning, and Omar looked up from the book he was reading and asked, "Where are you going so early?"

Her eyes watched to see his reaction, and she responded, "I'm going to visit Martin's church."

Putting his book down now, he looked up at her with eyes which reflected disapproval. "Why on earth would you go to Martin's church?"

Adeelah's eyebrows raised up and pulled together. And, with some apprehension, she replied, "It's part of our strategy to win acceptance from Martin's family for our relationship and for Martin to disclose his plan to become a Muslim. You know Martin has been attending the

Friday prayer services at our mosque. I'm curious to visit his church. We're hoping that, if Martin's parents get to know me for a while, they will find it more difficult to oppose our relationship, and that they will be more understanding when we tell them about Martin's decision to become a Muslim."

Omar still found it objectionable, but he didn't try to stop her. He simply commented, "It'll be interesting to see if your strategy works."

~.~

At eight o'clock, Sunday morning, Martin helped Adeelah into his yellow Mustang and put her wheelchair in the trunk. She wore a stunning blue dress which gracefully enhanced her slightly slender, but feminine figure. As they drove away from her home, Adeelah removed her hijab, so it would not be apparent she was a Muslim.

During the drive to church, Martin explained, "The orchestra's rehearsal this morning includes the music we'll play during the offertory as well as the music we'll play to accompany the choir."

"I'm definitely looking forward to hearing the orchestra."

When they arrived at Friendship Community Church, Adeelah sat in her wheelchair, in the sanctuary, near where the orchestra was located. The first rehearsal was with the choir, which sang *How Great Thou Ar*t.

As Adeelah listened, the first verse was a perfect expression of worship, which was entirely acceptable to Adeelah as a Muslim. However, when they sang the second verse, which acknowledged the deity of Christ, Adeelah found those words troublesome for her, since Muslims don't believe in the deity of Christ.

The orchestra then played the music planned for the offertory, entitled, *I've Got Joy*–a lively arrangement which Adeelah enjoyed immensely.

People were now entering to take their seats for the adult Sunday school class. Adeelah was surprised to see that men and women sat together in church, since services in a mosque require men and women to congregate in separate sections.

The Sunday school hour ended, and there was time before the morning worship service for people to enjoy some coffee and conversation.

Martin introduced Adeelah to Pastor Sawyer, who said, "Welcome, Adeelah. I like your name. It sounds middle eastern. Does it have any meaning?"

Adeelah smiled graciously and replied, "The name means equal, just, and honest."

"That's a wonderful name."

"Thank you."

"Well, I'm glad Martin brought you to visit us today. I hope you'll find this a good place to worship, but I'd like for you to know our service today is somewhat unusual. We'll start our morning worship service with a presentation from a folkloric group from Uzbekistan." The pastor purposefully did not mention that the group's members were Muslims.

Adeelah, with her gracious smile, replied, "How interesting! I'll very much look forward to this morning's worship service."

Pleased with Adeelah's response, Pastor Sawyer liked Adeelah, and it didn't occur to him that she was a Muslim.

Martin noticed that Rosalyn had spotted him with Adeelah. She stuck her nose up and scowled at them, making it apparent she was not happy to see them together. Martin bit his lip with concern and hoped it would not occur to Rosalyn to disclose that Adeelah was a Muslim. Fortunately, she did not.

The worship service would soon begin, and Martin introduced Adeelah to his parents and other church members who sat close to them. Everybody was quickly drawn to Adeelah's joyful, outgoing personality. Her quick, bright smile and the way she felt at ease with everybody was well-received, and most commented on how happy they were that she had come to visit their church. Martin's parents liked Adeelah right away and found her very charming.

Very surprised to see Adeelah in her church, Priscilla stooped down to face her in her wheelchair. With her eyebrows arched upward, she whispered in a tone which reflected repentance, "I want to apologize for the rude way I treated you at James' party last week. I hope you'll forgive me."

With tears in her eyes, Adeelah took hold of Priscilla's hands. "Consider all to be forgiven and forgotten. I meant it last week when I said I hoped one day you and I can be friends, and I hope today can be the start of a good friendship."

Now Priscilla fought back tears as well. "I can see Martin is lucky to have you in his life."

Noting Adeelah's slightly darker complexion, which she hadn't noticed before, Priscilla asked, "Martin has mentioned you are of Moroccan descent. Were you born there?"

"No, I was born here in Augusta, but my family immigrated here several years ago from Morocco."

"Martin tells me your parents have opposed your relationship with him. It appears they have become more supportive now."

"I'm glad to say they have become much more supportive. Our struggle to win their approval has been a major challenge. When I had my car accident, Martin was the first person on the scene, and he saved my life–I almost died. My parents were genuinely grateful to him, and they got to know him at the hospital. Little by little, they began to accept our relationship, and I think we've won that battle. Frankly, our main concern now is to win acceptance from your parents and you, of course. I must tell you, we love each other very much, and we very much want both of our families to be happy for us."

The morning worship service now began, and the folkloric group from Uzbekistan made a very well-done presentation. They showed a short video of some of the noteworthy things about Uzbekistan, and they demonstrated some of the culture which is uniquely associated with their country. They played some enjoyable music which is typical of their culture and talked about various foods which are unique to their culture as well.

Then, to the chagrin of Pastor Sawyer, they shared some of the things Islam has in common with Christianity. They emphasized that Muslims honor and believe in many of the same prophets as Christians. They also emphasized that Jesus is an important prophet in Islam, they believe in His virgin birth, they recognize Him as the Messiah, and that the Quran has an entire chapter dedicated to Mary, the mother of Jesus.

While the congregation enjoyed the presentation as a whole, their non-verbal feedback made it evident they were uneasy about the group's comments regarding Islam and Christianity.

The folkloric group concluded by asking if anyone had any questions.

Martin raised his hand and, when recognized, he asked, "What do you pray when you sit down for a meal?"

They raised their forearms to a position which was parallel to the floor, with palms facing upward, and responded, "Oh Allah, the most gracious, the most merciful, bless the food You have provided us and save us from the punishment of Hell."

To which, Martin replied, "I find your prayer very interesting because we Christians also find it very important to ask God to save us from the punishment of Hell. I trust God will grant to all of us the salvation which we request."

Pastor Sawyer's face went red, and he looked at Martin with an icy stare, which revealed he was not happy with Martin's question or his comments.

In his sermon, the pastor emphasized the need for people to put their faith in Jesus Christ in order to be saved, that without salvation through Jesus Christ, there is no hope of eternal life in Heaven. He also emphasized that the only true word of God was the Bible. He was obviously directing his message to the Muslim folkloric group. It was also obvious the folkloric group, and Adeelah, were uncomfortable with the pastor's message.

When the morning worship service ended, Pastor Sawyer was quick to corner Martin. And, in Adeelah's presence, he rebuked him emphatically, "Your question and your comments this morning were out of line!"

Martin smiled and replied with a feigned look of innocence on his face, "Really! And why is that?"

Pastor Sawyer shot back, "You know God will not hear Muslims' prayers for salvation or anything else because Islam is a false religion which worships a false god. So, God doesn't answer their prayers for salvation."

When he said this, Adeelah's face paled with embarrassment and consternation.

Martin raised his eyebrows, tilted his head to the side, and countered, "No sir, I don't know that. I know you believe that, but I confess I disagree with you."

Adeelah was offended but happy with Martin's response. Members of the congregation who heard this exchange were bewildered, surprised, and they were also unhappy with Martin for standing up to their pastor the way he did.

The pastor fumed as he responded through clenched teeth. "You cannot be a Christian without recognizing that Islam is a false religion."

With defiance in his voice, Martin asserted, "I am a Christian, and I disagree with you again."

"You and I need to talk."

"Pastor, I'd look forward to such a conversation. When would you like to meet?"

Caught off guard by Martin's response, the pastor asked, "When are you free?"

"Just about any evening this week. How about Tuesday evening?"

Pastor Sawyer checked the calendar on his phone and sternly said, "Tuesday works for me. Shall we say 7:00 PM?"

Martin nodded, and with a sly smile, he replied, "I'll come see you on Tuesday at 7:00 PM."

Martin's parents were visibly shaken and embarrassed about this confrontation.

As they walked toward their cars in the parking lot, David, Martin's father, asked with anger in his voice, "What's going on here?"

Martin, with Adeelah present, replied, "I don't know. I innocently asked a simple question, and we all heard an unexpected response. Do you find it ironic that Muslims would ask God to save them from the punishment of Hell?"

Dumbfounded, with an unfocused gaze, David replied, "Well, I must admit their response surprised me."

"Do you think God wants to save Adeelah here and other Muslims?"

"Of course."

"Then we can conclude that God's will is to save Muslims, right?"

David answered, with frustration added to his anger, "Yes. Yes! What's the point?"

Martin paused, faced his father, and gestured with his hand. "The point, Dad, is, as Christians, we believe God will grant the petitions people make to Him in prayer, when those petitions are in agreement with His will. These Muslims told us they ask God to save them from the punishment of Hell, a petition we understand to be clearly in agreement with God's will. Therefore, we must believe God is granting their petitions, and consequently, God must be saving them from the punishment of Hell."

Martin's response was totally perplexing to David, as well as Ellen, Martin's mother, and Priscilla. Adeelah was doing her best to subdue her glee at hearing Martin stand up for her religion.

David raised his eyebrows and puckered his lips. "Well, I bet you're going to have an interesting conversation with Pastor Sawyer. Are you and Adeelah going to join us for lunch?"

Martin responded, "That would be fine with me. Adeelah, can you have lunch with us?"

Adeelah brightened up and smiled. "Of course!"

They all went to Perkins Restaurant for lunch. By the time they got there, everybody had calmed down, and they had an enjoyable meal.

During their conversation, Priscilla, Martin's sister, asked, "Adeelah, what did you think about our services today?"

Adeelah pondered with a gentle smile, tilted her head, and cupped her chin in her hand. "I was surprised to hear so much music at your church. Is it always like that?"

Ellen's eyes brightened, and she straightened in her chair. "Actually, we usually have more singing and music. The special presentation today made it necessary to decrease the amount of singing and music we usually have."

"I think the music was the best part of the service for me."

Ellen responded, "I'm glad you liked it. I must say your question about our church's music surprises me. What is the music like at your mosque?"

Adeelah shrugged her shoulders. "Not anything like you have in your church."

David, Martin's father, leaned forward and commented, "Well, I want you to know you're certainly welcome to come back to our church anytime."

Adeelah smiled with friendly eyes. "Thank you. I believe I will come back."

David and Ellen found Adeelah's response both surprising and encouraging.

Ellen then commented, "Adeelah, I must say I didn't know quite what to expect when I learned I was going to meet you today."

With a playful smile, Adeelah lightheartedly responded, "Well, I hope you found me to be quite human. Martin's response after we first met was, 'I guess you don't come from some other planet.'"

Everybody at the table broke out into a hearty laugh.

Following up, Ellen continued, "Well, other than the presentation today by the Muslims from Uzbekistan, and now you, I have to say I've never had an encounter with Muslims before."

Martin put his arm around Adeelah and grinned, while Adeelah looked at him with adoring eyes. "As you get to know Adeelah, you'll find, as I have, that you quickly forget you're in the company of a Muslim. In Adeelah's case, I hope you'll come to see her as the wonderful woman she is–a woman who takes her faith in God seriously, yet a woman who just happens to be a Muslim. And I'm so glad she can sit at this table with us today. We're grateful we have gained acceptance from her family. My prayer is that you'll also find it in your hearts to accept Adeelah and the love we share."

David, Martin's father, now jumped in and said, "Adeelah, I think I speak for all of us when I say we're glad to finally meet you. I can easily see how Martin is so attracted to you. Frankly, the only challenge I see is the issue of our two religions and how this issue will play out if your relationship should lead to a wedding someday."

Martin leaned forward. "Dad, Adeelah and I understand this challenge very well, and we are committed to finding a workable solution which will be acceptable for both of our families. I must ask that you be patient with us and as open-minded as possible."

Priscilla changed the subject and asked, "So how's your recovery going, Adeelah?"

"My recovery is proceeding well. I'll still be in this wheelchair with these monstrous casts for a while yet, and I have a lot of physical therapy to complete. I have good reason to expect I'll make a full recovery during the next twelve months, thanks in a big way to this marvelous brother of yours who saved my life when I was a damsel in distress."

Wiping his mouth with his napkin, David responded, "Martin shared with us how serious your accident was. I see it as astonishing and providential that Martin arrived quickly on the scene to provide the first aid you desperately needed. And we rejoice to see you on the road to recovery."

As Martin took Adeelah back home, Martin's confrontation with Pastor Sawyer was on her mind, and Adeelah commented, "You certainly have set the stage for a challenging conversation with Pastor Sawyer. What do you think the outcome will be?"

"For me, the preferred outcome is that Pastor Sawyer would recognize that his belief about Muslims is wrong and that he should have a more tolerant attitude. But I confess I'm not hopeful he will change his position."

"What about your parents?"

"You saw how they enjoyed meeting you, and they like you. That is a definite step in the right direction. Moreover, it's obvious they had no basis to disagree with my reasoning about Muslims' salvation from the punishment of Hell. So, I'm happy with today's outcome. We'll have to be patient and see how things progress."

Adeelah was impressed with how Martin handled the day's delicate situation. She was glad she came with Martin to his church. She was proud of him and proud to be with him. More importantly, her love for him was deeper than ever.

# MARTIN FACES HIS PASTOR

On Tuesday, Martin arrived at the church at 7:00 PM, as he and Pastor Sawyer had agreed. Martin felt this meeting was crucial for the effort to win his church's acceptance of his relationship with Adeelah.

The pastor's demeanor was much calmer–no apparent hostility, and he asked, "Would you care for a cup of coffee?"

Martin replied, "I'd enjoy a cup of coffee. Thank you."

Now sitting on two comfortable chairs in the pastor's office, Pastor Sawyer asked, "What prompted you to ask the Muslim folkloric group about how they pray when they sit down for a meal?"

Martin tilted his head slightly, nodded, and gestured with his hand to make his point. "The fact is, I knew what their response would be, and I wanted the church to hear it."

The pastor put his coffee cup down, pulled his eyebrows together in a frown, and asked, "So, why was it necessary for you to get them to respond to this question?"

"Because I believe Muslims do worship the same God as we do, I believe God grants their request for salvation from the punishment of Hell, and therefore I believe they're saved."

With a quizzical smile, Pastor Sawyer cocked his head. "I don't know how you can say that, since you know very well, one must accept Jesus Christ as his or her Savior to be saved."

"I understand what you just said is one way to explain how one receives salvation."

"Explain yourself because I don't know where you're coming from."

As Martin had done with Adeelah and Imam Javed Rajput, he recounted to Pastor Sawyer about his experience in Morocco and his conversation with his Muslim firefighter friends who he worked with. Then he asked the same questions he asked his father, "Do you agree God wants to save Muslims?"

"Of course."

"Then, we can agree it is God's will to save Muslims, right?"

Pastor Sawyer raised his hand in a gesture of disgust that Martin should ask such an obvious question. "Yes," he retorted, with a tone of frustration in his voice, and then he quoted 2 Peter 3:9 from the Bible, "The Lord is . . . patient with us, not wishing that anyone should perish, but that all should come to repentance."

Martin shrugged his left shoulder and leaned forward as he responded. "A very important verse in the Bible! Moreover, as Christians, we believe God will grant the petitions people make to Him in prayer, when those petitions are in agreement with His will. Now, these Muslims told us they ask God to save them from the punishment of Hell, a petition we clearly understand to be in agreement with God's will. Therefore, we must believe God is granting their petitions, and consequently, God must be saving them from the punishment of Hell."

Pastor Sawyer replied, "I follow your reasoning, but I can't agree with your conclusion."

"Please explain why."

"Because I reiterate, Muslims believe in and pray to a false god. Therefore, since they aren't praying to the true God, He won't answer their prayers."

"What makes you think Muslims worship a false god?"

"Well, they use a false scripture which advocates violence against Christians."

"Have you read the Quran?"

With a scowl on his face and a voice which reflected derision, Pastor Sawyer replied, "Of course not! Why would I read a book which falsely claims to be the Word of God?"

Raising his eyebrows and shaking his head, Martin replied, "Then, Pastor, you don't know what the Quran says. I've read the Quran, and I find much of what I read to be edifying. There are passages in the Quran which authorize violence against Christians and others. However, when taken in context, it becomes very clear such violence is only authorized as a defense against violence initiated by Christians and others, and there are cases in history where Christians and others have initiated much violence against Muslims."

"And if you want to talk about the Quran and violence, there are numerous passages in the Old Testament where the Israelites initiated and committed genocide against their neighboring nations. They didn't just kill military men. They killed all the women, children, and, in some cases, all of their animals as well. If CNN had been around at that time, can you imagine how they would cover such a news story?"

Pastor Sawyer rolled his eyes. "Come on, Martin, you know as well as I do, God commanded the Hebrew people to attack their neighboring nations."

Martin put his coffee cup down. "I find it difficult to believe God would command such violence against innocent people."

"They weren't innocent! They worshiped false gods and refused to repent and turn to the true, living God."

"What you assert is the exact same argument which Islamist extremists use to justify their violence today–they also contend God commands them to commit their atrocities, and they are wrong. CNN justly condemns their atrocities. We Christians condemn their atrocities, and so do most Muslims."

Clearly upset, Pastor Sawyer almost screamed, "But that's what the Word of God tells us!"

Martin hesitated, leaned back, folded his hands behind his head in contemplation, looked Pastor Sawyer in the eye, and said in a soft voice. "In my mind's eye, I can see a young mother playing with her innocent son and daughter outside their home on a sunny day. They're laughing and having a wonderful time. And suddenly, out of nowhere, there appear these brutal monsters, called Hebrew soldiers, and they viciously slaughter them. As they perish, the mother and her children's laughter turns into screams at the horror inflicted on them. Psalms 137:9 aptly describes the soldiers' cruelty, 'Happy shall he be, who takes and dashes your babies against the rock.' Would our merciful, loving God really command them to commit such atrocities?"

"So, you don't believe the Bible is the Word of God!?"

Martin sat up straight, shrugged his shoulders, and lifted his hands in a matter-of-fact way. "I didn't say that. But I do find it challenging to accept those passages in the Bible which suggest that God ordered the Hebrew people to commit genocide against entire nations of innocent people. Moreover, not only did the Hebrew people commit such atrocities, both protestants and Catholics were guilty of committing torture and other atrocities against one another during the Catholic inquisition and the protestant reformation–both sides were convinced they were doing the will of God. And they were wrong!"

"I certainly reject the idea that the Quran should be accepted as the Word of God."

"Well, the Quran appears to be the basis for your assertion that Muslims don't worship the true God. But in the early years of the Christian church, before the Catholic Church decided which books should be included in the Bible, there were a wide variety of writings which many Christians deemed to be inspired by God, but the Catholic Church excluded them–writings which we describe as apocryphal today. And some Christians rejected writings which the Catholic Church included. But nobody accused such Christians of worshiping a false god, just because they didn't agree about which writings were divinely inspired by God. They called themselves Christians and took their faith in God every bit as seriously as you and I do. Consequently, the assertion that Muslims don't worship the true God, just because they regard the Quran as inspired, is ludicrous."

Rolling his eyes with a look of exasperation, Pastor Sawyer then asked, "Why is this so important to you?"

"Because I, like you, take my faith in God seriously, and it grieves me that we separate ourselves from others who equally take their faith in God seriously, just because they don't believe exactly as we do. And in a world which is increasingly ungodly, with no God-centered basis to promote peace, justice, and righteousness, our divisions weaken us as people of God and make us less effective. As Jesus said, 'A house divided against itself cannot stand.'"

"Christians and Muslims make up more than half of the world's population. Imagine the positive impact Christians and Muslims could have on our world, if we could overcome our differences, become united, concentrate on finding common ground, and promote the moral values which God-fearing people embrace."

"Do you think we should also unite with Hindus, who take their faith in their polytheistic religion seriously?"

"Hindus are polytheists–they believe in many gods. However, among the gods they believe in, they recognize there is one supreme God above all the other gods. Jews, Christians, and Muslims believe in only one God, but we also believe in angels. Angels are beings who are more powerful than humans. It appears to me that what we call angels, the Hindus call gods, in addition to their belief in the supreme God who is above these other gods. So, the difference between monotheists and polytheistic Hinduism is also not that significant either. What we call angels, they call gods."

Pastor Sawyer vehemently shot back, "But there are numerous doctrinal issues which clearly make Christianity and Islam incompatible."

"I understand that. And knowledgeable Muslims say exactly the same thing." As he explained to Imam Rajput, he reiterated to Pastor Sawyer. "In my opinion, we need to identify those beliefs which are absolutely essential and separate them from those beliefs which are very important. By absolutely essential, I mean that which is absolutely necessary to discuss with potential new believers, when we want to lead them to the assurance of salvation. Anything else may be very important, but not absolutely essential. By identifying those beliefs which are absolutely essential, I believe there is hope that Christians, Muslims, and Jews as well can break down the barriers which separate us."

"So, how would you classify the deity of Christ?"

"The deity of Christ is certainly a key issue which currently separates Christians from Muslims. Based on my definition of absolutely essential, however, the deity of Christ falls into the category of very important, but not absolutely essential."

"When we lead people to an assurance of salvation, we ask them to recognize their sinfulness and the penalty for sinfulness, and we tell them they must trust Christ for their salvation. They don't learn about the deity of Christ, the Trinity, the inspiration of the Scriptures, or any other doctrinal matters until sometime after they become a Christian. They are what the Bible calls 'babes in Christ' which can only handle the milk of the Word and not the meat. Moreover, if you had the opportunity to lead a Muslim to have assurance of his or her salvation, I have my doubts that you would include a discussion about the deity of Christ, which would totally alienate him or her."

Pastor Sawyer raised his hand to his chin in thought and replied. "I guess I'd have to agree with your last statement. But you would ask me to overlook the importance of the deity of Christ?"

"Not at all. I would point out to you, when the Apostle Paul addressed the Greek polytheists and idolaters at the Areopagus on Mars Hill, he said nothing to criticize their religion at all. In fact, he complimented them for being very religious. In his argument, Paul started with issues in which both he and the philosophers were in basic agreement. When he saw they had an altar to the unknown god, he began his most extensive sermon recorded in the New Testament, where he says in Acts 17:23, 'For as I passed along and observed the objects of your worship, I also found an altar with this inscription: 'TO AN UNKNOWN GOD.' What therefore you worship in ignorance, I announce to you.'"

"He said nothing about the deity of Christ or about Jesus being the only-begotten Son of God. In fact, he said in verses 29 to 31, 'Being then the offspring of God, we ought not to think that the divine nature is like gold, or silver, or stone, engraved by art and design of man. The times of ignorance therefore God winked at. But now he commands that all people everywhere should repent, because he has appointed a day in which he will judge the world in righteousness by the man whom he has ordained; of which he has given assurance to all men, in that he has raised him from the dead.'"

"Pastor, I emphasize that Paul referred to Jesus as a man, not God, and never even mentioned the need to accept Jesus Christ as Savior. His only goals were: One, to point these Greeks to the one true God, and two, to give them assurance of eternal life based on the truth that God raised Jesus from the dead."

"Pastor, I believe God still winks at the ignorance of so many people who take their faith in God seriously–Christians, Muslims, Jews, among others. Because our stubborn ignorance keeps us divided and keeps us from having fellowship with one another. This is not only an ignorance God still winks at, it's a divine wink at ignorance which God surely wants to eliminate. And I've found that when you make the effort to find common ground with Muslims, you discover it doesn't require that much effort, especially when both sides are willing to engage."

Pastor Sawyer hesitated and scratched his head. "I do see some validity to what you say."

Martin leaned forward, "Pastor, allow me to share one other important scripture. In I Corinthians 9:20-22, the Apostle Paul says, 'To the Jews I became as a Jew, that I might gain Jews; to those who are under the law, as under the law, that I might gain those who are under the law; to those who are without law, as without law (not being without law toward God, but under law toward Christ), that I might win those who are without law. To the weak I became as weak, that I might gain the weak. I have become all things to all men, that I may by all means save some.' If the Apostle Paul were alive today, he would certainly say,

'To the Muslims I became as a Muslim, that I might gain Muslims.' Why, Pastor Sawyer, should we do any less?!"

Pastor Sawyer replied, "You made your point very well, but you would deem the deity of Christ to be non-essential?"

"Well, let me bring up some more history that I'm sure you already know." Again, he reiterated a point he made to Imam Rajput. "In the early years of the church, there were many views about the nature of Jesus Christ. There were those who believed in the deity of Christ and those who did not. Among those who believed in the deity of Christ, there were questions about when Jesus became God. Some said at His birth, some when He was baptized, and some when He arose from the dead. There was also a dispute about whether He had a physical body or only a spiritual body. And some believed Jesus was a separate god. All of these views were held by Christian people who took their faith in God seriously. And the matter was not fully resolved until the fourth century by the Catholic Church."

"So, for four hundred years, there were Christians who had differing views about the nature of Christ and who He was. It took four centuries before the church decreed that the Trinity and the deity of Christ are Christian doctrines. It's absurd to think that massive numbers of God-fearing Christians during the early centuries of Christianity went to Hell, just because they disagreed about the deity of Christ."

"Well, I must say, I've never heard such an argument before."

Martin continued, "Moreover, there are Bible passages which can be logically interpreted to argue both sides of this issue. For such an important doctrine as the deity of Christ, it's difficult to comprehend that the Bible does not explicitly and consistently state that Jesus was God in the flesh."

"Virtually every epistle in the New Testament refers separately to God the Father and our Lord Jesus Christ, without saying anything about the deity of Christ. In fact, these scriptures distinguish between the two by calling our Heavenly Father God, and they call Jesus Christ Lord. Jesus said, 'God is a spirit, and they that would worship Him must worship Him in spirit and in truth.' The argument is made that, since Jesus was not a spirit, but a physical being, He, therefore, could not be God."

"And the Apostle John, who said, 'In the beginning was the Word and the Word was with God, and the Word was God;' (John 1:1) also said 'No man has seen God at any time.' And he said it twice–once in the Gospel of John and once in John's first epistle. John certainly did see

Jesus, so it can be argued from these verses in John 1:18 and 1 John 4:12, where John says exactly the same thing, that when John saw Jesus, he did not see Him as God. No wonder there were disputes about the nature of Jesus Christ in the early church! And for these same reasons, given these seemingly contradictory biblical passages, it's at least understandable how Islam recognizes Jesus as an important prophet but not God."

Pastor Sawyer, with anger in his voice, replied, "Are you trying to convince me that Jesus is not God?"

Martin stood and looked Pastor Sawyer in the eye. "No, Pastor. And I'm not denying His deity either. All I'm saying, as important as this doctrine is to most Christians, I believe, the controversial nature of this doctrine, especially in early church history, does not justify such a dogmatic view which keeps us from having fellowship with people who take their faith in God just as seriously as you and I do, but people who nevertheless differ with us regarding the Christian doctrine of the deity of Christ. Among such people are Muslims who ask God for salvation from the punishment of Hell. And I, for one, believe they are praying to the same God as we pray to, and that God answers their prayers, since there is no doubt that their requests are in agreement with God's will,"

Pastor Sawyer then commented, "But Muslims believe they earn their way to Heaven by good works."

"Yes. They do. But the fact is, since they're asking God to save them from the punishment of Hell, they're also acknowledging their good works are inadequate, and that God must grant them the salvation they need. Now, allow me to share a conversation I recently had with a Muslim imam about this very issue."

"This imam criticized Christianity from his perspective, saying that we Christians believe we can be saved and live any way we want to, without doing any good works. I replied that he was only partially right and he needed to understand Christian beliefs more fully. I quoted the Apostle Paul in his letter to the Ephesians, 'For by grace you have been saved through faith, and that not of yourselves; it is the gift of God, not of works, that no one would boast. For we are his workmanship, created in Christ Jesus for good works, which God prepared before that we would walk in them.' (Ephesians 2:8-10) Then I explained to him that Christians must do good works, not to earn our salvation, but because when we get right with God, He changes us in a way which compels us to do good works. So yes. As Christians, we can live any way we want. But, if we are truly Christians, God changes us so that we want to do good works."

"Then I pointed out to my Muslim friend that when Jesus said we must be born again, He was referring to this change which God does in us. And I also pointed out that a Muslim can observe this change when a new convert commits to become a Muslim–a change which is the result of God's grace. Now I tell you, Pastor, this had a profound impact on my Muslim friend, and I believe he now views his own faith as a Muslim in this new light."

Pastor Sawyer interrupted, "The Bible does say that God's plan of salvation requires an individual to believe that God has raised Jesus from the dead, and Muslims don't believe Jesus died on the cross and rose again."

"Pastor, I go back to my assertion that we should distinguish between what is absolutely essential from what is very important. Again, I deem the necessity to believe in Christ's resurrection to be very important, but not absolutely essential. Most passages in the Bible ask people to trust Christ for salvation, without mentioning the need to believe that God raised Him from the dead. In Jesus' own words we read, 'This is eternal life, that they should know you, the only true God, and him whom you sent, Jesus Christ.' (John 17:3) Here we see that Jesus explains how we can have eternal life and makes no mention of His resurrection or the need to acknowledge it. Muslims certainly know the only true God and Jesus Christ, whom God sent into this world. So, according to Jesus' own words, they have eternal life."

"I must tell you, however, as a Christian pastor, I can't accept your viewpoint."

Martin, with outstretched hands, pleaded, "Pastor, I don't ask you to accept my viewpoint. I only ask you to increase your level of tolerance regarding this issue."

Pondering their conversation, Pastor Sawyer replied, "I'll make this a matter of prayer."

In an effort to clear the air, Martin asked, "So, you're not going to kick me out of the church, are you?"

"I think we'll let you keep your membership. Just keep in mind please, many church members aren't going to understand your viewpoint, and, in fact, they will most likely find your views unacceptable."

"I do understand that. I'm glad we met to discuss these issues."

Pastor Sawyer replied, "I am too."

As he departed the church property, Martin called Adeelah. When she answered, she asked right away with an anxious voice, "How did your meeting with the pastor go?"

"It actually went better than I thought. I think there's hope that my family and church will ultimately accept our relationship."

"I hope you're right."

"We'll see. We still need to be patient. I'll be by to pick you up for work tomorrow. I love you."

"I love you too."

# Day Trip to Atlanta

Although she was progressing well in her recovery from her car accident, Adeelah was still not able to drive, due to the cumbersome cast she had on her left leg. The cast was so large that the steering wheel kept her from getting her leg into the car. So, there was no need for her to buy a new car yet. Consequently, she and Martin continued commuting together to work and back. On Fridays, Martin continued to go with Adeelah to the Islamic Center of South Augusta for the weekly midday prayer service, but now Adeelah also went to the Sunday services at Friendship Community Church with Martin. Both were increasingly accepted as a couple in both places of worship. Martin and Adeelah were now on a first-name basis with each other's parents.

So far, Martin had not made a decision to profess the *Shahada*, which would make him a Muslim, and Imam Javed Rajput was aware of this. Omar and Kareena were wondering when Martin would make this decision. On the other hand, Pastor Mark Sawyer, Martin's parents, and nobody else at Friendship Community Church had any idea that Martin planned to become a Muslim.

Adeelah had been confined to a wheelchair for the past three months. The cast on her arm was removed about a month ago, and her arm was quickly regaining strength, but the large cast on her leg did not allow her to use crutches. Today, Thursday, she had an appointment with Doctor Stewart at 3:30 PM to remove the cast on her leg–the last remaining cast. She had been undergoing physical therapy, which started soon after she left the hospital, and she was progressing well. Both Martin and Adeelah left work early, so Martin could take her to the 3:30 appointment.

With a small electric saw, Doctor Stewart prepared to cut through the cast. Although there were no complications when he removed the cast from Adeelah's arm, she was still quite nervous when she saw him come at her with the saw. When Doctor Stewart turned on the saw, its high-pitched, whirring, screaming sound startled both Adeelah and Martin. She grabbed Martin's hand and squeezed it. As the saw cut into the cast, it sounded like a dentist's drill as it penetrates a tooth. Afraid the saw might cut into her skin, Adeelah looked away, so she wouldn't see as the saw's blade sunk down into the cast. The smoke from smoldering plaster produced a pungent sulfur smell which made Martin and Adeelah grab their noses. The saw's vibration made her leg tingle. It took Doctor Stewart about fifteen minutes to remove the cast.

Adeelah found she had some significant joint pain in the leg because she was moving it for the first time since the accident. It didn't take long for swelling to occur around her knee and ankle. Comparing the leg to her uninjured leg revealed the obvious atrophy which had occurred. The muscles in her leg had decreased significantly in size, and the leg was so weak it was unable to support her weight. Additionally, there was a significant amount of dry, scaly skin around the leg. Adeelah appeared to be more concerned about the dry, scaly skin than the leg's atrophy and weakness.

As Doctor Stewart discarded the cast, he explained, "Don't be too concerned about the dry scaly skin. With a basin of warm water, not hot water, gently rub your leg with a flannel washcloth. Use a mild soap. The redness of your skin may increase, but don't be too concerned about that. Have a separate towel to dry your leg, and then wrap it in another towel soaked with cold water. Elevate the leg for at least five minutes. Remove the towel, dry off your leg, and apply a plain moisturizer to the skin."

"You'll also want to elevate your leg several times a day to help reduce swelling, and put a pillow or two under your leg when you sleep. However, don't elevate the leg continuously to avoid back pain. And don't sit with your leg hanging loose in the air."

The doctor provided Adeelah with crutches and cautioned her, "Now that you have these crutches, you'll want to be careful not to try to go too fast with them. A fall could cause a new injury to your leg, which could require a new cast and prolong the healing process. Do you have any questions for me?"

Adeelah was eager to ask, "When will my leg get back to normal?"

"I must tell you. Given the severity of your injury, it will take up to 6 to 12 months for full recovery, so don't be too concerned if your progress is slow. After a month or two, you'll be able to replace the crutches with a walker as your leg regains strength."

"Will I be able to drive now?"

"Now that we've removed your cumbersome leg cast, and since you can use your right leg without any impediment, there's no reason why you can't drive."

"Well, one reason I can't drive yet is I don't currently have a car."

"I understand," Doctor Stewart replied in jest, "but there's no medical solution for that. Any other questions?"

"Not right now."

"Good. The nurse will be in momentarily to set you up with your new physical therapy appointments. You can expect your physical therapist to put you through up to fifteen exercises per day, three days per week."

"Thank you, Doctor Stewart."

Martin looked at Adeelah and smiled. "With therapy three days a week, we'll have more time to spend together."

"Will you have the patience to do this three days a week?"

"For me, the biggest issue will be the time of day for the appointments. Other than that, I'm happy to be a part of your recovery team. What about you? You won't get bored with my presence, will you?"

Adeelah smiled flirtatiously. "I don't see that happening at all. You're kind of nice to have around."

The nurse came into the examining room and asked, "What time of day do you prefer to schedule your appointments?"

Adeelah replied, "My work schedule requires me to do evening appointments, if that is an option."

"Not a problem. Where do you work?"

"City Hall in Waynesboro."

"There is a physical therapist in Waynesboro. Each session will be about 30 to 60 minutes long. How does 7:00 PM sound?"

"Is 6:30 an option?"

"Yes. 6:30 it is. You can start on Monday."

"Sounds good."

As they departed Doctor Stewart's office, Adeelah discovered she would have to develop some proficiency with her crutches. Going out the door, she tripped and almost fell to the sidewalk, but Martin quickly caught her. Arriving at Martin's car was tediously slow, and she was sweating and out of breath when she finally plopped down in the passenger-side seat.

Martin commented, "I think we should celebrate now that you have your leg back. What do you think?"

"Well, I guess I have it back. It's just not too useful yet."

"Nevertheless, I'm sure you're happy to have your cast removed."

"Absolutely! What kind of celebration did you have in mind?"

"I understand there's a Moroccan restaurant in Atlanta called Marrakech Bistro. Have you been there?"

Adeelah's smile reached her eyes. "I have. But it's been a long time. They do have really good Moroccan food."

Martin looked over at Adeelah, feeling content that Adeelah liked his idea. "Great! I'm thinking we can leave early Saturday morning, and we can stop for breakfast along the way. I thought it might be fun to go to the World of Coca-Cola Museum in Atlanta, eat lunch at the Marrakech Bistro, and get back in time to have dinner with my parents."

"Sounds wonderful! Have you talked to your parents about dinner?"

"I'll mention it to them tonight. I don't think it should be a problem. But, if it is, we can always get an early dinner someplace when we return to Augusta."

When they arrived at Adeelah's home, Martin helped her up the steps to the front door with her crutches. She lost her balance twice, and he tightened his grip on her to keep her from falling. Martin stepped in for a moment to say hello to Omar and Kareena.

Omar looked up from his laptop computer. "Well, look at you! No more wheelchair."

Adeelah replied facetiously, "Yeah. But now I get to use these fashionable crutches."

"Still better than the wheelchair." And then he asked Martin, "I'm wondering when you might profess the *Shahada*?"

"I fully intend to take this step to become a Muslim. However, I still need to take some additional steps to prepare my family. While I believe they'll initially object, I'm confident they'll ultimately accept my decision, especially when they understand I'll also continue to be active as a Christian."

Omar looked at Martin over his glasses. "I hope you can take care of this soon. My friends at the mosque, including Imam Javed Rajput, are asking about this issue with increasing frequency."

Martin stroked his chin and stared into the air. "I'm glad you asked about it, Omar. I must confess, I'm somewhat reluctant about bringing this matter up with my parents."

"I can understand the difficulty you're experiencing."

When Martin arrived home, he called Ellen, his mom. He discussed the plan for Adeelah and he to go to Atlanta, and asked her, "When we return from Atlanta, would you mind if I brought Adeelah over for dinner?"

Ellen responded with a cheerful voice, "Not at all. We'd enjoy having her over."

On Friday, after work, and after her physical therapy appointment, Martin and Adeelah went to the Augusta Mall and had pizza at the Food Court. Afterward, Adeelah hobbled around with Martin to do some window shopping. But she tired quickly, so Martin got her home at around 8:30.

~.~

On Saturday morning, Martin arrived at eight o'clock to pick up Adeelah for their trip to Atlanta.

Now that Adeelah had the last cast removed from her leg, she saw it as an opportunity to look her best, and did she ever look her best! She wore a long black skirt with a very elegant white blouse which was trimmed with blue, red, and yellow flowers. The floral pattern was not too tight, so the prominent color was white. Her hijab was blue and matched perfectly the blue floral print in her blouse.

When Martin saw her, he grinned with happy eyes and exclaimed, "My! How elegant you look today, so very feminine, and kind of sassy too."

Adeelah was all smiles and very pleased that Martin saw her as the woman she was. She adjusted the way she was standing. "I just wish I didn't have to use these crutches."

"Well, you're so stunningly beautiful, I didn't even notice the crutches! I just hope you'll be able to get around all right with them."

Now Adeelah was blushing.

"I'm kind of surprised to see you're wearing a hijab."

"Well, if you're going to take me to a Moroccan restaurant, I want it to be clear that I'm a Moroccan woman."

"And that you are, and I am so proud to be seen with you, my Moroccan princess."

Adeelah laughed, socked him on the shoulder, and replied lightheartedly, "Now you're really laying it on thick!"

They were now exiting the City of Augusta, en route to Atlanta. It was a pleasant Fall day, and the autumn colors were at their peak. They opened the car windows to savor the pleasant temperature. Adeelah stuck her hand out the window and adjusted the position of her hand to let the breeze aerodynamically raise and lower it.

Martin asked, "Is there something I should try at this Moroccan restaurant which I may not have tried before?"

Tilting her head to the side and looking at him out of the corner of her eye, Adeelah asked, with a teasing look on her face, "Have you ever had lamb with prunes?"

Cocking his head and biting his lip, Martin paused. "Hmm! I can honestly say I don't think I've ever eaten prunes for any reason other than for their digestive benefits."

Adeelah laughed delightfully. "I think you'll be pleasantly surprised if you try it. The lamb is cooked until buttery tender with saffron, ginger, and onions, then topped with prunes which have been poached in syrup made with cinnamon and honey. It's then accompanied by crunchy fried almonds, which serve as a garnish."

In jest, Martin scrunched his face as if he smelled a foul odor. "Sounds exotic. I guess I'm willing to give it a try."

Seeing Martin's reaction, Adeelah stared out the front window and smiled.

When they arrived in Atlanta, they went straight to the famous museum known as the World of Coca-Cola. The museum was quite fascinating. One could see the variety of delivery trucks used over the history of the Coca-Cola Corporation and several different bottle designs, to include the story behind the classic Coca-Cola bottle shape. They watched a movie which showed key events in the history of the Coca-Cola Corporation and told the story about the highly secret Coca-Cola recipe. They also viewed an exhibit of the machinery used to fill bottles with Coca-Cola.

The best part for Martin and Adeelah was the tasting room, where they could try samples from among more than 100 different beverages produced by Coca-Cola around the world. They came across two beverages produced in Morocco called Pom and Hawaii Tropical Soda.

Adeelah's jaw dropped. "Oh my goodness! I haven't had these for some years." She filled a small paper cup with the Hawaii Tropical soda and offered it to Martin. "You really must try this. Both this and the Pom soda are really popular in Morocco. This one is made from a variety of tropical fruits. Pom is an apple-flavored soda."

Martin took the cup, gulped the soda down, shuttered, wrinkled his nose, and stuck his tongue out through a frown on his face.

Disappointment shaded Adeelah's face, and her eyebrows arched upward. "You don't like it!"

Martin looked at Adeelah with mischievous eyes and grinned. "No. Just kidding. Quite tasty actually! I do like it."

Adeelah socked him on the shoulder, raised her nose with an impish smile, and feigned displeasure.

Martin then tried the Pom soda, looked at Adeelah, and made the same face.

Adeelah socked him again.

They arrived at the Marrakech Bistro just before 12:30. Martin commented, "Wow! This is quite a restaurant. It looks very typically Moroccan, just like the restaurants I enjoyed during my work in Marrakech."

The restaurant's ambiance was not so formal. Instead, it was more like the kiosks which abound in the Medina area of Marrakech, with its fascinating bazaar ambiance. Canvas hung from the ceiling to emulate the tent-like structure typical of food kiosks in the Medina. The chef cooked and prepared customers' food in a kitchen located in the dining room in full view of the customers. The aroma of Moroccan spices and herbs was enticingly wonderful.

When the waitress came to their table, Martin said, "*As-salāmu ʿalaykum.*"

The waitress responded, "*Wa alaykumu s-salam.*" After taking a closer look at Martin, she looked at Adeelah with a confused expression on her face and asked in Arabic, "Is he Muslim?"

"Not yet, but he plans to convert."

Restaurant customers stared at them, just like they did when Martin and Adeelah first started eating together at the Good Day Café, with the same obnoxious whispers.

Martin did try the lamb with prunes, and commented, "This is really delicious. Do you know how to make this?"

"Sure. I have the recipe."

Martin pursed his lips and nodded. "Well, I must say I certainly see prunes in a different light now."

Adeelah laughed and thought, I'm so glad Martin likes to eat just about everything.

They also drank plenty of Moroccan tea and enjoyed baklava for dessert.

Martin and Adeelah took their time getting back to Augusta. If they saw something which caught their attention along the highway, they stopped to check it out. They quickly became aware that Adeelah's attire attracted a significant number of stares from the locals who lived in the small towns they visited. After their first stop, Adeelah removed her hijab, which made it much less obvious that she was a Muslim and reduced curious stares significantly. Nevertheless, her elegant attire stood out in a very dazzling way from the typical drab jeans and t-shirts which most women were wearing.

## MARTIN'S FAMILY LEARNS HE WILL BECOME A MUSLIM

Upon return from their trip to Atlanta, Martin and Adeelah arrived at the home of Martin's parents at about 4:30 PM.

When Adeelah hobbled in with Martin, Ellen said, "Adeelah, I'm glad to see you finally got your cast off. How long will you have to use crutches?"

"The doctor says about one or two months, but then I'll have to use a walker for about 6 to 12 months."

"That's a long time. I'll bet you'll be happy to put this episode behind you."

"You have no idea!"

Ellen then said, "Dinner will be ready at about five o'clock. Why don't you two take a seat in the living room."

Adeelah asked, "May I help you with anything?"

Ellen was pleased with the offer but replied, "Dressed so glamorously as you are, and being on crutches, what I'm doing in this kitchen would not be a good option for your help. Why don't you just keep me company?"

"I'd be glad to."

While they were conversing, Ellen asked, "What should I know about your relationship with my son?"

"Ellen, I think you know we're in love. Our feelings for each other are still a work in progress, but I like the direction in which they are going, and I think Martin would say the same thing."

Ellen added melted cheese to the asparagus. "Well, I think you two make a handsome couple."

"Thank you."

"Do your parents continue to support your relationship?"

Adeelah looked up at Ellen as she filled glasses with iced tea. With the iced tea pitcher in her hand, she tilted her head and shrugged her shoulders. "They do. How are you feeling about our relationship?"

Ellen stirred in some flour for the gravy she was making. "I've never seen Martin so happy in a relationship as he is with you, which makes me happy. I must confess, however, your different religions cause me concern."

Adeelah hopped on one foot to the refrigerator to get a stick of butter, hopped back to her chair, unwrapped it, and put it on the butter plate. "I'm sure your concerns are not so different from those of my parents. They still have concerns. All I can say is there are many interfaith couples who have found their faith in God has grown stronger, and they are quite happy together. Martin and I pray about this issue frequently, and I hope you will also pray for us."

Surprised at her request for prayer, Ellen turned around, walked over, and pressed Adeelah's head to her bosom. "You can count on my prayers for your happiness."

With a tear in her eye, Adeelah wrapped her arms around Ellen's waist and hugged her. "Thank you. In Arabic, I would say *Alhamdulillah*, which means, praise the Lord."

After some additional small talk and final dinner preparation, Ellen called Martin, David, and Priscilla to dinner, and they all sat down in the dining room together.

David said, "Let's give thanks." All bowed their heads, and he prayed, "Dear God, our Heavenly Father, we give you thanks for the food you have blessed us with, and please help us to honor you in all we do. Amen."

The meal consisted of tossed salad, roast beef, mashed potatoes and gravy, asparagus, sweetened iced tea, and peach cobbler for dessert.

Priscilla commented, "I love your outfit. It's really beautiful."

Adeelah smiled. "Thank you."

"How did your trip to Atlanta go?"

Martin finished buttering his bread and replied, "We had a great time. First, we went to the World of Coca-Cola Museum. Among other things, they have a tasting room where you can try more than 100 Coca-Cola beverages produced in various places around the world. Adeelah had me try two, which are popular in Morocco, Pom, an apple-flavored soda, and

Hawaii Tropical, a soda made from an assortment of tropical fruits. Afterward, we had lunch at the Marrakech Bistro to enjoy some Moroccan cuisine."

Adeelah added, "Martin tried the lamb with prunes."

David stirred some sugar into his tea and frowned. "That sounds rather unusual. I don't think I've ever heard of a dish which featured prunes before."

Martin replied, "That was my initial reaction as well, but the way they prepared the dish made for a delicious meal."

Their conversation was animated and enjoyable. While Ellen brought in the dessert, David asked Adeelah. "You've been coming to our church for some time now. Have you given thought to becoming a member of our church?"

Adeelah turned to Martin with a look of trepidation on her face, and Martin said, "Well, you know Adeelah is a Muslim. And for that reason, I must tell you, Adeelah can't join our church. In some countries, Adeelah could be executed for joining a Christian church."

Everyone looked at Adeelah, and she jumped in. "That doesn't mean I won't continue to attend your church. I've enjoyed the services."

There was a somewhat awkward silence in the room, which quickly became uncomfortable.

David put his fork down and broke the silence, "So, where is this relationship going between you two?"

Before either could answer, Ellen jumped in, "Adeelah assured me that her parents are supporting their desire to be together now. So, it appears their relationship is progressing well."

David, afraid of the answer he was about to hear, breathed deeply, and then asked, "How do you propose to deal with your religious differences?"

Martin wiped his mouth with his napkin and replied, "The short answer is, both Adeelah and I take our faith in God seriously, so we see no difficulties."

Priscilla chimed in, "That's very interesting, but I still think Muslims don't believe in the same God as we do."

Adeelah responded, "That's simply not true! There's only one God, and . . ."

Priscilla interrupted. "There may be only one true God, but our pastor tells us that the god Muslims worship is a false god."

Priscilla's comment offended Adeelah, but she prudently did not reply. Instead, with desperate distress, she looked at Martin with eyes which begged him to come to the rescue.

Martin spoke up and said, "I know we've heard our pastor make such comments in the past. You'll recall, I openly challenged that view when the Muslim folkloric group from Uzbekistan visited our church. I later met with Pastor Sawyer. And, as a result of our conversation, I don't believe you'll hear such comments in our church again. I'm convinced that Adeelah, as a Muslim, and we, as Christians, do, in fact, worship the same God."

Ellen then asked, "Is Adeelah saved?"

Martin leaned forward and crossed his arms on the table. "I believe she is saved. You'll recall, the Muslim folkloric group responded to my question about prayer before meals by telling us that, when they thank God for their food, as we do, they also ask God to save them from the punishment of Hell. And, Dad, you'll recall our conversation where I emphasized, since there's no doubt that it's God's will for Muslims to be saved from the punishment of Hell, and since Muslims pray that God will save them from the punishment of Hell, then God must be granting their prayers. And I can tell you Adeelah prays this same prayer when she sits down for a meal, so yes: I believe she's saved."

Priscilla then asked, "So Adeelah, do you believe in Jesus?"

Adeelah smiled and shrugged her shoulders. "Of course. The Holy Quran teaches that Jesus is the Christ, which is the Greek word for Messiah. So, I believe Jesus is the Messiah."

Still not convinced, Ellen commented, "But it's my understanding Muslims don't believe Jesus is God!"

Martin responded, "That's true. But the Bible doesn't say we must believe Jesus is God to be saved. In John chapter 5, for example, Jesus says, 'Most certainly I tell you, he who hears my word and believes him who sent me has eternal life, and doesn't come into judgment, but has passed out of death into life.'" (John 5:24) Then he turned to Adeelah and asked, "Do you believe in God, who sent Jesus Christ into the world?"

Adeelah, with a sense of relief, responded, "Of course!"

Martin then concluded, "So there you have it! Adeelah believes in Jesus Christ, and she believes in Him, which would be God, who sent Jesus. So, as Jesus Himself said, she therefore, '. . . has eternal life, and doesn't come into judgment, but has passed out of death into life.'"

David gestured with his hands. "Putting it the way you did, I guess we must accept Adeelah's testimony that she's saved."

Adeelah joyfully raised her hands and said, "*Alhamdulillah*!"

With a smile on her face, Ellen said, "That means, 'praise the Lord.'"

And Martin said, "And I praise the Lord with her!"

David then asked, "So Adeelah, how are your parents dealing with your relationship with Martin, as a Christian."

"They initially reacted much the same as you have, but they were more vehemently opposed to our relationship."

Martin added, "But they have now accepted our relationship, with the understanding that I will profess the *Shahada*."

Surprised, Ellen looked up. "And what is the *Shahada*?"

Martin looked at Adeelah, hesitated, took a deep breath, and then said, "When I profess the *Shahada*, I'll proclaim that I believe there is only one God and no other, and I'll recognize Muhammad as God's messenger. In so doing, I'll be recognized as a Muslim."

After another dreadfully difficult silence in the room, David folded his hands on the table and looked at Martin with a worried look on his face. "So, what you're saying is you'll no longer be a Christian!"

"No, Dad. I'll continue to be a Christian as well as a Muslim."

With a surprised look on her face, Ellen followed up, "How is that possible?"

"It is possible," and Martin explained how Reverend Paul Reynolds, a Methodist minister, came to see himself as both Christian and Muslim. "I see the rationale for his decision, so I have no problems in following his example to be both Christian and Muslim."

David then asked, "Have you discussed this with Pastor Sawyer."

"I haven't, and I'm not sure if I see such a discussion as necessary."

David rolled his eyes, took a deep breath, and exhaled. "Well, if he ever finds out about your profession of faith as a Muslim, you may find such a discussion will become very necessary."

In response, Martin said, "I guess I'll cross that bridge when I come to it."

Ellen put her hands on her cheeks, slid them down, and folded them under her chin. "I must tell you, I certainly wasn't prepared for this conversation today!"

Martin replied, "I confess that Adeelah and I have struggled with how to discuss this issue with you, and we didn't expect to have this conversation today either. But I think Adeelah would agree with me.

We're relieved that you now know of my intention to profess the *Shahada*."

Then Ellen asked, "If you two should get married, what will you do with your children?"

Adeelah responded, "There are many married couples where one is Christian and the other is Muslim. Typically, they share both religions with their children and teach them to embrace both. Martin and I have never discussed the subject of marriage, but I expect, if we were to get married, we'd follow this same course of action."

Again, another awkward silence. In an effort to lighten up the conversation, Ellen looked around the table, looked at Adeelah, and changed the subject, "If I were to visit your mosque, what would I experience?"

The tension in the room subsided, and Adeelah breathed a sigh of relief. "You may know, the Quran instructs Muslims to pray five times a day. The prayer times occur at dawn, noon, the latest part of the afternoon, just after sunset, and between sunset and midnight. Mosques are open at these prayer times, and Muslims are encouraged to come to the mosque for these prayers. But praying at the mosque five times a day is not obligatory. People may pray wherever they want, although they must face Mecca when they pray. On Fridays, however, the midday prayer is more extensive. In addition to the normal prayers at this midday mosque service, the imam also preaches a sermon. This service typically lasts thirty to forty-five minutes."

David, Martin's father, commented, "That's interesting. In addition to two worship services on Sunday and our Sunday school class, which you've experienced, we also have a midweek prayer meeting on Wednesdays. So, church occupies a significant amount of our time."

Ellen took a sip of her coffee. "I remember, after your first visit to our church, you expressed surprise with the amount of music and singing which occurs at our church. What is the music like at your mosque?"

"We don't have musical instruments in mosques. Muslims don't exactly sing songs in mosques either. We don't have congregational singing. However, we do chant verses from the Quran in a melodious manner."

Adeelah looked at her watch and commented, "It's getting late, and I need to get home since we plan to attend church tomorrow."

When they departed, David and Ellen continued to talk about the evening's provocative *Shahada* revelation well into the night, and both had a rather sleepless night. On the other hand, Martin and Adeelah rejoiced and were surprised that, one, this unplanned conversation occurred when it did, and two, the results were far better than they anticipated. They both slept well.

## Fahim Bakkari's Unexpected Appearance

Omar's phone rang. When he answered, Fahim Bakkari greeted him in Arabic, "Omar. *As-salāmu ʿalaykum*. Fahim here."

"Fahim! *Wa alaykumu s-salam*."

"I trust you're doing well. Please tell me how things are going with Adeelah."

"She's doing well. I'm sure you are not aware she had a very serious car accident several months ago. We were fearful for a while that she might die. Up until recently, she couldn't walk without the aid of crutches or a walker. She is only recently starting to walk on her own, but she still walks with a limp."

"I'm sorry to hear about her accident, but it sounds like she's recovering well now."

"She is recovering well, and I think she'll fully recover in another few months."

Fahim then asked, "I'm curious to know if she has also recovered from her relationship with the Christian man she was seeing."

With some reluctance, Omar hesitated. "The man's name is Martin, and I must tell you, Fahim, she's now seeing him regularly, and I expect one day soon they will announce their intentions to marry."

Fahim spoke with surprise, accented with notable resentment. "And you're okay with that?"

Omar noted Fahim's resentment and took a deep breath. "Well, Fahim, I have to tell you. I like Martin. He's shown a lot of interest in finding common ground between Islam and Christianity, and he has assured me he plans to convert to Islam."

"So, I understand he's not made that decision yet."

"That's true. He takes his Christian faith in God seriously, and I understand making a decision to convert to Islam is just as difficult for him as it would be for a Muslim who would contemplate conversion to Christianity. Many of the objections a Muslim family would have about such a conversion are the same objections that Martin's family would experience."

"I'm sure you understand the need for this Christian to convert to Islam, before the implementation of any plan for him and Adeelah to get married."

"I certainly do."

Hesitating for a moment, Fahim commented, "Well, the main reason for my call was to follow up on the possibility of a marriage between Adeelah and me. I conclude, for now, at least, this may not be an option."

"Given the close relationship between our families, it grieves me to say you're right."

"Omar, thank you for taking my call. Please let me know if anything changes."

"I'll certainly do that."

Then Fahim asked, "Is Habib there by any chance?"

"Sure! Let me get him for you."

Habib took Omar's cellular phone and said, "Fahim! *As-salāmu ʿalaykum*. It's good to hear from you."

"*Wa alaykumu s-salam*. Thank you."

After some small talk, Fahim asked, "How do you feel about Adeelah's relationship with this Christian guy?"

Habib walked away from his father and responded with some vehemence, "I don't understand how my family can tolerate their relationship. Adeelah is actually going to this guy's church with him."

"Really! That doesn't sound good at all. She certainly would face some serious consequences if she were to abandon her Muslim faith and convert to Christianity. What a disgrace that would be for your family!"

"I know. That really bothers me."

"You know, Habib, if this infidel remains a Christian, and if Adeelah marries him, many Islamic scholars would say she'd be guilty of fornication, which would condemn her to Hell. Moreover, if they were to travel to some Muslim countries, they very likely would be arrested and possibly sentenced to death."

"I do know that, but things are different in the United States, and my family may have to tolerate the possibility of her marriage with this Christian."

"I hate to see your family face such a disgrace. Maybe there's something you and I can do."

Habib sat down and asked, "What would that be?"

"I would still like to marry Adeelah. And if you and I could take her to a more conservative mosque in the United States, maybe we could get the imam there to marry us. If she and I get married, that would save your family from disgrace, and it might also protect them from more serious consequences. What do you think?"

Habib lowered his voice and looked around to see if anybody could hear him. "I could support that. If we're going to do such a thing, we need to act soon because their relationship is becoming increasingly more intimate."

"Habib, why don't you see if you can find an appropriate mosque for such a wedding? And I'll start making plans for a visit."

"I'll do that."

"Just keep in mind, nobody can discover what we're up to."

"I understand."

~.~

After contacting several mosques, Habib found a small mosque located in Camden, South Carolina and called Imam Waqas Gufran there.

When the imam answered the phone, Habib greeted him, saying, "*As-salāmu ʿalaykum*, Imam Gufran. My name is Habib El-Sayed, and I'm hoping you can help me."

The imam responded, "*Wa alaykumu s-salam*, Habib. What can I do for you?"

"My sister, Adeelah, was supposed to become engaged to a family friend, Doctor Fahim Bakkari, from Rabat, Morocco. However, she has gotten involved in a relationship with a Christian man, and I'm afraid they may soon announce plans to get married. Doctor Bakkari still wants to marry her and plans to travel here from Morocco, and we're looking for a mosque where Doctor Bakkari and my sister can be married. Can you help us?"

"Let me confirm my understanding. It sounds to me like your sister is not willing to marry this Doctor Bakkari. Is that correct?"

"My sister doesn't know anything about this plan, and I'm sure she wouldn't agree to this marriage willingly."

"Do you understand what you propose to do is very risky?"

"I do. But I'm concerned the disgrace for my family and the eternal consequences for my sister are far worse."

"I agree with you. I'm willing to help you, but we must be extremely discreet."

"We definitely want to be as discreet as possible."

"Fine. Make your plans and coordinate with me when you're ready."

"Thank you, Imam Gufran."

Habib got back with Fahim to update him, "We can take Adeelah to a small mosque in Camden, South Carolina–about one hour and forty-five minutes from Augusta. Imam Waqas Gufran will perform the marriage ceremony."

"Sounds good. I can be there in two weeks. When I arrive, I'll get a hotel room and a rental car. How can you arrange to pick up Adeelah with your car?"

"Because of her recovery from a recent car accident, Adeelah isn't driving yet. So, I think I can give her a call where she works and explain that something has happened to my father, and I'll tell her I'll pick her up and take her to the hospital."

"That should work. I'll meet you at the hospital, and we'll take her to Camden."

"We won't have to hurt her, will we?"

"No. I'll give her an injection of propofol, which will immediately put her to sleep. I'll have to give her at least two more injections before we get to Camden."

"Okay. We can probably stop in Columbia, South Carolina for the first injection. Let me know when you have the details for your travel plans."

"I will."

~.~

Two weeks passed, and Fahim called Habib on Thursday, "I'll arrive in Augusta on Monday. Let's plan our trip to Camden on Tuesday."

"Sounds good. I'll call Imam Gufran to let him know."

After ending his call with Fahim, he immediately called Imam Gufran, "We want to arrive this coming Tuesday afternoon for the wedding."

"Okay. I'll be ready."

Fahim called Habib on Monday, "I'm now in Augusta. Is everything ready?"

"Yes. I plan to call Adeelah at work tomorrow morning."

"Good! I Googled University Hospital, and I see they have a parking garage there. Give me a call early in the morning, so I can tell you where I've parked my rental car. Just bring her there, and I'll give her the injection to put her to sleep."

"What kind of car are you driving?"

"It's a green Mercedes-Benz."

"Okay."

On Tuesday morning, Adeelah answered a call from Habib, and he said to her, "Something's wrong with Dad, and Mom has taken him to the hospital. I'm on my way to pick you up."

Adeelah stood up with a worried look on her face, and she asked, "What's wrong with him?"

"We don't know for sure. It may be his heart, or it could just be nothing more than indigestion."

"Okay. I'll be ready when you get here."

On his way to pick up Adeelah, Habib called Fahim to find out where he was parked at the hospital.

Adeelah immediately called Martin. "Something's wrong with my dad, and my mom has taken him to the hospital."

Martin stood to his feet and replied, "Do you want me to come get you?"

"No. Habib is coming to pick me up."

"Okay. Give me a call when you get additional information."

"I will."

Adeelah also called Sarah Jefferson, the Human Resources Director, to let her know she had to leave right away for the hospital.

When Habib arrived, Adeelah grabbed her purse and departed with him.

Adeelah asked, "Do we have any new information about Dad?"

"No. Nothing yet."

Adeelah noticed Habib appeared to be nervous, but she concluded he was just worried about their father. They arrived at the hospital, and Habib drove into the parking garage. They approached Fahim's rental car, parked in a dark corner. Habib stopped, and, when Adeelah saw Fahim, she asked Habib, "What's he doing here?"

Before Habib could say anything, Fahim opened the car door and grabbed Adeelah. She began to struggle and screamed, "What are you doing!?"

Habib came around to the passenger side of his car to help restrain Adeelah, and he covered her mouth to stop her from screaming. Fahim, nervous, with glaring eyes and a devious smile on his face, said to Adeelah, "You and I are getting married today!"

Adeelah cried out with a muffled voice, "What! Are you crazy?!" And she fought back to get away.

Together, Habib and Fahim struggled to keep her from moving, and Fahim injected her with the propofol, which almost immediately put Adeelah to sleep. Habib removed Adeelah's cellular phone from her purse, and he and Fahim put her in the trunk of the Mercedes and threw her purse in the trunk with her. Habib parked his car, and they departed for Camden, South Carolina.

Concerned about Adeelah's father, Martin called Kareena, and when she answered, Martin asked, "How's Omar?"

Surprised with his question, Kareena replied, "Omar's fine. Why do you ask?"

"Adeelah told me you had to take Omar to the hospital."

Alarmed, Kareena said, "Just a minute," and she called Omar to the phone.

As soon as Omar picked up the phone, he asked, "What's going on?"

Martin answered with a quivering voice, "Something nefarious is going on. Just a little while ago, Adeelah called me to let me know Habib was picking her up to take her to the hospital to see you!"

Omar clenched his teeth and replied, "I'm obviously not in the hospital. I'm fine. So, what in the world's going on?"

"I have no clue. But I'm going to call the police. I know Adeelah has her cellular phone. So, they can track her location. I'll get back with you as soon as possible."

By tracking her cellular phone, Waynesboro police were able to determine that Adeelah was in South Carolina, approaching Columbia. They notified the Columbia Police Department to alert them that Adeelah might be in danger.

The Waynesboro police chief got back with Martin and said, "We've determined that Adeelah is on her way to Columbia, South Carolina."

Martin immediately called Omar back, "The police tell me Adeelah is in South Carolina, approaching Columbia. Do you have any idea why Habib would deceive Adeelah and take her to South Carolina?"

Omar, with trembling fear in his voice, replied, "I have no idea. I'm really worried now."

"I'll certainly keep you updated when I get additional information."

"Thank you, Martin."

~.~

After about forty-five minutes, Adeelah was awake and had fully recovered from the propofol injection. Habib and Fahim planned to stop in Columbia to give her another injection to put her back to sleep, but Columbia was still about thirty minutes away. Adeelah found her purse and noted that her cellular phone was missing, but she laid hands on her pepper spray, which she always carried with her.

Fahim pulled into a Denny's restaurant and parked in the back. He instructed Habib to sit in the driver's seat and said, "As soon as I give Adeelah this injection, we need to get out of here as soon as possible."

Adeelah noted they had stopped, and she was ready to act. When Fahim opened the trunk, she hit him with the pepper spray. Fahim fell to the ground in agony, and Adeelah got out of the Mercedes and limped as fast as she could to the restaurant's entrance. Habib went after her, but she made it into the restaurant before he could reach her.

Adeelah screamed, "Help! I've been kidnapped."

When Habib entered the restaurant, one of the customers tripped him, and he fell to the floor. Two others helped restrain him. The restaurant manager called the police, and two police cars showed up in less than five minutes with sirens blaring and blue police lights blinking. Police officers found Fahim in the parking lot, still choking from the pepper spray, and they handcuffed him. They also handcuffed Habib. After the police officers got back to the police station, the police chief in Columbia called Waynesboro police to inform them that Adeelah was safe, and they had two individuals, Habib El-Sayed and Fahim Bakkari, in custody.

The Waynesboro chief of police then called Martin to let him know Adeelah was okay and they had two individuals in custody.

Martin asked, "Can you tell me their names?"

The police chief responded, "Habib El-Sayed and Fahim Bakkari."

"Oh God," replied Martin, and said, "Please tell me where Adeelah is, and let her know I'm on my way to pick her up."

The police chief responded, "She was at the first Denny's Restaurant going into Columbia, South Carolina, and the police have taken her to the police station. I'll let the police in Columbia know you're on your way to pick her up."

"Thank you."

The Columbia Police Department returned Adeelah's cellular phone, and let her know Martin was on his way to pick her up. They also called in a doctor to examine her to confirm she was all right.

Adeelah immediately called Martin, and the first thing Martin asked was, "Are you all right?"

Adeelah was relieved to hear Martin's voice. "I'm fine now. My brother, Habib, was involved in a plot with Doctor Fahim Bakkari to kidnap me and force me to marry Fahim. I'm very troubled that Habib was involved in this and that he would do such a thing."

"The important thing for me is that you're all right. You know I'm on my way to pick you up, right?"

"Yes. The police told me. I love you."

"I love you too. You should hang up now and call your parents immediately. They're sick with worry about you."

Omar answered the phone, and the first words out of Adeelah's mouth were, "Dad, I'm okay."

Omar responded, "*Alhamdulillah*!" (Praise God) He then asked, "What happened?"

Adeelah explained, "Apparently, Fahim Bakkari convinced Habib to help kidnap me, and they planned to force me to marry him. Fahim gave me an injection to put me to sleep, and he put me in the trunk of his rental vehicle. They took my cellular phone and tossed my purse in the trunk with me, but they didn't see the vial of pepper spray I had in my purse. Shortly after I woke up, they pulled into a Denny's Restaurant here in Columbia. It's my understanding Fahim was going to give me another injection, and when he opened the trunk, I hit him with my pepper spray and ran into the restaurant to escape."

Omar now spoke with very mixed emotions, "I'm proud of you, and I'm so glad you had the pepper spray which I gave you." And then, with a trembling voice, he asked, "What will happen to Habib?"

"I'm sorry to say the police have arrested Habib and Fahim for kidnapping. They're now in jail, and I understand they'll have to go to trial. Unfortunately, there is a high probability that both will get prison time."

Devastated from what he just heard, he then said, "Here, Adeelah, talk to your mother. She's about to go to pieces."

"Hello, Mom."

"Adeelah! Are you all right?"

"Yes, Mom." After explaining what happened, she continued, "I was terrified by what happened, but I'm safe now. Martin is on his way to come get me."

"And Habib?"

"Unfortunately, as I explained to Dad, the police have arrested him, along with Fahim. Both are in jail and will have to stand trial for kidnapping. They'll most certainly have to spend some time in prison."

Those words brought tears to Kareena's eyes, and she cried out, "Allah, please help my children."

Omar now got back on the phone and asked, "How will you get home?"

Adeelah proudly said, "Martin is on his way to pick me up."

Hearing that, Omar was relieved to know his daughter would be in good hands, and he said, "Okay. I'll see you when you get back."

As she waited for Martin to arrive, news reporters accosted Adeelah and pressed her to tell her story. They had just gotten the details about the kidnapping and the plan to force Adeelah to marry Fahim when Martin arrived. When the reporters learned that Adeelah, a Muslim, was in a relationship with Martin, a Christian, they eagerly pursued this new dimension to the story. The television cameras did a close-up of Adeelah and Martin's passionate embrace, which would provide for the climactic end of the news story.

It was getting late, so Martin got a suite at the Embassy Suites Hotel in Columbia, which provided for separate bedrooms for him and Adeelah. They turned on the news and found all the major networks were covering Adeelah's misadventure.

The headline was, *Kidnapping Attempt Foiled in Columbia, South Carolina.* And the news report was as follows:

> *In Columbia, South Carolina, Adeelah El-Sayed successfully escaped her kidnappers after they abducted her in Augusta, Georgia earlier today. Allegedly, Doctor Fahim Bakkari, from Morocco, conspired with Habib El-Sayed, Adeelah's brother, to take her to a mosque in South Carolina with the intention of forcing Adeelah to marry Doctor Bakkari.*

*In Augusta, Doctor Bakkari gave Adeelah an injection to put her to sleep and placed her in the trunk of his rental car. They removed Adeelah's cellular phone from her purse but overlooked a vial of pepper spray which she also had in her purse. Later, they stopped at a Denny's restaurant here in Columbia, where Doctor Bakkari planned to give Adeelah another injection to put her back to sleep. When he opened the trunk, Adeelah hit him with the pepper spray, temporarily incapacitating him long enough for her to flee and get help in the Denny's restaurant.*

*Witnesses at the Denny's restaurant told reporters that Habib, Adeelah's brother, rushed into the restaurant to grab her, but patrons in the restaurant tripped him and restrained him until the police arrived, which occurred within minutes. Their quick response time was possible because Martin Webster, Adeelah's fiancé, discovered their plot and alerted police in Augusta. The police successfully located and tracked Adeelah's cellular phone, which led them to find and arrest Habib and Fahim. Both are now in jail without the possibility of bail.*

*Allegedly, Habib, Adeelah's brother, participated in this plot because Habib was concerned his Muslim family would face disgrace due to Adeelah's love relationship with Martin Webster, a Christian. Adeelah's parents, however, now rejoice and are thankful that Martin's quick action effectively intervened to thwart the planned forced marriage between Adeelah and Fahim. According to Javed Rajput, the imam at the mosque where Adeelah worships, Islam forbids such forced marriages.*

*Martin came to get his fiancé, and their happy embrace, as seen here, brought this terrifying incident to a happy ending.*

When they finished watching this report, Martin commented, "I never said I was your fiancé. Did you?"

"No. I never said the word 'fiancé.'"

Smiling, he said, "I think it's unfortunate the news story reported inaccurately that we're engaged."

Wondering why he would make such a comment, Adeelah replied, "I guess that's unfortunate."

"It startles me to think you might now be married to Fahim if these providential events had not occurred."

"I certainly am happy I'm not a married woman now."

Martin shrugged his shoulders. "I think we should do something to correct the inaccurate news story."

Adeelah tilted her head to one side. "What do you propose?"

Martin got down on one knee and said to Adeelah, "I propose marriage. Will you marry me, my love?"

Adeelah teasingly replied, "Are you just trying to correct the inaccurate news report?"

Grinning with a hopeful look on his face, he replied, "No! I'm trying to win your hand in marriage, so we can spend the rest of our lives together."

Now with tears in her eyes, Adeelah responded, "Then I happily agree to become your wife."

Martin then made the only appropriate response he could think of, "*Alhamdulillah*!" (Praise the Lord)

Then, in their hotel suite, with two bedrooms, they kissed, they hugged, and one of the two bedrooms was not used that night. So, they awoke in each other's arms in the morning. And while they struggled to resist the temptation to indulge in deeper intimacy, which would have dishonored Adeelah and her family, they did successfully resist temptation. So, Adeelah could truthfully testify, to use the biblical phrase, that she, "knew not a man."

# MARTIN'S DECISION

Martin and Adeelah returned to Augusta early in the afternoon on Wednesday, and he took Adeelah straight to her parent's home.

Omar and Kareena were desperate, anxious, relieved, and happy to see Adeelah; while, at the same time, it was clear they were experiencing very mixed emotions about what Habib had done–ranging from embarrassment and dismay to worry and anger.

Omar said to Martin, "Thank you for looking after our daughter."

"How could I do anything less for this daughter of yours who is such an important part of my life?"

Tilting her head to the side with an unsettled look on her face, Kareena commented, "We saw the news report about this ordeal, and they referred to you two as fiancés. Is there something you haven't told us?"

Martin looked at Adeelah, and both struggled to keep from grinning. "Well, until last night, the news report was wrong to refer to us as engaged, but we corrected that."

Leaning forward, Omar asked, "Really! How did you do that?"

Martin and Adeelah looked at each other again. Grins, no longer suppressed, broke out on both of their faces, and looking at Omar and Kareena, Martin shrugged and said, "I asked Adeelah to marry me last night, and she accepted, so now the news report is correct."

Omar and Kareena looked at each other and hesitated. They weren't quite sure they could say congratulations, so Martin followed up. "Omar, I'm hoping you can coordinate a meeting between Imam Javed Rajput, you, and me, so I can profess the *Shahada* on Friday when we attend the prayer service at the mosque."

That changed everything! Omar, Kareena, and Adeelah all brightened up. Kareena and Adeelah, with tears in their eyes, hugged each other. And Omar shook hands with Martin and said, "Despite yesterday's events, this is a very happy moment for us."

Omar agreed to make the necessary arrangements for Friday, and Martin then said, "I have some things to do. So, Adeelah, I'll pick you up for work tomorrow."

They kissed and embraced, and, when Martin departed, he went straight to the Augusta Mall, where he purchased an engagement ring. He also called Sarah Jefferson, Human Resources Director at the Waynesboro City Hall. When she answered, the first thing she wanted to know was, "Is Adeelah all right?"

"Yeah. She's fine, other than the huge disappointment for what her brother has done."

"Many of us saw the news story which reported that you and Adeelah are engaged. Is that true?"

"It wasn't true when the news report aired on television. But Adeelah and I corrected that last night by getting engaged."

"Really! That is so cool!"

"Sarah, could you arrange for some employees to gather around Adeelah's office tomorrow at about ten o'clock? I plan to surprise her with an engagement ring."

With excitement in her voice, she replied, "Not a problem! We can make that happen!"

Ending the conversation, Martin thanked her, saying, "That'll be good. I'll see you tomorrow."

Martin dropped Adeelah off at City Hall at eight o'clock and proceeded to his office at the fire station. Just after ten o'clock, people started arriving at Adeelah's office and expressed how happy they were that she was safe and that she was able to free herself from her kidnappers.

Then Martin arrived and made his way through the crowd which had gathered. When Adeelah saw him, she asked, "What's going on now?"

Martin pulled out the ring box, and Adeelah immediately recognized what it was. Her eyes filled with tears, and she put both hands together in front of her face with joy. Martin got down on one knee and said, "Adeelah, I want to make the decision we made Tuesday night in

Columbia official by asking you to accept this ring as a manifestation of my love for you and to formalize our engagement to be married."

Only her right hand now covered her face, while Adeelah extended her very willing left hand. And Martin slipped the engagement ring onto her ring finger. Everybody in the room burst into applause, and most of them also had tears in their eyes. Martin and Adeelah stood, kissed, and embraced, which only increased the exuberance of the crowd, and they applauded all the more.

After this most memorable event, Adeelah called Taslima. When Taslima heard Adeelah's voice, the first thing she asked was, "Are you all right?"

"I'm fine. I presume you heard the news report about my kidnapping."

"I sure did! And I've been so worried about you."

Adeelah exclaimed with a jubilant voice, "I can hardly wait to bring you up to speed on all the latest news. Martin has proposed to me, and I'm now wearing an engagement ring! And, tomorrow, Martin will profess the *Shahada* and become a Muslim. My parents are really pleased with Martin now, and they couldn't be happier about us, despite their disillusion with Habib. So, we anticipate we will have our wedding in just over a year!"

"Wow! I'm so happy for you. What an adventure all this has been for you. How are Martin's parents taking his decision to become a Muslim?"

"Martin plans to maintain that he is both Muslim and Christian. His parents know about this plan. And, while they're not thrilled with his decision, I understand they've accepted it."

"That's rather provocative. I've never heard of such a thing."

Adeelah told her about the Methodist minister, who also professed to be both Muslim and Christian, and explained, "Martin is going to follow that precedent."

"And Imam Rajput is okay with that?"

"He is."

"*Alhamdulillah*! What about your brother, Habib?"

"That's not such good news. He and Fahim have been charged with kidnapping, and they will soon go to trial. The police tell us they will almost certainly go to prison."

"I'm so sorry to hear about that. On the brighter side, I'm so happy to hear you now have to get ready for a wedding."

~.~

On Friday afternoon, Martin and Adeelah departed City Hall to attend the 1:30 prayer service at the Islamic Center of South Augusta. At the end of the prayer service, Martin, Adeelah, Omar, and Kareena went with Imam Rajput to his office.

Imam Rajput asked, "Martin, are you ready to profess the *Shahada*?"

Martin replied, "I am, with the understanding I'll now become both Muslim and Christian."

Imam Rajput responded, "That's fine with us. I just hope it will also be fine with your church."

"It will have to be fine with my church because I've made my decision."

Since the tradition is that the *Shahada* should be professed in Arabic, Imam Rajput coached Martin so he could say the Arabic words of the *Shahada* with a reasonably acceptable pronunciation.

Then, repeating after Imam Rajput, Martin uttered the following in Arabic, "*La ilaha illa Allah, Muhammad rasoolu Allah.*" (Which means, "There is no true god but God, and Muhammad is the Messenger of God.")

Adeelah hugged Martin, and Kareena exclaimed with excitement and glee in her voice, "I guess we now must plan for a wedding!"

After departing the mosque to return to City Hall, Adeelah asked Martin, "So how do you feel, now that you've become a true Muslim?"

"For some years now, I've recognized Muslims take their faith in God every bit as seriously as Christians, and I wholeheartedly believe we worship the same God. As you and I have discussed before, despite some significant doctrinal differences, I see common ground between the essentials that we believe, and I see virtually no difference in the way you and I pray and practice our faith on a daily basis."

Martin then quoted verses from 1 Corinthians chapter 9:20-22, "To the Jews I became as a Jew, that I might gain Jews . . . I have become all things to all men, that I may by all means save some.' If the Apostle Paul were alive today, he would certainly say, 'To the Muslims I became like a Muslim, to win the Muslims.' So, I see myself as following Paul's example, and I'm glad I don't have to give up my profession of faith as a Christian. I enjoy being around people who take their faith in God seriously, so I look forward to being recognized as both Christian and Muslim. *Alhumdulillah*!"

"So, what are you going to tell your family and the people at church?"

"As you know, my parents already know about my intention to become a Muslim and to continue to be a Christian. For them, nothing has changed. I'll simply let them know I have now made my decision. I'll continue to be active in my church, just as I have always been. If the church discovers I've become a Muslim, I won't deny it, and I'll explain the rationale for my decision, as I just did for you."

"What about our upcoming marriage?"

Martin took Adeelah's hand. "Our relationship has been no secret. It certainly must be obvious to anybody in my church who knows us that our relationship has been leading toward marriage. So, I don't see how our engagement can be a surprise to anybody. Therefore, I look forward to proudly announcing our engagement."

Adeelah gazed at Martin. "Should I continue to attend your church?"

Martin briefly took his eyes off the road to look at Adeelah. After getting his eyes back on the road, he slowly nodded. "That's a decision I'll let you make. However, my hope is that you'll continue to attend my church. My view is that we must support each other in our relationship with God. I know your faithful attendance at your mosque is as important to you, as my faithful attendance at my church is for me. I'll not just support you in your worship at your mosque, I'll continue to attend and worship there with you. And I hope you'll do the same with me. I hope our mutual attendance at our places of worship will be an important manifestation of our love for each other."

"Martin, you can certainly count on me to do the same."

Martin continued, "It's my understanding that the best relationship between God, a husband, and a wife is described by an equilateral triangle–that is, a triangle whose three sides are equal in length. God is at the top angle. The man and the woman are at the other two angles. In such a triangle, the goal is to make the triangle as small as possible and to keep all sides of the triangle at equal lengths. So, the closer the man and the woman get to God, the closer they will also be to each other. I'm sure you'll agree with me when I say, I wholeheartedly want our love and our marriage to be forever strong. So, let's do everything we can to make that triangle as small as we can. So, we'll always be very close to God and consequently very close to each other."

Adeelah looked at Martin with tears of joy running down her cheeks and said, "I love you so much, Martin."

"And I love you the same way. And, in fifty years, I want us to still be loving each other so much."

## IMPACT OF CULTURAL DIFFERENCES

Martin was anxious to share with somebody about his engagement with Adeelah, so he called his friend, James Landers, and they arranged to meet on Saturday morning at Starbucks.

Martin ordered a double espresso, James ordered a latte, and Martin paid the bill.

When they sat down, Martin commented, "I suppose you heard about Adeelah's kidnapping."

"I certainly did. I saw it on the news. What an ordeal for her. Is she all right?"

"She is all right. The biggest concern for her and her family right now is what will happen to her brother, Habib, who was one of the kidnappers."

"Why would her brother do such a thing?"

"You may recall I told you earlier that Adeelah's family had an arrangement with a family in Morocco for Adeelah to get engaged to their son, Fahim. The two families have been close friends since before Adeelah's parents came to live in the United States, well before Adeelah was even born. Fahim convinced Habib that Adeelah's relationship with me was a disgrace for his family, since I'm a Christian. Apparently, he also told him, that according to the Quran, Adeelah would be guilty of fornication if she were to marry me, and consequently, she'd go to Hell. The fact is, the Quran doesn't say such a thing. Nevertheless, Fahim convinced Habib to help kidnap Adeelah, with the plan to take her to a mosque in South Carolina and force her to marry Fahim."

Putting his coffee cup on the table, James rubbed his chin and said, "I find that wildly incredible. I don't think they could legally get a marriage certificate without Adeelah's signature, and I presume she wouldn't willingly sign for the marriage certificate."

"Certainly, you're right about getting Adeelah's signature on a marriage certificate. She'd never sign such a marriage certificate against her will. They must have planned to forge her signature with a female accomplice. On the other hand, Fahim came from Morocco for this crime. And Habib is young enough, so it's possible neither one of them knew better. Which means they may have set out to commit a crime which was destined to fail from its inception. And fortunately, it did fail."

"So, how's your relationship with Adeelah now?"

"Apparently, you didn't notice the news report about the kidnapping, which referred to me as Adeelah's fiancé."

With a look of surprise on his face, James crossed his legs and folded his hands. "So, you're engaged!?"

"We are now. The news report that referred to me as Adeelah's fiancé was inaccurate, but that prompted me to correct the report by proposing to Adeelah, and she accepted. So, yes! We're now engaged!"

"So, how are your families taking your engagement?"

Martin didn't disclose to James that he had become a Muslim but said, "As you well know, Adeelah and I have been dealing with family opposition almost since we met. Well before this incident that prompted us to get engaged, we had made some very good progress in winning our families' acceptance. I suspect both families have been anticipating an imminent engagement. So, as a matter of fact, Adeelah's family actually rejoiced at the announcement of our engagement. And I think my family will be pretty happy as well."

James leaned forward and changed the subject. "The two of you have some significant cultural differences. Her family is from North Africa. Yours is very European. She's Muslim, you're Christian, and there surely are some other very pronounced cultural differences between you two. Does that bother you at all?"

Martin paused briefly in contemplation, sat back in his chair, and put his hands behind his head. "The short answer is: No. As far as Adeelah's North African origin, her light olive-colored skin is absolutely no problem for me. In reality, her skin color is only a minor factor, which makes me find her so incredibly beautiful. And her femininity manifests itself in such an incredible way. It draws me to her and completes a part of me, which longs for and needs that femininity. As far as culture goes, different cultures fascinate me, and I've always enjoyed meeting and getting to know people of different cultures."

"The most difficult challenge is obviously our two religions. But even with respect to this very real challenge, the minor differences in the essentials of both of our religions are not insurmountable, and we're increasingly finding ways to reconcile them. The other big challenge has been to win our families' acceptance of our relationship. Other than that, we both take our faith in God seriously, we pray together, and we find no difference at all in our day-to-day walk of faith. How could I not love such a woman!"

"That truly sounds like a wonderful relationship."

Martin straightened in his chair, leaned his head on his right fist, and nodded. "She's wonderful, and I thank God for her."

As they ended their conversation, James said, "I expect I'll see you in church on Sunday."

"Of course."

~.~

Later that afternoon, Martin picked up Adeelah. Their plans were to go to the Augusta Canal, and they planned to have dinner together afterward.

As they walked together hand in hand along the canal, the sun happily danced its way through the tree canopy along the canal and bathed them in pleasant warmth, which competed with their enjoyment of the cool breeze which caressed them.

As they conversed, Martin commented, "We sure have experienced a lot together during this short relationship of ours."

"I see these experiences as proof of the strength of our love."

"It's funny you should make that very valid observation. I met with my friend, James, for coffee this morning, and he asked me if the cultural differences between us have bothered me at all. He emphasized our racial differences, cultural differences, and religious differences."

"How did you respond?"

"I'm happy to answer your question, but first, I'm curious to know how you would respond."

Adeelah looked down as they walked. "My main concern about racial differences has been my skin color and how you viewed me. I guess I also have had some concern about how others view us as a couple, but I never gave that much thought. Culturally, I was born in Georgia, so I don't see a significant difference between us culturally, except for the elements of culture my parents have preserved from Morocco. And you appear to have enjoyed our Moroccan culture, which makes me happy."

"The religious issues have obviously been the major source of our struggles. My experience at your church has changed my perspective about Christian people in general, and I'm grateful you take your faith in God seriously. I love your comparison of the relationship between God and us to an equilateral triangle. I believe and trust we will successfully reduce the size of that triangle throughout our lives together to keep us ever closer to each other and closer to God. The way things are turning out now with our engagement, I have absolutely no concerns about our relationship. I love you with all my heart."

Martin only responded, "I love you too."

After a brief silence, Adeelah put her hands on her hips and demanded. "Now you brought this subject up, I gave you my response, and you promised to share what you said to James. Now I want to hear it!"

Grinning, Martin replied, "I just wanted to see how curious you were." Then he proceeded, "In reality, my response wasn't much different from yours. You expressed some concern about how I view your skin color, so let me assure you that your light, olive-colored skin is absolutely no problem for me. In reality, your skin color is, as I told James, only a minor factor, which makes me find you so incredibly beautiful."

Martin's remark about her skin color relieved this hidden concern, which she had since they started seeing each other seriously. They had never talked about the differences in their skin color before. Adeelah was always pleased that Martin found her beautiful, and his comment caused her to blush.

Martin continued. "Again, I pretty much said the same things you just said. But there's something else I said which I want you to know. Adeelah, I find your femininity manifests itself in such an incredible way, which draws me to you and completes a part of me which longs for and needs that femininity, which is such a significant part of who you are."

That comment brought tears to Adeelah's eyes, and she reached out to Martin in need of an intimate kiss and embrace.

~.~

Martin was just beginning to learn what he had gotten himself into, now that he was engaged to a Moroccan woman. The first thing he learned was a Moroccan engagement lasts for at least a year. During that time, the woman's parents save up money toward the down payment for a home. The man's parents save up money toward the costs to furnish the home.

The first Sunday after Martin brought Adeelah back from her ordeal in South Carolina, they both attended the worship service at Friendship Community Church, which was now customary for them. Martin rehearsed with the orchestra, and they attended Sunday School.

When they met up with Martin's parents for the morning worship service, David asked Adeelah, "We saw the news item about your abduction. Are you all right?"

"Thank God, I'm fine."

"We couldn't help but notice the news report, which described Martin as your fiancé. Is there something you two haven't told us?"

Martin jumped in and said, "That news report was inaccurate at the time, but we have now taken steps to correct it." And he held up Adeelah's left hand to show off the engagement ring which now adorned her finger.

Adeelah was all smiles, and David and Ellen were both surprised and pleased. The main question in their minds was the Christian/Muslim issue. Nevertheless, Ellen hugged Adeelah and said, "Congratulations. I guess we have a wedding to prepare for."

Martin commented, "Yes. We do have to prepare for a wedding–a Moroccan wedding! I'm just beginning to understand what that entails. Now that we have announced our engagement, I understand our wedding will occur in just over a year."

David said, "Well, let's go to lunch after church, and you can tell us more about it."

"Okay. We're good with that."

As they finished their meal at the restaurant, Martin began discussing their upcoming wedding and said, "As I understand it, the bride's parents will begin saving money this year toward the down payment for a home. The groom's parents are supposed to save money toward the furnishings for the home."

Both David and Ellen put their coffee cups down on the table, looked at Adeelah and Martin with a dumbfounded expression on their faces, and David commented, "That's an interesting custom. Ellen and I will have to talk about how we'll do our part. How about the wedding itself?"

Adeelah explained, "The wedding is an event which takes three days."

Ellen exclaimed, "Three days! What happens over three days?"

Adeelah responded, "I'm not sure if I know all the details, but my mom will definitely get us up to speed."

# THE TRIAL

Since their crime occurred in Augusta, Georgia, the police in Columbia, South Carolina immediately made arrangements to transport Habib and Fahim to Augusta, where they were jailed at the Augusta police station. Shortly after their arrival, a prison guard conducted Habib and Fahim, dressed in orange prison jumpsuits, to a secure room where attorney William Everest was waiting to meet with them. William stood up when they entered the room, shook hands with them, and explained, "The State of Georgia has assigned me to be your defense attorney. Please take a seat."

As they sat down, the prison guard left the room and stood guard just outside the entry door.

William began, "I've reviewed the police report from Columbia. You are charged with kidnapping, and you probably know kidnapping is a very serious crime. There are two categories of kidnapping in Georgia. First degree, or aggravated kidnapping, which carries a prison sentence of 20 years or more, and second-degree kidnapping, which normally carries a minimum sentence of five years. Both categories are felonies. So, if you're found guilty, these crimes will affect you for the rest of your lives."

Because of Fahim's limited fluency in English, Habib served as translator. Both Habib and Fahim knew they were in serious trouble, but hearing their attorney's words physically made them feel as if they had received a blow to the stomach. It never occurred to them, they would likely spend some serious time in prison.

William then asked, "What was the motive which prompted this incident to occur?"

Fahim explained, "Some years ago, Habib's family and mine discussed the possibility for Adeelah, Habib's sister, and I to get married. Some time ago, Adeelah met a Christian man and started dating him. When her parents found out, her father forbade Adeelah from continuing her relationship with this man. During my visit shortly afterward, Adeelah made it clear she wasn't interested in marrying me, or anybody else, at that time. She explained she was recovering from her broken relationship with this man, which was imposed on them by her father."

Unaware that Martin and Adeelah had now announced their engagement to be married, and that Martin had now become a Muslim, Fahim continued, "Recently, however, Adeelah started seeing this man again, apparently with the acceptance of Adeelah's father this time. Their relationship appears to be leading toward marriage. Many Muslim scholars believe the marriage between a Muslim woman and a Christian man is forbidden in Islam. I still want to marry Adeelah, and Habib and I made arrangements to take Adeelah to a mosque in South Carolina, where I planned for us to get married. I must tell you. It never occurred to me that we were kidnapping her."

After Habib translated what Fahim said, William asked, "Correct me if I'm wrong, but it appears to me, you abducted her against her will because you intended to force her to marry you. Is that correct?"

This question made it much more clear to Fahim that he had acted very foolishly, and Fahim responded with remorse, "Yes sir. That is correct."

William continued, "First-degree kidnapping occurs when the victim is injured, is abandoned in an unsafe place, or is sexually assaulted. My review of the police report leads me to believe none of these occurred. So, I expect you'll be charged with second-degree kidnapping, which, as I explained earlier, normally carries with it a five-year prison sentence."

"The fact that Adeelah is an adult works in your favor regarding the amount of prison time you may actually have to serve, as does the fact that neither of you has any prior criminal record. On the other hand, if it can be established that confining Adeelah in the trunk of your rental vehicle made her vulnerable to excessive heat or carbon monoxide poisoning, which could have threatened her health or life, then the prosecutor could make the case that you should be charged with first degree kidnapping, arguing that you put her in an unsafe place."

"Most acceptable defenses for kidnapping in Georgia include the following: First, that you were protecting a child from imminent harm–obviously not applicable in your case, since Adeelah is an adult; and, therefore, not an option for you. Second, that the victim was not moved–again, not an option for you, since you moved her across state lines from Georgia to South Carolina. Third, that it was the result of a mistake–this is not the idea that committing the crime was a mistake. Instead, it must be a mistake in the sense that it was the defendant's belief that he or she was acting under the authority of the law and therefore had the right to capture the victim. I see nothing here which would lead me to believe you had a credible belief that mistakenly led you to think you had a legitimate reason under Georgia law to capture Adeelah. Finally, the last most prevalent defense is consent–which doesn't appear to be the case in this situation, since you put her to sleep with an injection and confined her in the trunk of your rental vehicle. Consequently, I believe your best course of action is to plead guilty, with the hope that we can convince the judge to be lenient on you. Do you have any questions or comments?"

Fahim's face reflected remorse and despair. He wrung his hands together and responded, "What if we believed we were acting under Islamic law. And, therefore, we believed we had the right to capture Adeelah?"

Attorney Everest rubbed his chin, paused, and then replied, "That's an interesting angle which did not occur to me. I'm not optimistic, but I'll look into that. I'd say your contention that you were acting under Islamic law at least justifies a plea of not guilty. Do you intend to plead not guilty?"

Seeing some hope of a finding of innocence, Habib and Fahim looked at each other, turned back to their attorney, and said, "We'll plead not guilty."

"Okay. That's the way we'll proceed. I also want you to know I'll try to get you out on bail."

William departed, and the guard took Habib and Fahim back to their prison cells.

~.~

William called Omar and, when the call connected, he said, "Mr. El-Sayed, my name is William Everest, and the State of Georgia has assigned me to be the defense attorney for your son, Habib, and Fahim. I don't think I need to tell you they're in serious trouble."

"I do know they're in serious trouble, and I thank you for taking the case to defend them. What do you think their chances are?"

"I think the worst-case scenario is, they will be charged with second-degree kidnapping, which is a felony which normally carries a minimum prison sentence of five years."

Visibly shaken by these words, Omar then asked, "Do you see any hope for anything better than that?"

"Actually, I do. Given that neither has any prior criminal record and given the circumstances of this case, I think a very possible outcome will be one to three years in prison and completion of the remaining five-year sentence on probation."

"Fahim asked me about the possible defense that they were acting under Islamic law, and therefore believed they had the right to capture Adeelah. If it could be shown they thought they were acting under Georgia law, that would be a possible defense which could lead to a finding of innocence. The same contention regarding Islamic law is tenuous at best but may be worthy of our consideration. What do you think?"

"I can see where he's coming from. They would allege that Islamic law does not allow a Muslim woman to be in a relationship with a Christian man, especially if the relationship will potentially lead to their marriage. And therefore, they took her against her will to keep her from breaking that law."

"I must tell you. I'm not too optimistic about this defense. However, I'd like to meet with you, your family, and the imam from your mosque to get additional information about the feasibility of this defense and to see if there are other facts and circumstances which might work in favor of Habib and Fahim. I can be available this week on Wednesday, Thursday, or Friday."

"Friday is not an option because it's a sacred day of prayer for Muslims. Let me see if our imam can make it on Wednesday or Thursday evening."

Imam Rajput agreed to a meeting on Wednesday evening at seven o'clock. Omar coordinated with Adeelah about the meeting and called Attorney Everest back to firm up the plan for Wednesday.

Omar, Kareena, Adeelah, Imam Rajput, and Attorney William Everest met at the El-Sayed home on Wednesday. Kareena served Moroccan tea and baklava. Attorney Everest's first question was for Imam Rajput, "Is there anything in Islamic law which would lead Habib and Fahim to reasonably believe they were acting to prevent Adeelah from breaking Islamic law, and that would, therefore, justify their actions to abduct Adeelah?"

Imam Rajput stood and covered his mouth with his hand as he pondered the question. Then he looked at Attorney Everest and responded, "First, let me say emphatically, it grieves my heart deeply that this incident has occurred. Now in response to your question, many Islamic scholars interpret Islamic law to allow for the marriage of a Muslim man to a Christian woman, but they contend that a Muslim woman may not marry a Christian man. Some Islamic countries would execute a Muslim woman and a Christian man who get married. That certainly wouldn't occur in this country. There are no definitive verses in the Holy Quran which address this issue. Islamic scholars who hold this view can only infer from the Quran the reasoning which backs up their views. And there are increasingly more Islamic scholars who don't share this view."

As he sat back down, Imam Rajput hesitated and continued, "One thing, however, is clear. While the Quran and Islamic law allow for arranged marriages, forced marriages are absolutely forbidden. Unfortunately, my understanding of the motives which led Habib and Fahim to kidnap Adeelah were to force her to marry Fahim. The other issue which is important here is that Martin Webster, a Christian, is now Adeelah's fiancé. Moreover, he gave Omar his word that he would convert to Islam if Omar would consent to allow their courtship to continue. And Martin has now converted to Islam. Given Martin's profession to be a Muslim, there's absolutely no prohibition recognized in Islam to forbid their marriage."

Omar pondered what he heard, hesitated, and added, "I must tell you, I informed Fahim well before this incident that Martin intended to convert to Islam."

Attorney Everest, after thanking Imam Rajput for the information he provided, informed him that he would prepare an affidavit for Imam Rajput's signature. He then turned to Adeelah and asked, "Can you share any details which would be helpful in my efforts to defend Fahim and your brother?"

The expression on Adeelah's face reflected both anger and worry. She set her teacup on the table, leaned forward, and replied, "I don't think I've ever been more terrified in my life. So, I have very little sympathy for Fahim. On the other hand, I don't believe my brother would do such a thing, unless he thought he was protecting our family and me in some way."

Omar stood, with a despondency which reflected his grief and dismay, and said to Attorney Everest, "I certainly agree Fahim has done a very horrendous deed, and I'm disappointed in my son that he would participate in such a crime. Nevertheless, it grieves me deeply that they'll face some severe punishment. Our two families are very close. So, I request you do your best to win any available mercy from the court for both of them."

Attorney Everest responded, "Based on what I've heard here, I don't see much hope for Fahim, but I believe mitigating circumstances might help Habib's case, so I'll arrange to meet with Habib alone."

Attorney Everest successfully got Habib released on bail. Because Fahim was deemed to be a flight risk, the court denied bail for him.

~.~

Meeting with Habib on Monday, he asked, "How did Fahim get you involved in this kidnapping?"

"Fahim referred to Adeelah's Christian boyfriend as an infidel. He warned me that, if Adeelah were to marry this infidel, the Quran says she would be guilty of fornication, which would condemn her to Hell. He also warned me, if she were to travel to Muslim countries with her Christian husband, some countries would arrest them and possibly execute them. I was afraid for my sister, so I agreed to help Fahim with his plan to marry her."

Habib and Fahim appeared in court in two separate trials, and both pled not guilty. Imam Rajput's affidavit made it clear that Islam prohibited forced marriages, and that this prohibition on forced marriages is well known. It also came to light that Fahim learned of Martin's intention to convert to Islam before implementation of his plan to kidnap Adeelah. These facts led the jury in both trials to reject the argument that they acted with the belief that Islamic law gave them the right to abduct Adeelah. The judge was moved that Adeelah's parents would ask for mercy for Fahim, despite his crime against their daughter. The judge also recognized how Fahim's influence instilled fear in Habib regarding the alleged severe consequences of Adeelah's relationship and potential marriage with a Christian man.

A security officer conducted Fahim into the courtroom. He was handcuffed and wore an orange jumpsuit. The judge asked the jury for the verdict, and they unanimously found him guilty. The jury foreman handed the verdict to the court clerk, who delivered it to the judge. In Fahim's case, the judge commented, "The crime of kidnapping is one of the most serious offenses you can commit, not only in this country, but in any country."

"I don't buy your contention that Islamic law justified your abduction of Adeelah to keep her from marrying, Martin Webster, a Christian man. What motivated you was strictly your desire to marry her. Moreover, it is clear now, that before this crime occurred, Mister El-Sayed informed you of Martin Webster's intention to convert to Islam. So, you knew there was no reason why Adeelah could not marry Martin. And your intention to force Adeelah to marry you is clearly forbidden in the Quran, as Imam Rajput testified in his affidavit."

"The jury has found you guilty of second-degree kidnapping. The penalty for second-degree kidnapping is normally at least five years in prison. I have the discretion to convert some of your prison time to probation. In your case, I'm considering two factors in my decision about an appropriate punishment. One, you are a first-time offender. Two, Adeelah and her family have asked for mercy regarding your punishment. Therefore, I believe five years in prison is excessive. So, I sentence you to three years in prison and two years of probation."

The judge slammed his gavel down on the judge's bench. The gavel's sharp sound startled Omar, Kareena, and Adeelah and made them jump. Fahim showed little emotion. Omar, Kareena, and Adeelah watched as the security officer led Fahim away.

Also handcuffed and dressed in an orange jumpsuit, a security officer brought Habib into the courtroom. In Habib's case, the jury also found him guilty of second-degree kidnapping. The court clerk passed the verdict from the jury foreman to the judge. Commenting on his case, the judge said. "The penalty for second-degree kidnapping is normally at least five years in prison. I have the discretion to convert some of your prison time to probation, and I've decided to exercise my discretion in your case."

"I understand the other defendant in this case convinced you to help him with this crime by telling you that you were acting on religious grounds to protect your family and your sister from disgrace and divine punishment. Your sister, Adeelah, testified you are a good man, and it's admirable that a young man of nineteen years of age takes his faith in God seriously. But, unfortunately, that doesn't excuse the crime you've committed. I, therefore, sentence you to one year in prison and four years of probation."

Kareena let out a short scream when she heard the verdict, and Omar, dismayed, put his arm around her.

When the judge slammed his gavel down on the judge's bench, it startled Habib, who had tears in his eyes. Kareena sobbed and dried her eyes with a white handkerchief. Omar embraced her. Adeelah also had tears in her eyes. And they watched with sorrow and shame as the security officer led Habib away.

Meeting afterward with the El-Sayed family, Attorney William Everest said, "I want you to understand, the judge, in both cases, was as lenient as she could be under the law. I know you don't want to see your son and Fahim go to jail, but I honestly believe the outcome could not be better."

Omar shook hands with Attorney Everest and replied, "I thank you, sir, for all of your efforts."

Kareena, with a quivering lip, also replied, "Thank you."

# THE ONE-YEAR WAIT

Wedding preparations had now begun. On one Sunday, just after the evening service at Friendship Community Church, David informed Pastor Sawyer that Martin and Adeelah were engaged to be married.

Right after the evening Service, Pastor Sawyer sought out Martin and said, "Your father tells me you and Adeelah have become engaged. Do you have a few minutes? I'd like to meet with you briefly in my office."

Martin replied, "Sure. May I bring Adeelah with me."

"That shouldn't be a problem."

After the pastor finished greeting people as they departed the church, Martin and Adeelah accompanied him to his office.

Pastor Sawyer began, "First, congratulations on your engagement."

Martin and Adeelah both said, "Thank you."

The pastor hesitated and chose his words carefully, "Adeelah, I saw the news report about your kidnapping. While I'm certainly happy you successfully escaped your captors, I recall the news report revealed you are a Muslim. This troubles me only because it's my understanding that the Islamic religion requires non-Muslims to convert to Islam if they want to marry a Muslim." Stroking his chin, he turned to Martin, with a distressed look on his face, and asked, "Martin, have you, or will you, convert to Islam in order to marry Adeelah?"

Martin paused, pressed his lips together, which expressed his uneasiness with this confrontation, and replied, "Yes. I have professed the *Shahada,* which makes me a Muslim."

With very obvious distress on both his face and in his voice, Pastor Sawyer responded, "So, you have renounced your Christian faith!?"

"No. I haven't renounced my Christian faith." Martin explained how Reverend Paul Reynolds, a Methodist minister, came to see himself as both Christian and Muslim. "I see the rationale for his decision. So, I have no problems in following his example to be both Christian and Muslim. I made it clear to Adeelah's parents and to Imam Javed Rajput at the Islamic Center of South Augusta that I too will profess to be both Christian and Muslim, and they have accepted this."

"How is it possible to profess to be both Christian and Muslim?"

Martin leaned forward. "You'll recall our earlier conversations in which I distinguished between that which is absolutely essential from those issues which are very important, regarding areas in which Christians and Muslims are not in agreement. From my point of view, it isn't difficult to reconcile those issues between Islam and Christianity that are absolutely essential. I'm satisfied with that. Differences I deem to be very important but not essential are simply areas I choose not to worry about. Such differences don't affect our daily walk of faith. Adeelah and I pray together, we seek to live in ways which please God, we both take our faith in God seriously, and we continually seek to have a closer relationship with God."

Now conflicted, Pastor Sawyer replied, "That's a very provocative position."

"Well, Pastor, as I emphasized before, I believe God still winks at the ignorance which separates people who take their faith in God seriously. Moreover, I believe God winks when love and religion become rivals, which clearly occurred in our case. So, I'm not convinced that my position is so provocative."

Pastor Sawyer turned to Adeelah and asked, "How do you feel about this?"

Martin leaned back and put his arm around Adeelah as she responded, "I agree with Martin. As he just said, we both take our faith in God seriously. We pray together. We love each other. Not only that, but we see no conflicts in our day-to-day lives as we seek to live our lives in submission to God's will. We both respect each other's religion, and we've agreed to be active together in both Christian and Muslim forms of worship."

"What about your children?"

Martin gestured with his hand. "We'll teach them to take their faith in God seriously and to hold in high esteem both religions. We'll ensure they understand what salvation is and how God saves us by His grace.

We see these things as consistent with both religions, again, as you and I discussed previously."

Pastor Sawyer then commented, "Martin, my concern is that you're venturing into a situation which will turn out to be troublesome for you."

Martin replied, "I expect you would have that concern. The question I have for you is: Does anybody need to know about this conversation?"

Pastor Sawyer sat up in his chair. "Why do you ask?"

Martin leaned forward and looked Pastor Sawyer in the eye. "I ask the question because I don't see it as necessary to discuss it with anybody. I'm hoping you'll accept my decision and our marriage, even if you can only do so reluctantly. And it may be difficult for you to justify your acceptance, if this conversation should come before the members of our church."

"What if it does come before the members of our church?"

"Then we'll deal with it as necessary."

Pastor Sawyer then replied, "As is the case with any church member who comes to talk to me, let me assure you our conversation today will remain confidential."

Martin took Adeelah by the hand. They both breathed easier now, and Martin concluded, "Thank you. We earnestly seek to do God's will. Please keep us in your prayers."

Pastor Sawyer replied, "I'll certainly do that."

When they got to Martin's car, Adeelah commented, "I'm glad we had this conversation. Thank you for including me in it."

Martin looked at Adeelah and took hold of both of her hands. "Shall we pray about this?"

"Yes."

Bowing their heads together, Martin prayed, "Dear God. We seek to live our lives in a way which pleases You. Please make Your will clear to us, guide us, and bless us. May our upcoming marriage honor you, and help us to honor You in all we do. Amen."

Adeelah added, "Inshallah." (As God wills.)

~.~

Events now centered around two things: one, preparations for the wedding, which was planned to occur sometime after Ramadan. And two, trips to the Richmond County Correctional Institution to visit Habib, Adeelah's brother, and Fahim. Martin occasionally joined Adeelah's family during these visits, and both Habib and Fahim ironically developed close friendships with him. If all went well, Habib would get out of prison in time for the wedding.

While they experienced significant shame due to Fahim's crime to kidnap Adeelah, Omar successfully convinced Fahim's parents, Mustafa and Soraya, to come from Morocco for the wedding, so they could both attend the wedding and see their son, Fahim. Both families regretted the crime their respective sons committed. Adeelah's family, and Adeelah herself, were quick to communicate to Mustafa and Soraya that they forgave Fahim, and they emphasized that the friendship between their families was far too important to let this crime, serious as it was, destroy their friendship.

Soraya quickly became actively involved in the wedding preparations. Kareena asked Soraya to function as one of the negafas (wedding planners), which, in Soraya's case, meant she would take charge of procuring the four changes of clothing which a Moroccan bride wears during her wedding. The typical garments for the bride are called *takshitas*, the first of which must be white, the second red, and the remaining two may be in colors selected by the bride. Adeelah chose green and yellow for the third and fourth *takshitas*.

Kareena asked Soraya, "Could you also bring a *dishdasha* for Martin?"

"Of course. Are you sure Martin will be willing to wear one?"

"I think he will. He seems to appreciate our Moroccan culture."

"What color should Martin's *dishdasha* be?"

"Let's make it white."

To ensure Martin knew what his role would be during the wedding, Adeelah explained, "Our wedding will consist of two parts. The administrative part, which takes very little time, and the celebration part, which is what takes three days, as I mentioned to your parents."

She continued, "As with anybody who gets married in Georgia, we have to get a marriage license. Then you, I, and two witnesses must appear before Imam Rajput, and he completes the necessary paperwork to make our marriage legal. In the Islamic tradition, there is a wedding contract, which includes a requirement called *meher*. The *meher* includes two gifts which you must give to me. The first gift is called the prompt, which these days is the ring you put on my finger on our wedding day. The second gift is typically a gift of jewelry, and it's a token which promises security and freedom in marriage for the bride."

"Then there is the *nikah* ceremony, in which you formally propose marriage to me. Finally, as at other weddings you have witnessed, there will be vows you and I will make to each other."

"The three-day celebration consists of three parts. The *hammam* day occurs on day one and consists of ceremonial baths for the bride. The *henna* party occurs on day two, which primarily involves women, but the men typically also get together–separately, of course. During this party, *henna*, a type of ink which is burnt orange in color, will be used to draw intricate designs on my hands and feet. Your name will be hidden within the artwork, and you'll later have to find your name during the festivities on day three, which is delightfully fun. The third day is the culmination of the wedding celebration, and there will be a banquet and several ceremonies during that celebration. During the festivities on day three, I'll change my clothes three times, and you'll change clothes once from a regular suit to a dishdasha during the final ceremony. After that ceremony, you'll change back to your suit."

Not knowing how Martin would react to all of the festivities, Adeelah wrinkled her forehead with a hopeful look in her eyes. "What do you think?"

Martin hugged her, gazed into her eyes, and took Adeelah by both hands. "First, I'm sure we'll have a good time. Second, I believe, after three days of such festivities, there'll be no doubt that we will be thoroughly and truly married. Third, I'm sure this memorable occasion will be something we'll always cherish."

Adeelah took a deep breath, and, somewhat surprised, she replied, "I'm so glad you have such positive things to say. I was afraid you might find it all to be excessive."

Martin hugged Adeelah again. "Don't you worry. I promise you, I'm looking forward to everything."

~.~

Now that wedding plans were underway, Martin and Adeelah decided, with some urging from their parents, it was time for their families to finally meet each other. Usually, such family meetings would occur much earlier. The earlier meetings didn't occur simply because of the mutual family opposition to Martin and Adeelah's relationship.

The decision was made for the parents to meet at Adeelah's home at 6:00 PM on Saturday. Adeelah suggested to Martin that everybody should dress well but casually.

When Saturday came, Ellen wore a new dress, which was a very pretty navy blue in color, with white shoes. David wore tan wool trousers, black, highly polished shoes, a black long-sleeved shirt (without a tie), and a conservatively patterned beige sport coat which coordinated well with the trousers. Martin wore a white pair of trousers with a brown belt, a well-tailored dark blue, long-sleeved shirt, and brown shoes. Kareena wore an elegant long medium green dress, salmon-colored shoes, and a salmon-colored hijab with a green floral pattern which matched the green in her dress. Omar wore dark gray trousers, black shoes, and a Latin American style white, long-sleeved guayabera shirt. Adeelah wore a long pink skirt with shoes and hijab to match, along with an off-white, long-sleeved blouse which contained a floral pattern which matched the color in her skirt and hijab.

David drove, and Martin gave directions. When they arrived at the driveway of Omar and Kareena's home, it immediately became apparent to David and Ellen that Adeelah came from a wealthy family. As it occurred when Martin saw their home for the first time, David and Ellen were awestruck when a servant asked them to remove their shoes, showed them into the very elegant living room, invited them to take a seat, and served each of them a cup of Moroccan tea.

Shortly after their arrival, Omar and Kareena descended the staircase and walked directly to the Webster family–Omar with an outstretched hand, ready to shake hands with David. The Websters stood as Omar and Kareena approached. David and Omar shook hands, and Martin made the introductions. They all then took their seats in the living room, and the servant brought tea for Omar and Kareena and replenished the tea for the Websters.

Omar said, "Welcome to our home. It's so good to finally meet you."

Adeelah then made her entrance, gracefully descending the staircase in a way which made her look like she was floating on air. She immediately caught Martin's attention, and she enjoyed how Martin's loving gaze very obviously revealed how much he proudly admired her very feminine beauty.

A servant stood ready to give Adeelah a cup of tea.

After David and Ellen expressed their thanks for the invitation to come to Omar and Kareena's home, they engaged in light conversation, which was initially a bit of a struggle as they worked on breaking the ice. Martin and Adeelah were happy to see their religious differences didn't become a topic of conversation.

To overcome their struggling efforts to make conversation, David said to Omar, "We know Adeelah was born in Augusta. I'd find it fascinating to learn how you and Kareena came to immigrate here from Morocco."

Omar explained, "I came here on a student visa to study at the University of Georgia in Athens. After graduation, I returned to Marrakech to marry Kareena, and we were fortunate enough to get resident visas to come to live here permanently. We eventually took steps to become United States citizens."

David, who also graduated from the University of Georgia in Athens, was surprised to learn both he and Omar graduated in the same year, and they began what was to become a close friendship.

While David and Omar talked about their college days, Kareena showed Ellen a video of a previous Moroccan wedding, as well as various photos on the internet which exemplified the clothing Adeelah and Martin would wear for their wedding.

Ellen's face expressed amazement when she saw the video, and she exclaimed, "Wow! All the pageantry is stunning."

Ellen and Kareena got deeper into the details for the upcoming wedding. Martin and Adeelah made their way out to the pool to let their parents get to know each other better.

A maid announced that dinner was served. They all enjoyed a very typical Moroccan dinner of roast lamb with dates, couscous, and a pumpkin, cranberry, and red onion tagine. There was plenty of Moroccan tea, and they enjoyed Moroccan orange cake for dessert.

Omar and David ended up shooting several games of pool well into the evening, and Kareena and Ellen happily got back into the details of Adeelah and Martin's upcoming wedding.

Martin and Adeelah rejoiced to see that their parents were hitting it off very well, so they stayed out of the way and let nature take its course.

# Mosque Massacre

Ramadan was now starting, and Martin participated for his first time as a Muslim in the month-long, daily fasts, which limit food and drink to two meals a day–one before sunrise and one after sunset. Martin and Adeelah attended special evening services on Fridays during Ramadan at the Islamic Center of South Augusta.

These services consisted of a prayer time at sunset, and afterward, all gathered in the courtyard to break their fast and enjoy a good meal together, known as an *iftar*. During one Friday service, a visiting imam, a Christian pastor, and a Jewish rabbi spoke to those in attendance. They emphasized the common ground all three religions shared, and they stressed the importance of tolerance and solidarity among the three religions. As is the usual practice in Islam, men congregated with men and women with women. The month-long Ramadan fast gave Martin an excellent opportunity to develop some new friends at the Islamic Center, and he was impressed with the great camaraderie which united Muslims from several countries around the world.

Soon after Ramadan ended, Martin and Adeelah departed City Hall on Friday to attend the regular weekly afternoon prayer service at the Islamic Center of South Augusta. When they arrived, they met up with Omar and Kareena. Since they arrived early, they happily discussed some of the details for the upcoming wedding.

They stored their shoes in the cubbyholes in the mosque's entryway. And, while they did their ablutions, Omar announced, "Habib should be released from prison on time to attend the wedding." This was news which all four rejoiced to hear. Then Martin went with Omar to pray with the men, and Adeelah went with Kareena to pray with the women.

Shortly after the prayer service started, a man burst into the main entrance and made his way into the ***muṣallá*** or prayer hall. He wore a battle fatigue military uniform, a bullet-proof vest, and a nylon stocking over his head. He carried a high-powered assault rifle with a high-capacity magazine, and he immediately opened fire on the worshipers. Walking back and forth, the shooter indiscriminately fired at people. Whereas moments ago, there was the blessed peace of worshiping people in prayer to Allah, now the strident crack of gunshots thundered out dread and doom. Panic, screams, shrieks, and chaos erupted as people did their best to flee. But, in just a few minutes, the shooter had gunned down several people, and they lay bleeding on the floor.

Two armed security guards rushed to try and stop him. The shooter killed one, but the other guard stopped the shooter with bullets to the chest and head, and the shooter dropped to the floor, bleeding and motionless.

A haunting, momentary, eerie silence was soon interrupted by the shrieks and cries of worshipers which now occurred, as people began to discover loved ones who were victims of this mass shooting. The scene was grisly and grotesque. A smoky haze hovered in the prayer hall from the gunshots which were fired. The acrid smell of gunpowder permeated the air, and there were spent gun casings strewn on the floor. The sounds of sirens now pierced the air as well.

Martin found Omar. Both were uninjured. They immediately went to find Adeelah and Kareena. Adeelah sat stunned, motionless, with a blank stare on her face–blood spattered on her blouse. In front of her, in a pool of blood, was the lifeless, contorted body of Kareena, her mother. The eyes on her mother's face were open but saw nothing. They only revealed the blank stare of death. Omar arrived and immediately reached out to her. He didn't just weep, he wailed as he held his beloved wife in his arms with no life in her.

Martin embraced Adeelah, and she began to stir. As the vivid macabre image of seeing her mother drop to the floor from a gunshot wound came back to her, she clung to Martin and sobbed–a cry which emanated from deep within her soul. Martin had never experienced such heart-wrenching wailing and cries of despair, and he felt hopeless to do anything except hold Adeelah close to him. He also reached out and put his arm around Omar, who did not resist his touch. Instead, he welcomed

Martin's human warmth. Martin perceived correctly that no words at this moment were adequate to console Adeelah or her father. So, he said none. He just prayed silently for them.

Worshipers everywhere were dealing with the same tragic trauma. Wailing and cries filled the room. Mothers held dead children to their bosoms, rocking back and forth in grief. Both husbands and wives wept bitterly over the bodies of their dead spouses. Looks of deep despair were etched on their tear-stained faces. Others tried to help their injured loved ones, and there were many. Above the widespread wailing, worshipers throughout the mosque cried out, "*Ya Ilahi*!" (Oh my God.)

Police and ambulances now started to arrive. The twerp, twerp, twerp of a helicopter hovered overhead. News media also began to arrive. The priority was to get the injured to hospitals, remove the dead, and provide solace for the survivors. Some tried to cling onto their loved ones, and first-responders had to pry them away. Others just stared in horror and disbelief. The helicopter landed to pick up the most seriously injured and take them to the University Hospital in Augusta.

Reporters began gathering information for their news reports. They knew, however, that now was not the time to interview survivors, and they respected that.

On the evening news, they reported,

> *A shooter, wearing a military uniform and carrying an assault rifle with a high-capacity magazine, burst into the Islamic Center of South Augusta today and opened fire on innocent worshipers. According to police, nine people are dead, and twelve have been injured. The gunman is described as a white supremacist and a military veteran, who suffered from post-traumatic stress disorder after the violence he experienced in Afghanistan. He acquired his weapon at a local gun show, from a vendor who failed to obtain the necessary background check. We have learned that a background check would have kept the shooter from purchasing the assault rifle used in the crime.*
>
> *The police have classified this as an obvious hate crime. Two security guards confronted the shooter. The shooter killed one of the security guards. The other security guard shot and killed the shooter, and averted further death and injury.*
>
> *The imam at the Islamic Society of Augusta has assured worshipers at this mosque in South Augusta that they are welcome to worship with them until necessary repairs can be made to the Islamic Center of South Augusta.*

*Several churches in the area have reached out to make their facilities available as well and to provide any assistance wanted or needed.*

*John Woods, Mayor of Augusta, Georgia, condemned this attack on the Muslim community in the Augusta area and commented, "It grieves me deeply to hear about the loss of life and injuries which occurred today at the Islamic Center of South Augusta. It is a sad day when such a deplorable hate crime occurs in our city or anywhere else."*

On Saturday, despite the tremendous shock from the previous day's massacre, Imam Javed Rajput stoically began funeral preparations for the nine people who lost their lives during the shooting. Islam requires that every effort should be made to bury the dead within two days. The Imam at the Islamic Society of Augusta worked closely with Imam Rajput to make the necessary arrangements. Together, they organized the required washings of the dead bodies.

Adeelah and Omar discussed who would wash Kareena's body. Omar expressed his preference that Adeelah should do the washings. Adeelah was willing to do them, but she had very strong mixed feelings. On the one hand, she was simply squeamish about handling a dead body, and she found it especially traumatic to be working with the body of her dead mother, which was grotesquely marred by a bullet wound. On the other hand, she saw it as an important responsibility and an honor to prepare her mother for burial. She asked her friend, Taslima, to help her. Taslima also found this task to be difficult, but she did not hesitate to help her friend, Adeelah.

Islam requires that a body must be washed at least three times. If, for some reason, three washings are insufficient, at least two more washings are necessary because there must be an odd number of washings. Additionally, the body must be washed in the following order: Upper-right side, upper-left side, lower-right side, lower-left side. Adeelah also had to wash and braid Kareena's hair into three braids.

Next, Adeelah and Taslima had to shroud the body with three large white sheets. The body must be placed on top of the sheets. They then had to dress Kareena in an ankle-length sleeveless dress and head veil. Next, they placed Kareena's left hand on her chest, and the right hand was placed on the left hand, as in a position of prayer. Afterward, they folded the sheets over the body, first the right side, then the left side, until all three sheets completely wrapped the body. Finally, they secured the shrouding with ropes, one tied above the head, two tied around the body, and one tied at the feet.

As they completed these tasks, Adeelah had to stop from time to time to deal with her grief, with sobbing and cries, as she lamented the surreal loss of this woman whose body lay in front of her–the cherished mother she loved so dearly. Also grieving, Taslima did her best to be a source of comfort for Adeelah.

Omar stepped into the room as they were finishing. And, when he saw the shrouded body of his dead wife, reality set in. It was more than he could bear as he realized that the woman who was so important in his life–the woman who he loved so deeply for so many years, would no longer be by his side. He didn't just weep, he wailed with profound grief, his head shaking, his eyebrows arched in deep sorrow, with tears flowing down his face. He and Adeelah hugged each other, and both felt some relief from the tears they shed together and the warmth of their embrace.

Now that they completed the preparation of the body, Adeelah contacted Imam Rajput, and he sent a hearse to transport the body to the Islamic Society of Augusta Mosque. Imam Rajput, his face pale from the burden of his horrific responsibility, informed them with a low, sorrowful voice. "*Salat al-Janazah* (funeral prayers) will occur tomorrow morning in the courtyard of the Islamic Society of Augusta Mosque at 9:00 AM. Afterward, all nine individuals who perished will be immediately transported to the cemetery for burial. We've also organized a reception at the Islamic Society of Augusta Mosque tomorrow evening at 7:00 PM."

While all this was going on, Martin contacted his parents early Saturday morning about Friday's massacre at the Islamic Center. He was simply too traumatized to contact them on Friday. When his dad, David, answered, Martin said with a broken voice, "I'm sure you heard about Friday's massacre. It occurred at the mosque which Adeelah attends. She, her parents, and I were present when the attack occurred. And it grieves me to say, Adeelah's mother was among those who lost their lives."

David was devastated and immediately informed Martin's mother, Ellen. Then he replied, "I must tell you, it never even occurred to us that you might have been at this mosque during the shooting. Please express our deepest condolences to Adeelah and her father. Is there some other way we can express our condolences?"

"Yes, there is. Muslim tradition calls for a quick burial with very few people in attendance. Afterward, however, there will be a reception

Sunday evening, and that would be the right time for you to attend and express your condolences." He then said, "I need you to know also that Adeelah and I won't be in any of our church's services on Sunday. Will you please let the orchestra director know I'll be absent?"

"I'll do that."

"Thanks."

Martin visited Adeelah and Omar late Saturday afternoon, and both were grateful for his visit. Omar expressed his regret that his son, Habib, would not be able to attend his mother's funeral.

Martin immediately grabbed his cell phone, called the Richmond County Correctional Institution, and spoke with one of the corrections officers, "I'm hoping you can help me. You have a prisoner there whose name is Habib El-Sayed. His mother is one of the people who were killed during the massacre which occurred at the Islamic Center of South Augusta on Friday. She'll be buried tomorrow. Can we get him released with an escort so he can attend his mother's funeral?"

The corrections officer replied, "I don't know what we can do with such short notice, but let me look into it. I'll get back to you as soon as possible."

"Thank you," Martin replied, "Please know, the family would be deeply grateful if their son could attend the funeral."

About twenty minutes after they hung up, the corrections officer called back and said, "The arrangements have been made. Habib will be able to attend his mother's funeral. We have a Muslim corrections officer who will escort him. I just need some details."

"The funeral will occur at the Islamic Society of Augusta Mosque at 9:00 AM. All funeral events will conclude by Sunday evening."

"Okay. Habib El-Sayed will be at the Islamic Society of Augusta Mosque at 9:00 AM tomorrow."

"Thank you very much." Martin then turned to Adeelah and Omar and said, "Habib will be at the funeral tomorrow at nine o'clock. A Muslim corrections officer will escort him, and take him back to the Richmond County Correctional Institution after the reception tomorrow night."

With profound gratitude and tears in their eyes, Omar and Adeelah thanked Martin.

On Sunday, a very large gathering from among the Muslim community attended the *Salat al-Janazah* (funeral prayers) at 9:00 AM.

Despite their heavy grief, Omar and Adeelah rejoiced that Habib was able to be with them.

Omar explained to Habib, "I want you to know it was Martin here who made the necessary last-minute arrangements, so you could be here for your mother's funeral today."

Habib hugged Martin and said, "*Shukran.* (Thank you) I'm grateful that you would do this for my family and me, and I'm humbled. I hope you can forgive me for the grief I caused you and my sister."

Martin warmly tightened his embrace. "I'm happy to forgive you. I'm happy you can be here, and I hope our friendship will only get stronger."

Habib's tears flowed freely. "I'll certainly do my part to make that happen."

From that point on, they would be very intimate friends indeed.

After the funeral prayers, family members proceeded to the cemetery for the burial. In Islam, only men typically go to the grave site for a burial, but given this unique tragedy, women went as well. Martin and Adeelah stayed close together throughout the burial proceedings, and Martin's shoulder was a welcome place for Adeelah to express her profound grief for her mother's death–she wept bitterly.

In the evening, they met for the post-funeral reception at the Islamic Society of Augusta Mosque. Normally, only close male family members and friends attended this traditional reception. That would not be the case for this reception. Martin's parents, David and Ellen, were among those who attended, and they both expressed very heartfelt condolences to Adeelah and her father, Omar.

Ellen especially found it difficult to contain her grief at Kareena's death. Despite her very recent first encounter with Kareena, they had quickly bonded into a friendship which held the promise of growing deeper with time.

Food was generously provided by many in the local Muslim community, and large numbers from the Muslim community attended the reception as well in a show of solidarity.

In all the events during the day, members of the press were permitted to attend, but they had to agree to refrain from taking photos and videos.

The TV news on Sunday evening reported:

> *Today nine people, brutally killed on Friday during the massacre at the Islamic Center of South Augusta, were laid to rest, as parents, sons and*

*daughters, husbands and wives, and other friends and relatives grieved for the loss of their dear loved ones.*

*John Woods, Mayor of Augusta, Georgia, had this to say, "I condemn in the strongest way possible this senseless killing and hold in utter contempt those who label themselves to be white supremacists, for the hatred which they promote toward innocent human beings who are simply different in skin color, culture, and religion–innocent people in this most recent case who gathered peacefully to worship and pray on Friday. My prayers are with the families who lost loved ones this past Friday. And I pray for the speedy recovery of those who were injured."*

As soon as possible, Martin called Frank Washington, the Waynesboro City Manager. "I'm calling to let you know that Adeelah's mother was among those who died during the massacre at the Islamic Center of South Augusta."

"Thanks for letting me know, Martin. I'm so sorry to hear that. I'll let the City Council and city staff know about Adeelah's loss."

When she returned to work on Monday, Adeelah's mood was very somber. Nevertheless, she graciously received visits from the Waynesboro mayor, city council members, the city manager, and several other employees, including Martin, of course. They all expressed their dismay at what happened and rallied around Adeelah to show their support and solidarity for her.

When Martin and Adeelah met for lunch at the Good Day Café, several restaurant employees and customers, who had become Adeelah's friends, came over to pay their respects as well. Most in the restaurant shed tears when they learned that Adeelah had lost her mother. This warm outpouring of compassion deeply moved Adeelah, and contrasted starkly with the stares and whispers which occurred during Adeelah's first visits to the café.

The news media covered this atrocity internationally. In the United States, it quickly resurrected the issue of gun violence. As with other similar, recent mass shootings, there was the promise of regulation to combat gun violence. But again, elected officials vacillated, and nothing was done. And soon, indifference resumed. But there were two families, among many, which were cruelly touched by this senseless tragedy, one Muslim and one Christian–the El-Sayed and Webster families. And they would forever be united and zealous in their support for effective gun regulation. Kareena's memory would ensure they would never waver on this issue.

# THE MOROCCAN WEDDING

After two weeks went by, with no mention at all about their wedding, Martin began to be a little concerned. Everything between Martin and Adeelah seemed to be good, so he wasn't exactly worried. But one day, he finally asked, "When will we once again talk about our wedding?"

Adeelah explained, "As Muslims, we traditionally mourn for at least forty days after a funeral. I contacted Mustafa and Soraya, Fahim's parents, to let them know about my mother's death. My mom and Soraya have always been very close friends, and Soraya took the news pretty hard. Soraya will be bringing some things from Morocco for the wedding, so I also confirmed for them that our wedding would obviously be delayed. I tell you this because they need adequate time to make their travel plans. So, I'd like to propose a wedding date for the last week in June."

"As far as I know, that should be fine. I'm sure you as well as I will need to coordinate with our families to ensure that the last week in June will be a good date."

After making necessary coordination, the wedding date was confirmed and set to start on the last Wednesday in June. Habib was scheduled to complete his one-year prison sentence, and a wedding in the last week of June would make it possible for him to attend.

As Omar had stipulated earlier, he required Adeelah to get a medical examination and a certificate to confirm she was a virgin. Disappointed again that her father would require this certificate, she nevertheless reluctantly agreed to the medical examination and received the certificate which confirmed Adeelah was, indeed, a virgin.

The last week in June approached quickly. Mustafa and Soraya Bakkari arrived during the weekend before, and Omar happily opened his home to them during their visit. The time they spent with their son, Fahim, at the Richmond County Correctional Institution was bittersweet, but they were glad to hear he was described as a model prisoner. Soraya found it difficult to be in Kareena's home and to face the reality that she was gone. Soraya's tears and her presence also brought tears to Adeelah's eyes. Mustafa and Soraya were grateful for Omar's hospitality, and they wholeheartedly helped with wedding preparations and implementation.

The wedding events were now upon them. The religious marriage ceremony would occur on Wednesday, and the three days for the wedding celebration festivities would start on Thursday and conclude on Saturday.

On Wednesday, Martin and Adeelah met at the Islamic Center of South Augusta with Imam Rajput and two witnesses, which were members of the Islamic Center's congregation. David, Ellen, Priscilla, Omar, and Habib were also in attendance. While they all rejoiced to see this day come, the day was nevertheless touched with a somber sadness due to Kareena's absence. Consequently, along with the great and real joy of the wedding events, there were also some tears of lamentation.

Martin presented the *meher*, a wedding contract which, among other things, specified two gifts for Adeelah. The first gift, referred to as the prompt, was the wedding ring, which he placed on Adeelah's ring finger. The second gift was a very elegant gold necklace with an emerald pendant, which Martin would give to Adeelah later.

The *nikah* followed, in which Martin formally stated the details of the *meher*, knelt on one knee, and formally asked Adeelah, "Will you take me as your husband?"

Both Adeelah and Martin responded to the *nikah* by repeating three times each the word, *qabul*–an Arabic word which means "I accept." Then Adeelah, Martin, and the two witnesses signed the marriage contract, making the marriage legal according to civil and religious law. In keeping with tradition, Adeelah and Martin fed each other a date.

Next, Martin and Adeelah prayed together the words of the first Surah from the Holy Quran, "In the name of Allah Most Gracious Most Merciful. Praise be to Allah the Cherisher and Sustainer of the Worlds. Most Gracious Most Merciful Master of the Day of Judgment, Thee do we worship and Thine aid we seek. Guide us in the straight way. The way of those on whom Thou hast bestowed Thy Grace, to those whose portion is not wrath and who go not astray."

Imam Rajput then led them to pronounce the wedding vows.

Adeelah smiled and looked into Martin's eyes with tears of joy. "I, Adeelah, offer myself to you in marriage in accordance with the instructions of the Holy Quran and the Holy Prophet, peace and blessing be upon him. I pledge, in honesty and with sincerity, to be for you a loyal and faithful wife."

Martin also gazed into Adeelah's eyes, smiled, and took her by the hand. "I, Martin, pledge, in honesty and sincerity, to be for you a faithful and helpful husband."

Imam Rajput concluded the wedding ceremony by stating, "By the authority vested in me by the State of Georgia, and with the blessings of Allah, it is my pleasure to announce that you are husband and wife. Martin, you may now kiss your bride."

Martin and Adeelah then shared their first passionate kiss as husband and wife. But they didn't start married life yet. While they were legally and religiously married, the wedding was not considered "final" until after the three-day wedding celebration.

Day one started on Thursday with the *hammam* party. Taslima, Soraya, and other female friends gathered together to complete the customary ceremonial baths for Adeelah. They washed her hair with *ghassoul* (a type of clay), and they scrubbed, massaged, and perfumed her body.

Day two, on Friday, was the *henna* party, which again focused primarily on Adeelah. *Henna*, a red/orange ink, was used to create intricate decorative designs which were applied to the hands and feet of Adeelah and her attending guests. The geometric and floral designs had several meanings which emanate from ancient Egyptian culture, including protection from evil spirits, bringing good luck, and increasing fertility. In Adeelah's case, the designs included Martin's name, which was hidden among the designs in a way which made it difficult to find. During the festivities on day three, Martin would have to look over the designs on her hands and feet to find his name. The ink is temporary and eventually washes off.

Day three on Saturday was the culmination of the wedding celebration. Both Martin and Adeelah's parents cooperated to hold Saturday's formal dinner and festivities in the Rose Room at the Marion Hatcher Center in Augusta, and they contracted with caterers to provide food and beverages for these events.

The Marion Hatcher Center occupies an elegant home, which dates back to 1835, and was perfect for the wedding events. The original structure was a three-story Georgian style home and was the family residence of John Phinizy, a wealthy Augusta merchant and businessman. The original home, in addition to the three floors, also included an oval two-story porch and observatory located on the west side of the building. The Phinizy home had an outside kitchen, connected to the main house by a covered walkway. Stables and four smaller homes once occupied the site where the parking lot is currently located. The Rose Room has a capacity for 299 people, and there is a library area which is attractively decorated, to include a comfortable sofa, several easy-chairs, a vintage carpet, and other furnishings which handsomely reflect the 19th-century charm of the home.

The celebration itinerary consisted of varied festivities, along with a formal dinner, for the guests to enjoy. The wedding guests arrived at 7:00 PM. The bride and groom planned their entrance to occur after all guests had arrived.

Adeelah sat on a very elegantly constructed platform, called an *amaria*, which contained elaborately decorated columns to support an ornate roof. The floor of the *amaria* was covered with a large emerald green cushion. Adeelah wore a white, elegant Moroccan *takshita*, which resembled a long, flowing wedding dress, but more elaborately designed and adorned by an abundance of different brilliant-colored stones. Heavy makeup applied to her eyes made them look twice as large as they were. Her hair was piled high on her head in braids and interwoven with gold chains and colored stones. *Henna* designs adorned her hands and feet. Martin found her exotically beautiful. He wore a suit and led the way, followed by four men, the *amaria* bearers, who picked up the amaria and danced their way into the Rose Room, where the guests were assembled. The dancing *amaria* bearers made the *amaria* oscillate from side to side.

As this procession took place, musicians played continuous loud Moroccan music which featured various types of drums, oboes, *rababs* (fiddles), *ouds* (lutes), *kamenjahs* (a violin-style instrument played vertically on the knee), *qanunas* (zitheras), *darbukas* (metal or pottery goblet drums), *taarijas* (tambourines), flutes, and other typical Moroccan instruments. The predominant instruments heard were the various drums, oboes, violins, and tambourines. Moroccan women used their tongues to produce a high-pitched yodel-like sound, while Moroccan men sang with their unique Arabian voices. Many of the guests were dancing.

After lowering the *amaria* to the floor, Adeelah stepped out of it and went to sit with Martin on a highly decorated sofa, elevated well above the guests. Guests took turns sitting beside them for pictures. Everybody watched with delight as Martin tried to find his name among the *henna* designs on Adeelah's hands and feet.

The loud music, the yodels, and the singing continued.

Martin looked over Adeelah's left hand and then the right to find his name, hidden in the henna artwork, and said, "This is taking way too long. Can you give me a hint?"

Adeelah laughed and said, "No hints! Don't worry. We're having a great time watching you deal with your dilemma."

When he tried to look for his name on her feet, Adeelah stopped him and said, "Don't worry about my feet. I would never put your name on my feet, which would be seen as an insult."

He finally found his name on Adeelah's right hand, and asked, "Is there some significance that my name is on your right hand?"

While everybody laughed heartily, Adeelah told him, "The custom to hide your name on my right hand is to esteem you as my noble and honorable husband."

When it was announced that dinner would be served, Adeelah went to change into a deep red *takshita*, also heavily adorned, to wear during the dinner.

The menu consisted of lamb with prunes, dried apricots, and sesame seeds. Side dishes included saffron rice, and *loubia* (Moroccan stewed beans with garlic, tomato, cilantro, and other Moroccan spices). The main beverage was Moroccan tea, and baklava was served for dessert.

Martin asked David, Ellen, and Priscilla, "So how do you like the lamb with prunes?"

All three found the lamb with prunes delicious, and David commented, "I must say, I'm pleasantly surprised."

The remarkable thing about this wedding dinner was the various Christians and Muslims who were among the guests. Many of the Christians experienced their first significant interaction with people of the Islamic religion. With very few exceptions, most of the Christian and Muslim guests got along very well.

After dinner, Martin and Adeelah visited the tables to say hello to all the guests and to thank them for coming. They also danced to the music.

At the appointed time, Adeelah went to change into an emerald green, regal looking *takshita* called a *lebssa fassia*. It was beautiful but heavy with much more extensive adornment, and it covered almost every part of her body except her face. With the crown placed on Adeelah's head, she looked every bit like an Arabian princess. This outfit was worn specifically for the tour in the *mida*, another platform (unroofed this time). Martin also changed his clothes and wore a traditional Moroccan *dishdasha–a* garment which was very similar to typical Arabian attire for men, but more ornate with embroidered gold-colored designs. He also wore an ornate turban. Martin and Adeelah each sat in separate *midas*. They were then lifted up and paraded around the room. As with the amaria bearers, the men who carried the *midas* also danced during this procession, with various loud drums and more abundant music, singing, and yodels. Martin and Adeelah only had eyes for each other, as they merrily enjoyed this uniquely Moroccan custom.

The celebration came to a close when both Martin and Adeelah changed clothes again. Adeelah changed to a yellow *takshita*, and Martin put his suit back on. Guests enjoyed the wedding cake, as did Martin and Adeelah as well. Martin and Adeelah danced one last time and departed. The celebration continued for the guests.

As they departed in a limousine for a suite at the Marriott hotel, Martin smiled and commented in jest, "That was a wonderful celebration, but I'm now exhausted! What happens now?"

Adeelah socked him, looked at him with a broad smile, and flirted with her mischievous, double-sized eyes. "We get to go do something we've been denying ourselves for far too long. I hope you're not too exhausted!"

Martin grinned. "Well, I find your words very invigorating. You've given me new-found energy. So, I think I'm ready to proceed to this glorious part of our wedding day celebration."

"I'm very glad to hear that. You know in times past, Moroccan tradition required two men be appointed to come by our abode in the morning to see if there's blood on our sheets and thereby confirm the virginity of the bride."

"Really!" Martin exclaimed, "I trust that custom is no longer observed."

Adeelah lightheartedly responded, "I guess we'll find out in the morning. Nevertheless, we don't want to disappoint them, do we?"

"I, for one, don't want to create any controversy, so let's make sure we don't disappoint them."

When they arrived at the suite at the Marriott Hotel, Martin carried Adeelah in his very muscular arms across the suite's threshold. That night their marriage was happily, thoroughly, and duly consummated.

Nobody came to check the sheets in the morning.

# Honeymoon

In preparation for their honeymoon, Martin and Adeelah ensured their passports were in order for their planned travel to Morocco. Since Adeelah, of Moroccan descent, was now married to an American, Imam Rajput thought it prudent to provide them with a letter with his signature, which testified that Martin had converted to Islam.

On Sunday, before church, following Islamic tradition, Martin gave Adeelah the gold necklace with the emerald pendant, which was the second gift Martin promised during the *meher* contractual part of the religious wedding ceremony. Adeelah received the necklace with child-like joy, hastily put it around her neck, and Martin fastened it for her.

She hugged Martin and exclaimed, "I love it! Thank you."

Martin replied, "It looks much more classy, now that I see it on you."

They departed on Monday night, and their travel plans gave them a three-day stay in Paris, which they enjoyed immensely. They had accommodations at the Hôtel Opéra Richepanse, located within walking distance of the Eiffel Tower.

When they arrived at the Paris Orly International Airport early Tuesday morning, they were surprised to find prayer areas for Catholics, Protestants, Muslims, and even for those who did not identify with any religion. A Protestant service was only available on Sundays, but they were able to visit the mosque located at Level -1, room A 726, where they participated in the pre-dawn prayer service.

Neither slept well during their all-night flight, and they were hungry. So, before leaving the airport, they enjoyed a continental breakfast which included an assortment of breads, fruits, cheeses, yogurts, and coffee.

The breakfast left them feeling somewhat refreshed–especially the two cups of coffee they each drank.

Exiting the airport an hour later, they encountered a bustle of activity. Many people competed for the relatively few taxis which were available at this busy time. Martin and Adeelah's efforts to get a taxi were hopeless. Adeelah saw a metro sign, and, with an animated sense of adventure, she suggested, "Let's take the subway!"

Martin, somewhat intimidated about her subway idea, asked, "Do you think that's a good idea?"

Adeelah shrugged. "I'm sure there are many Parisians who agree it is a good idea, especially since there are no taxis to be had."

Still a little reluctant, Martin replied, "Okay. Let's go for it."

They went back into the airport to exchange dollars for euros and dragged their luggage onto the escalator which took them down to the subway station. Being of Moroccan descent, where French is widely spoken, Adeelah had some minimal capability with the language, so she identified what she believed to be the right train to take. She was wrong! And they got totally lost underneath Paris.

Martin's earlier reluctance now tended toward panic, and Adeelah asked, "Martin, where's your sense of adventure?"

"I think I left it back at the airport."

While the Parisian people have an undeserved reputation for being snobbish toward foreigners, they found the people underneath the city were not only friendly but helpful. And, with Adeelah's limited French, they finally boarded the subway train which dropped them off within walking distance of their hotel.

After checking in at their hotel, they took a 2-hour nap. Feeling better after the much-needed nap, they could hardly wait to get to the Eiffel Tower, where they enjoyed their first introduction to French cuisine at the Jules Verne Restaurant. They delighted in the stunning view of Paris, while they dined at 410 feet above the city. In addition to savoring more French cuisine at other fine restaurants during their visit, they also visited the Arc de Triomphe, took a river cruise on the Seine River, visited the Pont Neuf Bridge (built in 1578), and explored the Grevin Wax Museum. While at the wax museum, they took selfies with Marie-Antoinette, Léonardo de Vinci, and Pablo Picasso.

Each night, they walked hand-in-hand down the Champs-Élysées, famously acclaimed as the world's most beautiful avenue. They found the lighted, picturesque avenue with its sidewalk cafés and fountains to be a mesmerizing kaleidoscopic sensation. Overwhelmed by the seductive aromas which emanated from the various bakeries and cafés, they were especially enchanted with the Ladurée café, which opened in 1863 and featured quintessential Parisian decor. They sat in the outdoor patio and happily watched the parade of people pass by on the famous avenue, while they savored the café's famous macarons, which caressed them with a pleasant almond aroma and heliotrope essence. They found the refreshing night air and the macarons to be a delicious combination.

They arrived in Marrakech on Friday. While their passports indicated they were United States citizens, they also had to disclose their religious and ethnic origins. So, both disclosed that they were Muslims. Martin disclosed that his ethnic origin was primarily of English European descent, and Adeelah disclosed that she was of Moroccan descent. This raised the question about whether Martin was indeed a Muslim. So, Martin also showed them the letter Imam Rajput had written. This eased their situation somewhat, and customs officials allowed them to proceed to their hotel but required them to stay in the hotel while they confirmed the veracity of Imam Rajput's letter.

They made their way to the Al Fassia Aguedal Hotel, where Martin had stayed during his previous visit to Marrakech as an Air Force officer. Despite their lack of freedom to leave the hotel, they enjoyed their stay, to include the excellent meals they had at the hotel's five-star restaurant. Their plans called for them to visit some of Adeelah's relatives in and around Marrakech. After being confined to the hotel for two days, Moroccan officials informed them they were now free to do as they pleased.

They were invited to a party organized by Adeelah's Aunt Badaya, and Adeelah took Martin to the Medina in Marrakech to buy some gifts for Badaya, Kareena's sister, and her husband Said, in whose home the party was to take place. The Medina was founded in the year 1072. It is surrounded by high stone walls and is divided into plaza-like squares. Each square has a mosque, a bathhouse, a communal bread oven, a madrasa, and a water fountain.

Also in the Medina are traditional marketplaces called Souks. Martin marveled at the assortment of herbalists, spice sellers, metalworkers, tanners, and food markets, which were concentrated on trade-specific streets. Speedy mopeds snaked up and down the narrow alleys, dodging mule carts and wagons. Consequently, Martin and Adeelah found the narrow alleys to be a precarious place to walk.

Martin observed with amusement as Adeelah haggled with the merchants. Adeelah explained, "The vendors typically are disappointed if you don't haggle with them."

They found a nice assortment of scented soaps for Badaya, a soccer ball for their son, and a Disney picture book for their daughter. An appropriate gift for Said was more challenging.

At one of the kiosks, Martin commented, "Here's a nice pocket knife. Do you think that would work?"

Adeelah took the knife, returned it to the vendor, and immediately said, "No! In Morocco, giving a knife to somebody signifies you want to cut off your friendship with them."

"Well, we don't want to do that! How about this nice fountain pen?"

"That would be a good gift."

On the way to Said and Badaya's home, Adeelah warned Martin, "Try not to use your left hand any more than necessary, especially when eating. Also, you'll note that everybody removes their shoes, and we'll want to do that as well when we enter their home."

"No problem," Martin replied, "I should be used to that custom by now. Every time I come to your parents' home, the servants zealously ensure I remove my shoes."

When they arrived at Said and Badaya's home, Martin was surprised to see that the home was built around a courtyard, which was entirely surrounded by the home. So, the only way to get to the courtyard was from one of the rooms in the home. The courtyard itself had no roof, and virtually every room in the home had a door which opened into the courtyard. Furniture, attractive small trees, and other plants in the courtyard provided for a comfortable place to sit and relax.

Adeelah spent some time with her Aunt Badaya, and they looked at photos of Badaya and Kareena which were taken during the sisters' youth. It was the most bittersweet part of their visit in Morocco.

They had a good meal, and everybody in Adeelah's family was curious to meet Martin. Language issues made it difficult for Martin's participation in the conversations. People nevertheless tried to talk to him, and he, who didn't understand a single word, frequently turned to Adeelah with a sheepish look on his face. Adeelah translated as well as she could.

~.~

Mustafa and Soraya had returned to their home in Rabat just before Martin and Adeelah's arrival in Marrakech, and they invited them for a visit. Martin and Adeelah booked first-class accommodations on a very modern train operated by the Moroccan Railway. The trip took just over three and a half hours, and a good portion of the journey took them along the scenic Atlantic coast of Morocco.

They enjoyed their stay with Mustafa and Soraya in their comfortable and spacious home. They visited several interesting places in Rabat, to include: Chellah, a medieval fortified city located in the heart of Rabat; Kasbah des Oudaias, the original site of the City of Rabat, with breathtaking ocean views; and the Old Medina, which was similar to the Medina in Marrakech, but not quite as hectic and chaotic. Martin decided that the more hectic, chaotic ambiance of the Marrakech Medina made for a more memorable experience. After their three-day visit, they returned to Marrakech.

During the remainder of their visit to Morocco, Martin and Adeelah took a three-day trip to the Atlas Mountains, went for a camel ride in the Palm Grove of Marrakech, enjoyed meals in many great restaurants, and re-visited the Marrakech Medina several times.

Martin found it fascinating to see several Berber villages during the three-day trip to the Atlas Mountains. Adeelah explained, "Many people in rural areas live in clay houses with no electricity or running water. Others live in small towns in the Atlas foothills, where they enjoy a quasi-modern lifestyle."

When they went for the camel rides, Adeelah laughed delightfully as Martin climbed on his camel. After figuring out how to sit on the camel's back, the camel got up with both of its hind legs first, which unexpectedly threw Martin forward. It was all he could do to hold on, until the camel got up on its front legs. The ride itself consisted of a jerking motion in which the camel oscillated between front to back and side to side. After his ride, in which he straddled the camel's very wide back, Martin experienced symptoms of seasickness and had to spend some time recovering from the pain in his groin.

One of the best parts of their time in Marrakech was their visits to the Medina. In addition to shopping opportunities, there was an abundance of street performers, musicians, acrobats, snake charmers, monkey sellers, food kiosks, and tea vendors. Loud, aggressive vendors, Moroccan music, and diverse aromas from the food kiosks made for a truly exotic experience.

One of the snake charmers displayed a quote from Psalm 58:3-5, which read, "The wicked go astray from the womb. They are wayward as soon as they are born, speaking lies. Their poison is like the poison of a snake, like a deaf cobra that stops its ear, which doesn't listen to the voice of charmers, no matter how skillful the charmer may be."

Martin commented, "I had no idea how long snake charmers have been around."

One of their more fascinating dining experiences was at the Comptoir Darna Restaurant, which featured excellent Moroccan cuisine, music, and exotic, attractive female dancers, who did not in any way adhere to modest Muslim dress standards. Two of them, in their scantily clad outfits, descended an elegant staircase with large platters of fruit balanced on their heads. Others, also scantily clad, performed exotic belly dances to the tune of Arabian music, which Martin found provocatively sensuous. Martin relished his opportunity to enjoy camel steak.

Amazed with the dancers' seductive moves, Martin lightheartedly asked Adeelah, "Can you dance like that?"

Adeelah surprised Martin when she teasingly replied, "You ain't seen nothing yet."

Pondering her provocative comment, he exclaimed, "I must say, I never expected such a seductive promise to come from the mouth of my Muslim wife. You have awakened within me a sense of breathless anticipation."

With a playful and mischievous smile, Adeelah added, "A seductive promise for your eyes only."

Frequent lovemaking during their honeymoon was poetically pictured by the bride in opening verses of the Holy Bible's Song of Solomon 1:1-5:

*Kiss me with the kisses of your mouth;*
*For your love is better than wine.*
*Your perfume has a goodly fragrance;*
*Your name is as an aromatic oil.*

*Draw me near; bring me into your chambers;*
*We will be glad and rejoice,*
*For our love is such sweet wine.*
*Rightly do I love you.*

# ADEELAH'S TESTIMONY

Back home from their honeymoon, Martin and Adeelah attended the Friday prayer service at the Islamic Center of South Augusta, and on Sunday they went to church with Martin's parents, where they attended both the morning and evening services.

Pastor Sawyer congratulated Martin and Adeelah on their marriage. And, after the morning service, he asked them to be prepared to say a few words during the evening service.

Surprised that Pastor Sawyer would ask them to speak, Martin coordinated with Adeelah after they left the church's morning service. "I'll introduce you to the congregation as my wife, then I'll let you say what you wish to say, and I'll speak after you."

Adeelah replied, "I'd like to talk about what unites us as people of God. Will that be all right?"

"I think that will be fine, and I, for one, will look forward to hearing what you have to say."

During the evening service, Martin simply said, "I'm now very happily married to this stunningly beautiful Moroccan woman, and we're happy to be back from our honeymoon in Morocco. We look forward to praying together, to following God's will, and to serving Him together. Please listen to Adeelah's testimony."

Adeelah then stood to speak, "I stand before you Christians and profess that I'm a Muslim woman, and I am now the wife of my Christian husband, Martin."

Offended by Adeelah's opening statement, a deacon stood and angrily shouted, "Pastor Sawyer, make this heathen shut up and sit down!"

Very disappointed, and with dismay, Pastor Sawyer responded firmly, "I will not tolerate such vicious comments in this church! Adeelah has been worshiping with us for some time. We are Christians, and we'll treat anybody who comes to worship with us with love and respect. Now I want to hear what Adeelah has to say."

The deacon stomped out of the church.

Adeelah trembled after hearing the deacon's offensive comment but continued, "The word Muslim is an Arabic word which describes anyone who submits to the will of Allah, which is the Arabic word for God. So, if you submit to the will of God, by that definition, you too are Muslims. I take my faith in Allah seriously and seek to submit myself wholly to Him. I recognize Muhammad as Allah's messenger. I understand you may not agree with me on this. But I also recognize Jesus Christ as Allah's messenger. The Holy Quran states, 'O Mary! Allah giveth thee glad tidings of a Word from Him: his name will be Christ Jesus, the son of Mary, held in honor in this world and the Hereafter and of the company of those nearest to Allah.'" (3:45)

"The Apostle John, in the Christian New Testament, quotes Jesus in chapter 17, where He prayed for His disciples, which includes you and me. In His prayer, Jesus said, 'This is eternal life, that they should know you, the only true God, and him whom you sent, Jesus Christ.' (John 17:3) These words are very similar to the *Shahada*, which one must profess to become a Muslim. In the *Shahada*, one recognizes the only true God and Muhammad as His messenger. And I testify with great joy that I, as one of Jesus' disciples, believe in, trust, and know the only true God and Jesus Christ, whom God has sent–who came for our salvation that we might have eternal life, and that we might have it more abundantly, as Jesus asserts here and as He promised in John 10:10."

"The Apostle Paul explained this salvation as follows, 'For by grace you have been saved through faith, and that not of yourselves; it is the gift of God, not of works, that no one would boast. For we are his workmanship, created in Christ Jesus for good works, which God prepared before that we would walk in them.' (Ephesians 2:8-10) By these verses, I understand that the source of my salvation is God's grace. And that I must do good works because God's grace compels me to do them, not because they will earn me my salvation. I also value what James said in the following verse, ' Yes, a man will say, "You have faith, and I have works." Show me your faith without works, and I will show you my faith by my works. You believe that God is one. You do well. The demons also believe, and shudder. But do you need to know, you fool, that faith apart from works is dead?'" (James 2:18)

"I see these scriptures as consistent with Surah 1 in the Holy Quran, which I pray daily." Adeelah then lifted her arms to just below her shoulder height, and with the palms of her hands facing upward, she invited the congregation to join her as she prayed, "In the name of God Most Gracious, Most Merciful. Praise be to God the Cherisher and Sustainer of the Worlds. Most Gracious Most Merciful Master of the Day of Judgment, Thee do we worship and Thine aid we seek. Guide us in the straight way. The way of those on whom Thou hast bestowed Thy Grace, to those whose portion is not wrath and who go not astray. Amen."

Few began with her in prayer, but all in the congregation ended with her in prayer. Adeelah then continued, "I recognize the need to say this prayer to Allah because my own efforts are inadequate for my salvation, and I, therefore, must trust God to guide me in the straight way. Therefore, I take comfort from Paul's words when he says, 'For by grace you have been saved.'"

There were now tears in the eyes of many in the congregation.

"You as Christians and I as a Muslim have our differences, but I hope you'll see that I, a Muslim, worship the same God as you do, and I take my faith in God seriously."

Martin then stood and said, "You've heard Adeelah's testimony, in which she affirms to us that she has the assurance of eternal life, based on Jesus Christ's own words–His promise to her. Very recently, Adeelah lost her mother in the tragic shooting which occurred in the mosque where she and her family go to pray. Despite the great sorrow she endures because her mother is no longer with her now, she also has the great hope that she will one day see her mother again in Heaven."

"We were recently shocked when our pastor invited the folkloric Muslim group from Uzbekistan to make a presentation in our church, and we were also shocked to learn that they ask God to save them from the punishment of Hell, as we Christians also do. So, it should be abundantly clear to us now that, while we follow our separate faiths in different ways, we nevertheless believe in, worship, and serve the same God. I hope you'll continue to make Adeelah, my believing wife, feel welcome as we worship here with you. Yes. There are things which Christians and Muslims believe differently. But I hope all of us will take comfort and instruction from the Apostle Paul, who clearly elevated love above all else, including our faith, when he penned the following words, known as the love chapter."

> *"If I speak with the languages of men and of angels, but don't have love, I have become sounding brass, or a clanging cymbal. If I have the gift of prophecy, and know all mysteries and all knowledge; and if I have all faith, so as to remove mountains, but don't have love, I am nothing. If I give away all my goods to feed the poor, and if I give my body to be burned, but don't have love, it profits me nothing.*
>
> *Love is patient and is kind. Love doesn't envy. Love doesn't brag, is not proud, doesn't behave itself inappropriately, doesn't seek its own way, is not provoked, takes no account of evil; doesn't rejoice in unrighteousness, but rejoices with the truth; bears all things, believes all things, hopes all things, and endures all things. Love never fails. But where there are prophecies, they will be done away with. Where there are various languages, they will cease. Where there is knowledge, it will be done away with. For we know in part and we prophesy in part; but when that which is complete has come, then that which is partial will be done away with. When I was a child, I spoke as a child, I felt as a child, I thought as a child. Now that I have become a man, I have put away childish things. For now we see in a mirror, dimly, but then face to face. Now I know in part, but then I will know fully, even as I was also fully known. But now faith, hope, and love remain—these three. The greatest of these is love." (1 Corinthians 13)*

"Every description of love in this great love chapter cries out and demands tolerance."

Martin continued, "Among the altars on Mars Hill, where Greek philosophers once worshiped their many gods, they erected an altar to the unknown god. The Apostle Paul introduced these philosophers to this unknown god–the only true God of the universe. And regarding their ignorance for worshiping so many false gods, Paul told these Greeks, 'The times of ignorance therefore God winked at. But now he commands that all people everywhere should repent.'" (Acts 17:30)

"In the love chapter, which I just quoted to you, Paul, who God inspired to give us so much of the New Testament, admits, 'For we know in part and we prophesy in part.' So even the Apostle Paul recognized that his and our current, inescapable, stubborn ignorance makes us incapable of understanding perfectly the truth of God, as He has revealed it to us. It is this ignorance which leads us to divisions and disagreements.

And, as God winked at the ignorance of the Greek philosophers on Mars Hill, I believe He winks today at this stubborn, insidious, inescapable ignorance which causes divisions among the various peoples of God–good, God-fearing people who take their faith in God every bit as seriously as we do."

"In I Corinthians 9:20-22, the Apostle Paul writes, 'To the Jews I became as a Jew, that I might gain Jews; to those who are under the law, as under the law, that I might gain those who are under the law; to those who are without law, as without law (not being without law toward God, but under law toward Christ), that I might win those who are without law. To the weak I became as weak, that I might gain the weak. I have become all things to all men, that I may by all means save some.'"

"If the Apostle Paul were alive today, he would most certainly say, 'To the Muslims I became as a Muslim, that I might gain Muslims.' The Apostle Paul is not alive today, but I am. And to the Muslims, I became as a Muslim, and I have won a Muslim who I now cherish as my wife–the love of my life."

# ABOUT THE AUTHOR

Michael Wright tells multicultural stories about women who find Mr. Right. He attributes his passion for writing multicultural romance novels to his military service, where, as Captain Wright, the Air Force took him to five of the seven continents on the planet and introduced him to the good people of many nations, cultures, races, and religions. He spent six years working in various countries in Latin America, where he met Dalys, his Panamanian wife. His other multicultural romance novels include: A Balmy Breeze from Two Seas and Teresa's Tale. Please visit his website at www.thewrightauthor.com to own these novels and to enjoy Michael's poetry.

www.ingramcontent.com/pod-product-compliance
Lightning Source LLC
LaVergne TN
LVHW050627100826
845148LV00011B/1758

* 9 7 8 1 7 3 6 4 1 1 4 6 9 *